⌐⌐ GIRL
IN
THE EMPTY DRESS

a Bennett Sisters novel

LISE MCCLENDON

Also by Lise McClendon

Blackbird Fly: a Bennett Sisters Novel (#1)
All Your Pretty Dreams

The Alix Thorssen Mysteries:
Bluejay Shaman
Painted Truth
Nordic Nights
Blue Wolf

The Dorie Lennox Mysteries:
One O'clock Jump
Sweet and Lowdown

writing as Rory Tate:
Jump Cut
Plan X

Lawyrr Grrl

Where a woman can grrowl about the legal profession

BLOG—Sistrrs in Law
Tagged *family matters, vacation, kvetching, screaming inside, ulcer time*
Posted June 13

Grrls, it's confession time. You may have guessed from posts over the past year that I have four sisters and all of us are trained attorneys. Kinda crazy, but there it is. Our father and his father before him were also lawyers. The law is in our blood. We grew up debating, arguing, holding mock trials over dishwashing duties, deposing each other, trying to best one another around the dinner table and running to Daddy's law books if we were stumped.

We sisters are all different and use our legal training in various ways: profit, non-profit, corporate, non-traditional. I'm not going to tell you exactly what we do or where we live. I *will* tell you this: being a non-lawyer in this family was a non-starter. Eventually we all fell into lock step. Some are happy troopers, some not so much. Some enjoy cracking the whip, some like taking a beating. We all have our strengths.

So we're going on a trip together! No lounging around five-star hotels or cruise ships for us. No, we're walking through the countryside, reading maps like explorers, getting spider webs in our hair, perspiring like champs, losing our way. Sounds like a bonding experience, huh? I mean, what the hell? We don't wear zip-off pants and hiking boots. We wear power suits and stilettos. We're lawyers: we have manicures for f••kssake!

And yet. Grrl sigh. Not going is also a non-starter. I will report in, or lose my shit, or both.

1

Cresting the hill on the dirt road, Merle Bennett felt the ache of her calf muscles and paused to adjust her backpack. She wasn't breathing that hard, just needed a second to catch her breath. Four days on the trail in the French countryside, plus all that jogging she'd done this spring made her feel strong.

Her oldest sister pulled up next to her, a little red in the face but smiling. Annie was fifty-four, bearing down on Social Security, she joked, but looking fit in cargo shorts, hiking boots, and a tie-dye T-shirt from a CSNY concert. "This is so great, isn't it? Look at that old ruin up there, all Castle Grimly."

Merle followed her gaze. "It belonged to Lord Byron, they say. Very gothic."

Francie arrived puffing, auburn tendrils stuck to her face and freckles blurred by exertion. Sister number four, she was too young to be a reluctant hiker. Forty-three was nothing. Just wait until she turned fifty.

Fifty. It had hit Merle hard. Fifty and alone: the words circled her brain. Even with James. Somehow he didn't change things where it counted, deep in her heart. *Was James not a keeper?* No, no mind games, not today on the top of a beautiful hill in the Dordogne surrounded by orchards and vineyards and cows with the sun on her shoulders and the scent of lavender and roses on the breeze. This was a good day. Her sisters were here, helping her celebrate being a big, fat fifty.

Focus, Merle. Smile, Merle. This is your life, Merle Bennett.

Stasia was ahead, walking down the hill beside Elise. Number two and number five, the sisters were the same height and walked the same way. Their hips swayed just so, and they swung their arms enthusiastically. Elise had dark brown hair like Merle, but Stasia's was lighter with well-maintained highlights. Merle was the middle sister. The Tent Pole they called her, possibly because of her Olive Oyl figure. The running, the worry, and Harry's death were responsible for that.

"Where the fuck are we?" Francie gasped, pulling out her map.

"Right here, right now, Miss Francine honey," Annie said, smiling like the Dalai Lama.

"That's what you always say."

"And I'm always right," said Annie. "Come on." She linked arms with Merle and Francie. "Let's truck down this hill. We're off to see the—"

"No singing," Francie hissed.

"Tell that to your friend," Merle muttered. She squinted down the hill. Francie's friend Gillian was dressed in safari classic, khaki head to toe with an asymmetrical hat that made her look like Crocodile Dundee. *What was she trying to prove with that get-up?* She hadn't made a good impression on the Bennett sisters. Merle hated to dislike people in general. Everyone had at least one good quality. Lawyers were trained to find the overlooked, that one detail that would set the case back. They just hadn't found that detail, something positive, in Gillian yet. Her presence had upset the sister dynamic, throwing off the finely tuned, five-spoke spin. But it was too late to get rid of her.

Merle sighed, pledging to herself to try harder. She didn't want to *try* to like someone on her vacation. It didn't seem quite fair.

Since they arrived in Paris together, on the plane, on the train, and on the trail, Gillian had remained aloof. She didn't answer when asked a question, didn't listen, didn't offer help or information. She acted like she was doing *them* a favor by going on the trip. Merle had given Gillian a pass for a couple days, but it was the singing that pushed her over.

She had a nice voice, that was true. Besides Annie's folk guitar days, none of the Bennett sisters were musical. They would be walking along, talking and laughing, and Gillian, not participating in the conversation, would nonetheless pick up on some phrase or word and burst into song. Usually Tony Bennett or Frank Sinatra—if someone remarked on the moon, she rang out with all the verses of "Fly Me to the Moon"—which was weird for a woman of 30-something. No one knew how old Gillian was. She seemed older than Elise, who was also celebrating a birthday on this trip, her 40th. Elise, the baby, always seemed young.

But, dear lord, the singing. It drove Merle bat-shit crazy. She was trying hard not to let it show. There were five more days on the trail to go.

Stasia, in a wide-brimmed hat decorated with wildflowers, rolled up pants, and a pink shirt, stopped next to Gillian. Elise pulled off her backpack and laid it on the dirt. A break was in the offing even though they'd only walked for an hour. They'd never make it back to Malcouziac tonight at this rate.

Gillian was staring at something in the ditch, hands on her hips. Merle frowned. There wasn't supposed to be a sixth member of this trip, but Francie hadn't gotten that memo. She'd invited her law firm colleague to go walking through France with them. Francie was the type who always needed a pal at her side, reinforcing her specialness. She was the prettiest sister, auburn hair streaked with sunlight, beautiful skin, the tallest. Pulling in the biggest salary too. But right now she was just one of the hiking Bennett sisters. She'd been cranky from the start.

When they arrived at the bottom of the hill, Gillian was crouched low in the grass, hand extended. Elise turned to them, eyes wide. "It's a dog. Hurt or something. Gillian found it."

They gathered around a filthy liver-and-white dog curled on its side, head up, brown eyes sad. A poodle maybe or a mix, a small one, its curly hair matted. When Gillian reached out a hand to pat its head, the dog thumped its tail.

"Don't touch it," Stasia said. "God knows where it's been."

"Aw, sweetie dog," Gillian cooed, ignoring her. Merle looked at Stasia, who wiggled her eyebrows. This was a new wrinkle, the fuzzy side of Gillian. Stasia had tried to befriend her at the start of the trip, being a pal, calling her Gillie. She'd been corrected.

"He's hurt. He's all bloody on that hip," Elise said, peering down. "I bet he can't walk."

"We'll carry him," Gillian announced. "How far to the next village?"

"Hold on," Merle said. "We can send somebody back for him."

"It's a mile at most." Francie consulted her map. "Loiverre. Not super tiny."

"So they might have a vet." Gillian walked around the back of the dog. "I'll carry him. Stand back."

"Wait, Gillian. Stop." Stasia held up a hand. "He'll bite you if you pick him up. Then we'll have two injuries."

Gillian handed her backpack to Elise and scooped her arms under the dog while clucking in his ear. The dog whimpered, his injured leg twitching, but laid his head back against his savior. Gillian gave Stasia a look of victory—or possibly *fuck you*—and walked out of the grassy ditch toward the village.

"She won't make it." Stasia marched beside Merle, shaking her head. "So bull-headed. What was Francie thinking? Gillian is ruining everything."

At five-four with an athletic build, toned arms, and muscular legs, Gillian was strong and fast. The rest of them struggled to keep up with her, even with a dog in her arms. Francie skipped ahead to try to help. Elise carried the extra backpack and offered encouragement.

"She must hit the gym more than the lawyers I know," Merle said.

"Don't hold that against her," Annie said.

Stasia laughed. "Oh, I've got a dozen other grievances, counselor."

In fifteen minutes they'd reached Loiverre and gathered in the central square to reconnoiter. Gillian lowered herself to the stone steps by a statue of a soldier and the French flag, cradling the dog in her arms. Annie volunteered to go ask about a veterinarian.

Elise jumped up and they took off together for the post office before Merle could say anything. She'd never found postal employees helpful in France, especially if you didn't speak perfect, colloquial French.

Sandwiches were eaten in silence as they waited. Gillian soothed the dog, talking baby talk. Annie and Elise returned and led them down a side street to the entrance of a medical office. "No vet," Annie explained. "But the doctor treats animals sometimes."

The receptionist in the doctor's office begged to differ. Her eyes widened at the sight of the smelly dog. Merle asked in her re-tooled French if there was someone around here who treated dogs.

"*Ah, oui, madame*," the young woman said, dashing into a back room. She returned with an older woman, apparently a nurse. She was tall, silver through her dark hair, and had kind eyes. Merle explained their situation.

"She says she can take him home and treat him," Merle told her sisters. "We can leave him with her. She'll try to find the owner."

"No," Gillian said, still attached to the animal, clutching him tightly. "I want to take him with us."

The sisters looked at each other. "Be reasonable," Francie said. "We're on vacation. What are we going to do with an injured dog?"

The nurse bent down beside Gillian and talked to the animal soothingly in French. The dog seemed very sweet, considering the pain he must be in.

The nurse stood and addressed Merle. "Tell your friend not to worry. She can come back for *le chien* in a couple days if she wants."

The walk that afternoon was hot and dusty. They were mostly on farm roads but veered off onto a trail marked with little pink slashes on fence posts, through woods, and next to a creek. The shade was delicious. The French sun could be brutal in June, baking the hillsides. The roses in the hedgerows grew limp as did the Bennett sisters. Gillian marched off moody and alone, back to her silent self.

The walking was meditative for Merle, calming her overactive mind. Her job in New York helping Legal Aid get Big Law backers kept her spinning in circles. Or maybe that's just the way she rolled, booked to the max, going 110 percent all the time. At any rate, she was back to her mind-set of lists and calendars. Nearly a week in France hadn't cured her of that. She would stay on for a couple extra weeks though so there would be time to unwind. It worked last year in this soft European time, where no one has anything more important to do than buy fresh croissants. She'd looked forward to getting back in the golden light for months. It really was a shame Gillian had to come along with her negativity.

Stop. Calm. Family. Tristan. She said it like a mantra. *Dinner tonight at Albert's. Wine. France. Calm. Wine!* There was a happy thought. Her throat felt parched, even with the last few lukewarm gulps from her water bottle. A cold Sauvignon Blanc would go down nicely.

By late afternoon, they were close to her adopted town. The approach to the walled village of Malcouziac filled her with pride and a kind of longing. Here was her piece of the Earth, a rocky, forlorn shard of charm. Harsh, unknowable, foreign. And yet, she belonged to it. Down a deep valley choked with brambles then up the other side, past high cliffs where the Saint Lucretia shrine guarded them all, around the butte, down another hill and there they were, the golden stone of the *bastide* walls, framed against the sky, curved and delicate, yet sturdy, and satisfyingly permanent. As much as the village had despised her last year, she loved it in all its messy glory. Centuries of fighting, clan against clan, duke against king, outsider against local. The walls of Malcouziac had lasted seven centuries. They would endure long after the petty quarrels of today's inhabitants.

The past year had taught her so much: patience, tolerance, forgiveness. If she could practice those things on herself, she could sure as hell offer it to the unfortunate citizens of Malcouziac. They had a new mayor and *gendarme*. She'd only been in the village a couple days before the walking tour, but there was a new air of friendliness.

They rounded the cliffs, tall and chalky on their right. An image of Harry sprang into her head, something that didn't happen often anymore. Her husband died last year of a heart attack and set her world on end. He would have enjoyed this though, in his curmudgeonly way. She could see him waddling along in his fancy loafers, tie loose, suit coat draped over a shoulder, moaning about the heat. If he wasn't already dead, the heat would have killed him.

"What are you smiling about?" Annie asked her.

"Nothing." Merle took her sister's arm. "Everything."

"Harry or Pascal?"

Pascal: last summer's curative to her broken spirit. She hadn't told him she was back in France. It would be awkward with James around. It seemed less complicated to just forget about Pascal.

"You know me too well."

Annie squeezed her hand. "Will we have to go back for that damn dog?"

Merle laughed. "Yes, oh wise one. I think we will."

2

The multi-paned door to the house on Rue de Poitiers stood wide open, a gust of wind rattling its dry shutters against the stone. Merle stood on the threshold, heart thumping. Tristan was alone in the house. He'd forgotten to lock the door. Panic shot through her. How close disaster had been last summer.

Laughter in the back garden reassured her. The cache of wine was gone. The bad guys were locked up. She took a breath. Why was she still so jumpy? She and Annie were the last two hikers to arrive. The sisters had felt the need for fresh air. That was all.

The ancient stone house still smelled stale from the winter, its thick walls cool and a little slimy in spots. It needed airing. The blue shutters were old and cracked but freshly painted. The orange tile roof had been repaired and survived the winter intact. *Everything* was intact. No need for worry. In the main room with its huge trestle table and a worn horsehair sofa, she knocked on a window sash and pushed it up. A breeze from the vineyards carried in the scent of fruit and musk.

Stasia called from outside. "Bring the wine, Merdle!"

When Merle arrived after a year away, she'd been worried her garden would be a mess, both from neglect and from last year's modernizing. But her neighbor Josephine—who lived here long ago—had delivered on her promise to keep things tidy and growing. She'd watered the grapevine and the espaliered pear tree, trimmed the roses, and swept dead leaves off the gravel patio. Merle was looking forward to thanking her at dinner tonight.

Stepping through the tiny kitchen into the sunshine, Merle felt the same rush of pleasure at the sight of the garden as the first time—an electric charge of wonder: her oasis, her pleasure grounds. Stasia had scoffed when Merle described it, calling her a romantic. How could a small garden be *all that?* When she saw it, Stasia admitted she was wrong. It was a special place. There, where she and Pascal danced that last night. There, the old rock *pissoir*, a soon-to-be converted outhouse with a vine climbing over the mossy roof. The wooden water cistern, still used for laundry and gardening, stood guard on its ten-foot legs surrounded by lavender. The roses were all in bloom, the red one busting its guts.

It was all so quaint and harmless and *French.*

Such a contrast, this little paradise surrounded by hard, weathered rock walls. Inside, they were softened by wisteria and clematis and grapevines. Outside, the world could be hard and cold. But in here, everything was safe and calm.

She delivered the bottle of wine as her sisters took off boots and swilled liquids then went to hug her son.

Tristan and Valerie sat at *Père* Albert's kitchen table, playing cards. Her son had met the girl last summer. She was the reason Merle got Tristan to come back to France with her. Her great-uncle Albert was round and cheerful, a former priest with the sort of beatific air that made you forget not to call him Father. His head injury from last year had set him back a little. He'd lost weight, Merle noted, and was less sure of climbing the ladder to pick his beloved plums for *eau de vie*. But he emerged from the sitting room with a big grin and open arms.

"*Bien venue*, Merle. How was the walking?"

"Lovely. The weather couldn't have been nicer. We stopped for a few *gustations* along the way." The wine tastings only worked at the end of the day of walking, otherwise there was much weary carping. But Merle only smiled. Albert wasn't interested in bickering.

"And your feet? Okay?"

"Not one blister."

"What about Aunt Francie?" Tristan said, his eyes on his cards. "No blisters for Queenie Franceenie?"

"Well, yes. She got a couple." And bug bites, thorn pricks, sunburn, and scraped elbows. Disaster seemed to follow Francie on the trail, at least from her perspective. Each sister's personality blossomed on the trail. That morning Merle had made a mental list of each one's travel mojo.

Annie: Everybody has a good time, right now!

Stasia: Follow the plan or I shoot you.

Merle: I just hope nobody stabs anybody.

Francie: This cheese is so freaking awesome! Ow! Look at me! Pass the wine!

Elise: If you tell me what to do I will pout all day.

And the plus one:

Gillian: My mind is too beautiful to share.

Two days in Malcouziac resting, then they would hit the road again for three more days in a loop off to the North. The thought of it made Merle queasy. Her sisters were getting along all right, but the togetherness sometimes put a strain on things. If anybody bailed, Stasia would be livid.

Merle turned to Albert's niece. "Have you and Tristan had fun, Valerie?" She put her hands on her son's shoulders. Maybe this was all the hug she'd get. Her boy was sixteen now.

"*Oui, madame. Nous*—pardon, I am to speak English." Valerie rolled her eyes. "It sounds terrible to me."

"It sounds great," Tristan said. "I love your accent."

Valerie gave him a playful punch. "What accent?"

At fifteen the girl had already perfected the French pout, the ammunition against men for centuries. She turned up her nose, folded her arms, smirked, and burst out laughing. She was going to be a handful, if she wasn't already.

"Thanks so much for looking after my boy, Albert," Merle said.

"Valerie took charge of activities. I only feed the man." Albert wagged his finger. "Not a boy any longer. So tall!"

"And handsome," Valerie chimed in. "With big shoulders." Her violet eyes flashed at Tristan again.

Merle tapped his big shoulders. "Come say hello to the aunties, Tris." As he got up, Valerie did too, straightening her chic print blouse that clung to her chest and tugging down her mini-skirt.

"Oh, *madame*, I will love to practice my English on them!"

"Dinner at nine," Albert called as they trailed through the back garden to the alley and through Merle's garden gate.

The women dressed for dinner, changing into summer dresses. Merle had been able to rent her neighbors' house as her own was too small for all of them. They had been very generous. Elise, Francie, and Gillian were staying in Yves and Suzette's house next door. It was much more modern than Merle's, with a full bathroom on the second level and everything very chic. It made Merle's tiny *maison de ville* look medieval.

When the younger three showed up in the garden for wine before heading to Albert's, they looked refreshed, shampooed and powdered. Elise, youngest and shortest sister, wore a flowered skirt and crisp, white blouse. Francie had on a fitted dress with the kind of low neckline she liked. Gillian had transformed herself with a short lilac dress with black lace insets better suited to New York than rural France. She'd worn it to dinner twice already, with her thick brown hair twisted artfully on her head. She took a glass of wine and stepped away without speaking, as if fascinated by the ripening pears as she tottered on four-inch heels.

"How much do you think that dress costs?" Stasia whispered in Merle's ear.

"Whose?"

"Gillian's. I saw it at Fashion Week. It's couture, some Italian designer."

"Looks expensive."

"Pucci. That's it."

"Really? I thought he did all those blocky, colored things."

"Look at you, fashionista. That's why this dress stood out. Isn't it divine? I checked it out at Bergdorf's. I lusted after it." They watched Gillian move carefully over the dirt, bending to sniff the roses. The black lace seemed to glow. The dress *was* kind of amazing.

As assistant managing editor at *Gamine*, a trendy women's magazine, Stasia had access to all sorts of insider perks. Last winter, she'd arrived at Merle's with an armload of sweaters and let her take her pick. "Wouldn't *Gamine* give you one?"

"Are you kidding? I can't believe she has it. Of all people." Stasia leaned closer. "Way too pricey. Eight-thousand."

Merle sloshed her wine. "Dollars?"

"I have a personal limit for a single item. Kinda way over."

Merle stared at the dress. It fit Gillian like a glove. Those shoes look spendy too. Who would pay eight-thousand dollars for a dress? "She must be making some serious cash," Merle muttered. But Stasia had moved away to talk to Elise. Their youngest sister was already on her second glass of wine. She'd twisted her ankle the first day out, not bad enough to stop walking. No one saw any swelling. But Elise took it as a sign of doom. She used to be such a sunny person before she went to law school.

Wine and *Franglais* flowed freely at dinner between Valerie, Albert, Tristan, the sisters, Josephine, and Gillian. Josephine wore her ever-present pearls and brought a huge terrine of cassoulet rich with duck sausage. Not a usual summer dish, she explained, but one she'd made so often she could make it with her eyes shut. They were all sated with food and wine when Gillian stood up, clinking her glass with her knife.

"Thanks for dinner. It was good." She nodded gravely at the old people. Merle blinked, fatigue slowing her reflexes. Was Gillian making a speech? "I can't go to that church or whatever it is you've cooked up for tomorrow." She looked at Albert. "We found this little dog, hurt, by the side of the road today. He's in a village with an old lady. I don't trust her. I have to go get him."

She sat down abruptly. Francie recovered first, sitting on her left. "I'll go with you. I don't think I can stomach another church."

"I found him. I want to go by myself."

She glared at Francie who blinked, confused. "I didn't—"

"I'll go, and Valerie can too. I love dogs," Tristan said, carrying dirty plates.

Valerie pouted. "I am to leave tomorrow. Back to Paris."

"Well, I can go. Can I go, Mom?"

Gillian folded her arms. "I don't need anyone to go with me. I just need to use the rental car." She looked up at Tristan, appraising his worthiness or manliness or something. Merle felt a shiver. Gillian squinted against the candlelight. "All right. He can go."

Rapport de Police, Midi-Pyrénées. 18 June.

M. Jean Poutou, resident of St-Paul, Lot, called to report a stolen dog. Poutou, age 82, was confused and upset. Wailing heard in the background. Claims expensive dog used for truffle hunting was released from its pen and taken from grounds. Unsure of date of incident, possibly as long as three days ago. No explanation for why dog was unattended for such a long time. Dog belongs to grandson not currently on premises and has imbedded ID chip (dog, not grandson.) Advised that *les policiers* do not look for lost dogs and to call insurance agent.

Patrick Girard, Commissariat de Police, Toulouse

In the Italian Piedmont

Bettina Dellepiane arranged her silver hair in the intricate way she always did, sitting at her dressing table. She lowered her arms and sighed, peering into the mirror. The lines on her face were deeper. She hadn't been sleeping well. Worry about the business had reached a pitch that it buzzed in her ears all day and night: Bankruptcy. *La Famiglia.* Land gone. Legacy lost.

She must save it. It was on her own neck that things had taken such a turn. She had mismanaged, miscalculated, or something. She had no choice. That hurt the most, that because of her actions, her grandchildren might never experience the richness of this beautiful country with its oaks and olive trees, never take their own children by the hand and trek with the dogs in the age-old treasure tradition that was *ricerca del tartufo*, the truffle hunt.

She stood, straightened her old back, and went to work on the accounts. The sorting sheds were silent now. The truffles would not come for several months, depending as always on the weather. What if the land was depleted? Truffles took years to mature, to acquire that unique pungency, the flavor of the woods. The inferior Chinese truffles that some *tartufai* mixed into their bags proved that. And the ridiculous Americans who had begun seeding oaks in that country: they made her laugh. Their great-grandchildren might benefit.

At mid-morning she sipped an espresso and stepped into the sunshine. A warm breeze blew down from the hilltop. When the telephone rang, she shook herself out of a reverie of days past, her husband young and vibrant, her boys tumbling and playing, the dogs of legend, straining leashes at the scent.

"*Signora,* we have bad news."

Bettina closed her eyes. "*Sì?* Tell me."

"The dog has escaped. We will find her but it will take longer. We know where she went."

Maldestro idiota. Maybe she was the idiot to think those two olive pickers would come through. She had given them five-hundred euros that she'd never see again. She remembered the rheumy eyes on the one called Hector, the twitch in the unshaven cheek of gimpy Milo. They were *difettoso*—defective.

She felt her temper rise and let out a curse. "And how will you find it?"

"The microchip. It sends a signal. We must buy a gadget, what do you call? We will need money for that. We—what's that?"

Milo, talking in the background. Curses flying.

Hector returned. "*Mi dispiace, signora.* The chip is gone. Milo removed it so the owners could not trace the dog."

Bettina sat heavily on a hard chair, staring at the phone before putting it back to her ear. She had been so desperate for a good dog. She promised them five-thousand euros if they brought back an excellent truffle dog, one she heard about last year. Two days before, they had been successful. Her hopes had risen. It was not right, stealing, but for the cause of saving the estate for the grandchildren, a necessary evil. And now this. It was hard to see this as anything but the end of *la famiglia.*

"She can't go far, *signora.* She is a little thing. Good nose, but small and skinny. A highly trained dog, the best, all the people say so. We will find her. You can count on us."

4

A horn honked insistently on rue de Poitiers. Merle was upstairs, catching up on email. She frowned at the noise. Finally, she walked to the front window and opened the glass panes wide. The little blue Renault they'd rented in Bordeaux was parked on the street below. Gillian sat behind the wheel, jamming on the horn. She looked up, saw Merle, and stuck her head out the window.

"Come on. We have to get the dog to Bergerac before they close. Hurry!"

Minutes later, having scooped up her translator, Gillian flew out of Malcouziac, skidding tires on the cobblestones. Merle hung on to the Renault's door handle as they jack-knifed onto the narrow highway, a road built for oxen. Tristan slid across the back seat with the dog in his lap.

"I'm going to get sick as this dog if you keep that up," he said. Gillian slowed but rapped her fingers on the steering wheel nervously. The story emerged that they'd found the dog feverish and limp and felt it was their duty to rescue her from the clutches of the evil nurse. Beyond that neither Tristan nor Gillian appeared chatty so Merle just waited until they reached Bergerac. The industrial town on the plains of the Dordogne probably wasn't listed as one of the Beautiful Villages of France, but its commerce was decent. And they had veterinarians.

It was nearly noon when they reached the office of Jules Fabien,

Docteur en médecine vétérinaire, in an old building in the center of town. Much of the old town had been demolished years before, but his building looked medieval with whitewashed stone and red shutters. They double-parked and rushed inside with the dog in Tristan's arms. An old woman with a tiny white Bichon let out a squeak and clutched her puppy to her breast.

Merle rang the bell. When the assistant showed up things went surprisingly fast. They were whisked into an exam room where the veterinarian saw them within minutes. The French did love their dogs. And their sacred lunch breaks which often lasted until three. The vet was adamant: they must leave the dog, and she must have IV antibiotics for the infection. Gillian looked distraught, hugging the animal, but agreed.

They found a café with outdoor tables three streets over in an old square and ate hearty country lunches, their appetites spurred by the morning's drama. *Salade paysanne,* the enormous peasant salad with meat and eggs for Merle, plus a glass of rosé and an omelet for Gillian. Tristan made quick work of his *croque monsieur* and fries. By two they were back on the road. The sisters were already back from their excursion to see an enormous clock in a nearby cathedral.

Gillian parked the rental car and glanced at Merle. She seemed reluctant to trust anyone, and now she had to accept both the vet's advice and Merle's translation. "What did he mean that she was near death?"

"I think you got her there just in time. She had a high fever and the wound was infected. That's why they put her on the IV."

"It was such a small wound. Was it an accident? Could he tell?"

Merle hadn't translated that part for her. She wasn't sure she heard it right at the vet. But a quick check in her French/English dictionary proved she wasn't wrong. They stepped into the street. Merle looked at Gillian sympathetically. "He thought it might be a gunshot wound."

"What? Who would—?" Her eyes welled. She ran into the neighbor's house, her hand over her mouth. Tough-as-nails Gillian seemed the last person to cry on this trip. Some of her sisters were well-known for tears. Tristan watched, eyes wide, as Gillian slammed the door and disappeared.

"Did she run over her dog or something?"

Merle put her hand on his shoulder. "I have no idea."

The front door was open wide again and the sound of voices came from the garden. Someone had dusted and rearranged the chairs. A vase full of fresh flowers dressed the heavy dining table. Tristan flopped on the sofa, making it squeak, and pulled out his summer reading. *Catcher in the Rye* was on the agenda.

"Holden Caulfield. What a douche," he declared.

Stasia stood in the kitchen doorway with a strange smile. "Got something for you. Come on." She grabbed Merle's hand and pulled her out toward the garden.

She saw the black T-shirt first and stumbled on the gravel. He had his back to her, waving his hands while talking to Francie and Annie. Francie was giving him full-on, cleavage-baring attention until she saw Merle. Then she smirked, straightening.

He turned, smiling. Pascal looked exactly the same, as if a year hadn't passed since they were in this garden together. His black hair still curled over his collar, his jeans still fit, and his sunglasses were parked on his head, holding back that lock that always fell across his forehead.

He stepped toward her, taking her shoulders in his rough hands. "My little blackbird, you flew home." He leaned in to kiss her cheeks, not twice, but three times. She counted.

His voice cut through her like a warm knife. She'd spoken to him a few times over the winter but the conversations were always short. He was working on a big case, she needed to be somewhere. There was never time. And what could they talk about? They hardly knew each other.

But if the physical reaction her body was sending was a clue, that didn't matter. Oh holy Jesus. James was coming in a few days. And here was last summer's *l'aventure* in all his Yves Montand, swarthy, earthy Frenchness. She couldn't speak.

Annie came to her rescue. "Pascal was telling me and Francie about the night the thieves tried to steal your wine, Merle. You forgot a few details when you told it."

Francie's eyes fluttered. "Wow, Merle. You saved the day."

"It wasn't really—" Her voice caught.

"Yes, it was." Pascal took her hands. "You look fantastic, Merle. Your hair has grown. I like it."

She pulled her hands away, embarrassed. Her sisters watched like cackling vultures. "You, ah, too. Are you back in town?"

"For a few days. Annie didn't tell you?"

Merle squinted at her oldest sister. Her wavy, graying hair was threaded with lavender blossoms like a hippie princess. She wore a white peasant blouse with cargo shorts and seemed quite pleased with herself. "She forgot to mention it."

"What kind of wine do you have, Merle? Never mind, I'll check." Annie launched herself toward the house. "Francie, get glasses. Stace, do we have olives or something? Let's celebrate. Pascal is back!"

After they disappeared inside, Pascal took Merle's hands again, smiling. "Charlie's angels are on the case."

She rolled her eyes. "More like herding cats. Annie invited you?"

His lip twitched. She'd forgotten about that, a sly, endearing smile revealed in a tiny twitch. "Are you mad?"

"No, of course not."

"But you didn't tell me you are coming to France."

"I'm sorry. I know." She looked up at his face and couldn't resist touching his chin. A three-day beard, scratchy, flecked with gray. "Things are complicated."

"Are they?" He kissed her quickly on the mouth. "I hadn't noticed."

He was pulling her close for a serious kiss as Tristan's voice broke in. "Pascal! You're here, man!"

They spent the afternoon drinking wine and getting caught up on the legal woes of the thieves from last summer. One was in a French jail, one in a British one, one got a slap on the wrist and lost his job as mayor. That news, that the awful mayor of Malcouziac had only lost his job, that nothing could be held against him, made Merle's blood boil. He was the sort of slippery, corrupt elitist she had way too much experience with in New York.

"Is he still around here?"

"I believe so. I've been on the Côte d'Azur most of the winter." He smiled smugly. "It's a tough life."

"What about the sister of the vineyard owner?" Merle asked.

"She got a short sentence," Pascal said. "I think she runs the vineyard now. She was able to hang onto it."

"How did she manage that?"

"We are keeping an eye on her," He patted Merle's arm. "A strong sense of justice, this one. But all the sisters are lawyers. You are all this way?"

"She's the worst," Elise said. "Everything is black and white with Merle."

"That's not true," Merle protested.

"Remember the time Elise stole a piece of candy from Nelson's Store and you made her march back and pay for it?" Francie asked.

"She cried the whole time," Stasia said.

Francie giggled. "And wet her pants!"

"You had to carry her," Annie said.

"By her heels," Stasia laughed.

"I was only three," Elise said. She threw her hair back and stuck her chin out. "You were meaner than Mommy, Merle."

And you were the baby. Merle looked into her wine glass. She wasn't going to be drawn into an argument, especially in front of Pascal.

"You know what they say," Annie said. "It takes a village."

"Takes a village for what?" Pascal asked.

"Never mind." Merle stood up, grabbing his hand. "Come on. I miss my long walks already."

The alley sported a mossy strip down the middle, so neat and tidy. Merle was still holding Pascal's hand. It reminded her of his work on her roof and in her bed. Like its owner it was hot, muscular, and a little rough around the edges. She stopped abruptly, facing him.

Pascal had put his sunglasses on. He skidded to a stop and looked over them, his dark eyes flashing under unruly eyebrows. "Everything okay?"

Merle took a breath and looked at her feet, trying to process what was happening. Should she tell him about James? Did it matter, really? She would be here for nearly three weeks. Pascal—who knew? Days, hours? James had insisted on coming against her advice. Should she feel flattered he couldn't stay away or annoyed? Then there was Gillian, also uninvited. And Pascal, in all his manly now-ness. Holiday crashers all.

His hand cupped her cheek. "What is it, *mon petit merle?*"

She thought of the things she should say: her sisters, the togetherness, the bickering, the love she felt for them, the interloper, the walking, the stray dog. Tristan, growing up too fast. Her job, demanding all her energy and dwindling charm. She wanted to tell him all of it, but it was too much. Time had gone by and here they were again, alone together, two strangers in a small town in France.

She bit her lip and looked into his brown eyes. They were just as warm and open as she remembered. What else could she say?

"I've missed you."

LAWYRR GRRL

WHERE A WOMAN CAN GRROWL ABOUT THE LEGAL PROFESSION

BLOG—That Girl
Tagged *vacation, blisters, wine, whine*
Posted June 18

Turns out there is an extra along, not just the five sisters. It's a dog! Found by the side of the road, injured, and suddenly we are the Doggie Samaritans. Is anyone more dog-crazy than Americans? A brown-and-white mutt, filthy, whiny, and bleeding: what a pathetic sight. But the Sisters have come to the rescue like the angels of mercy we are.

Plus That Girl.

Yes, a real sixth wheel. One of the sisters invited along a friend. A law colleague. What was she thinking, throwing the poor thing into the cat house like an injured mouse? She seems capable enough but the girl is not a mixer. Doesn't even try. And by now she's alienated even the nice sisters. (The not-so-nice sisters took against her from the start.)

To be fair to the sisters, That Girl has made her bed. She's not warm or friendly in the least. And so private it makes you wonder what she's hiding. Hard worker and all that, always walks the fastest, but standoffish. Turns out she's really into lost dogs, so how bad could she be? The sisters should warm up to her, if she ever gives them the chance. Right now she's off somewhere moping.

Oh, wait. Drama ensues. Oldest sister, rock of flippin' Gibraltar, has just raised her voice. She's the calm, Zen sister no more. She is calling out another sister for whining. Love it! I see tears coming! Now she's calling out another sister for being bossy. Another one is getting it for inviting That Girl along and messing up the 'delicate karma of sisterhood.' The last one gets it for something lame, can't even be bothered to repeat it. Just equal opportunity ragging.

A hush falls over the crowd.

Then somebody opens a bottle of wine and it's over.

Texts between Annie Bennett and her father, Jack.

Annie: *Find out anything on Gillian Sargent? She's messing with my head. Got a contact at Ward & Baillee?*

Jack: *From the website: Colorado Law, 98. Playing golf with attys on Saturday. Will ply with liquor. Jack, Ace Detective*

Jack: *Finally got a source at W&B. Somebody there dubbed her 'The Girl in the Empty Dress.' Nobody knows a damn thing about her.*
Curiosity piqued. Background check?

Annie: *Hold off. She hasn't done anything*

And one from Francie.

Francie: *M&D: Why didn't you tell me about Camembert? You've been holding out on me! Thinking of cheese biz. My friend Gillian is driving us crazier than we are already. Must drink wine to hold tongues! Sisters having fun!*

Bernadette: *Remember, dear, cheese is very binding. Mother.*

5

The market at Uzès was bustling in the morning sun, red umbrellas lining the sidewalks to the Place des Herbes, the central square. Vegetables, nuts, spices, bread, sausage, and a vast array of clothing, dishes, and souvenirs beckoned to the two middle-aged men. Hector loped slowly by the stands, dragging his worn boot heels, hands in his baggy trousers. Everywhere he turned, the Dutch: tall blond people with small, blond rug rats. Milo munched on a *croissant chocolat* and complained about the heat.

It took them thirty minutes to determine that no one was selling truffles. Wrong time of year. Truffle-hunting was a winter sport and most markets ran January to March. The markets at Lalbenque and St.Paul-Trois-Châteaux had been equally disappointing. Tourists everywhere, Hector thought, spitting out the stub of his cigarette. Nothing but tourists.

If only they could speak to a single *truffière*. The truffle hunters were a close-knit and closed-mouth bunch. But they might gossip about a dog on the loose. But the markets were hopeless, endless stands of tablecloths, *courgettes*, and old shoes.

Milo wanted a beer. The heat was wicked and he was parched but Milo must not have a beer. Hector bought him a bottle of water and led him back to the truck.

Driving north, Hector looked for the dog along the roadsides. She would be injured, bleeding, thanks to Milo. She couldn't go far. He kept to the secondary roads, winding around the hills, along the rivers. Milo began to snore.

It took several hours to get to Sarlat. Crowds at the market had thinned but it was still lively. Again no truffles for sale. Such a specialized product, one mushroom seller told him. So pricey. Ask the duck and goose people.

One seller of *foie gras* remained in his stand under a large, green canopy. He was an old man with scarred hands from handling temperamental fowl. The drawing of a fat goose hung on a mural behind him. Hector waited for him to sell a small tureen and three jars of *foie gras* and duck *confit*.

"Excuse me. *Bonjour, monsieur.*" Hector doffed his cap and waved toward the mushroom merchant. "*Monsieur des cèpes* has advised me to ask if you have heard anything of my poor dog. My little Julie was taken from her pen. Did you hear of it? My truffle dog was stolen."

The old man's wrinkles deepened around his eyes. He squinted at Hector and Milo. Not his usual customer, no tourist or rich *Parisienne*. He wore a Greek sailor's cap and a dirty navy blue apron over his white shirt. His jowls were legendary, as were his forearms, exposed with turned-up cuffs, muscular and hairy. Milo was coughing into a dirty handkerchief. When that was over, the old man eyed Hector.

"I hear things."

"I'm afraid someone will try to sell her. She is one of the finest noses—*plus coûteux*—in the Dordogne. In France! Tell me. Where was she seen?"

The old man crossed his arms, taking another look at Milo then back at Hector's sweat-stained striped shirt and dirty hands. "You are the owner then?"

"*Oui, oui.* I have been searching for her day and night. I am most anxious."

"*Quel dommage.*" *Too bad.* He shrugged and turned his back.

Hector's hopes sunk. The old man didn't believe him, the hard country nut. He reminded Hector of his grandfather, gnarled, suspicious, and coldhearted. Where could he try next? Périgueux? It was nearly four o'clock. It would be another night on the ground under the truck. At least they still had a few of the *signora's* euros to get a decent meal.

Then the old man was back. He stood across the table full of preserved duck and liver of goose, a sheet of blue paper in his hand. Hector reached for it as the old man asked, "How much will you offer?"

In large, black lettering, the paper announced a reward for a truffle dog stolen from a farm. A grainy photo showed her from the side, ears flapping in a breeze. There she was, the scrawny, whimpering mutt they had held in their arms three days before. The one who had wiggled the latch on the crate while he and Milo drank a few celebratory Kronenbourgs.

RÉCOMPENSE [REWARD]
Chien Volé [Stolen Dog]
'Aurore'
10,000 €
Pas des questions [No questions asked]

Milo clucked. He could only read the numbers. "Ten-thousand?"

"When did you get this?" Hector asked the old man.

"Yesterday. The owner was desperate. His grandson raised the dog, trained her himself. He can't afford that much but he has no choice." He squinted at Hector. "And now your dog, also stolen. Must be a ring of thieves."

Back in the truck Milo asked Hector what the old man said. "But that is more than the signora will give us. Much more."

"*Sì, sì, sì.*"

"What should we do?" Milo poked a stubby finger at the sheet. "He pays much more. Will the *signora* be offended? I never cared for her myself. Beautiful, yes, but, *pffft*. She is a miser with the wages."

Hector started the truck. "Stop babbling. Let me think. I am the thinker. When I decide, I will tell you."

Ten thousand euros. The money was in his mind, in his hands, already spent.

6

Bettina Dellepiane learned the news that same day through the world of truffles. There were only a handful of operations like hers, owners of truffle grounds who were also buyers, sorters, and distributors. One was her neighbor and fierce competitor, Gianluca Gribaudi. That he was her late husband's distant cousin was perhaps inevitable; the family owned all this land at one time.

Gianluca and her Furio never were friendly. There had been a feud when they were boys with lingering bad feelings. So it was suspicious when Gianluca drove his new black Land Rover onto the courtyard that afternoon as the sun beat hard on the gravel. Bettina re-pinned a loose strand of hair as she watched his quick, happy step toward her door.

She smiled at him. "Come inside out of the heat."

He kissed her cheeks. "How are you, Bettina? Are you well? I've not seen you for many weeks."

Months, to be sure. Since the harvest fair in March. His white hair was thick and swept back from his tan forehead now creased with lines. He was still proud of his physique, the way he hitched his pants to show his prowess. He wore fancy sunglasses, a pressed purple shirt, white linen slacks, and leather loafers. He smiled at himself in the mirror in the hall.

She ushered him into the parlor and offered him a glass of chilled wine. Was he just being polite by this visit or did he hope she had taken ill and would sell out? She didn't trust a word from his mouth. He made small talk about the weather and the price of truffles. He inquired about the grandchildren. When she had poured each of them a tiny glass of wine, he got to the point.

"I heard your beloved Pompeo has gone." He sat forward, eyes sad. "I know how hard that is. My sincere condolences."

Bettina felt the loss of her dog once more, like a knife. Pompeo had been her faithful partner for twelve years until the cancer came. The best dog, best friend, best truffle hunter: *il suo buon tartufaio.* He softened the loss of dear Furio and made every day sunnier. She couldn't cope with putting him down, but in the end, she couldn't watch her loyal companion suffer either.

She gathered herself. "It's been two months. Time heals the wound." She sipped a little wine. "But I appreciate your sentiment, Gianluca." Even so late, she did.

"Has it been so long as that?" His hand flew to his heart. "I apologize. I should have come sooner."

She gave him a conciliatory smile. He was probably too busy celebrating the loss of her money-maker. Pompeo's nose was known far and wide. Gianluca had many dogs but none in the same league as her Pompeo.

"Have you looked for a new dog?" he asked. She nodded. "And—success?"

"I've seen a few. But none close to Pompeo."

"An impossible standard." His extravagant eyebrows twitched. "I wonder. Pardon. I thought it might be too soon but since you say it is two months... I saw this in the village and thought of you."

He extracted a white sheet of paper from his pocket and unfolded it. Smoothing it against his knee, he passed it to her. A photograph she had seen before on the Internet in an article about top truffle dogs. The sheet, from the *Ente Nazionale per la Protezione degli Animali* and the *Carbinieri*, announced a reward for a dog stolen in France. She read the name and felt a chill of fear. She straightened her back and turned to Gianluca, arranging her face.

"What do you suggest?" She tried to laugh brightly. "That I go searching in France for this dog?"

He smiled. "No, no, Bettina. But you could contact this owner. Offer to pay the reward and buy the dog in one single step."

She glanced again at the picture of the dog. She had already done that, more or less. Carefully, hand shaking, she passed the sheet back. "I don't think so. But a very creative idea. Very creative indeed."

"Please, keep it. Maybe you will change your mind. I have heard of this dog. They say she is very capable."

He didn't stay long, sensing perhaps she wanted to get rid of him. As she closed the door, she fell against it in anguish. The owner was offering twice the money for Aurore. Her olive pickers would know this by now. She must call them right away before they found the dog and returned it to the owner.

Her forehead thumped against the solid old door. She cursed Gianluca, then Furio for leaving her with this. How dare he die so young? She let out a little groan. How was she to come up with ten thousand euros? Because there was no other solution now.

7

Tristan arranged the pillows in the basket, gently setting the dog's head on a pink velvet heart that Valerie had left with Albert. She was still weak, her leg bandaged, but she looked better. Her tail thumped as he patted her head.

"Don't worry," he whispered to her. "I'll take good care of you."

Behind him the women were arguing. Gillian had her hands on her hips and a scowl on her face. "I don't see why you want the dog over here. I can take care of her better than any of you. I know how to give pills to a dog."

"Honestly, Gillian," Francie said. "It's not rocket science. A little peanut butter and you're good to go."

"You think you can find peanut butter in this village?" Gillian said.

"Nutella," Annie suggested.

Merle said, "Actually the vet said cheese, which we have in quantity. I already gave her a pill. She likes gruyère." She looked at the basket her son had set up in the corner of the main room. A shaft of sunlight warmed it. The dog looked comfortable, clean, and well-loved. Why was Gillian making such a fuss? She seemed to have two settings: silent and brooding or hot and bothered. "Besides, we don't have permission to have a dog at Yves and Suzette's."

Tristan stood up. "I don't care if you give her the pills, Gillian. All I want is for her to get better." Merle smiled at him. Somebody had to be an adult here.

Gillian had her dark hair pulled into a ponytail. She wore a short khaki skirt that exposed her muscular calves with a black T-shirt covered with white hairs from holding the dog in the car. She'd been frantic to get the dog back this morning, talking the vet into releasing her into their care.

She tossed back her hair and sniffed. "That's all I want too. Of course."

"The vet told me something different today, Gillian, about the wound." Merle had her attention now, bright, dark eyes. "It wasn't a gunshot wound."

Gillian melted a little, relieved. "What was it?"

"It was too small for a bullet," Merle continued. "But it wasn't an accident. Based on where the wound was, the size and depth of it, he thinks it was a computer chip. An identification chip."

"Someone took it out?" Gillian asked.

"And not very neatly," Merle said.

"Eeeeuw," Francie squealed helpfully.

"If he's right," Merle said, "she was probably stolen. The chip was removed so the owner couldn't trace her."

"So she's a girl dog?" Elise was kneeling by the basket, petting the dog. "Poor baby."

"The vet told us. We've never had a dog. Are you leaving tomorrow for the next part of the walk, Mom?" Tristan looked at his aunts gathered around the living room, eyes twinkling. "Because I can hang here and take care of Tartuffe." He flashed his boyish smile. That smile was the only thing of Harry Merle saw in her tall, lanky son. "That's what I named her. Tartuffe."

Gillian blinked. "You named her?"

"Sure. Why not?" Tristan went back into his crouch by the basket.

Gillian let a *hmmph* escape her mouth and rolled her eyes. Annie said, "Let's not fight over a dog. Please."

"We're not fighting," Gillian said, still very much in combat mode. "We're discussing what's best for the dog."

"We don't have to call her 'the dog.' Tartuffe," Tristan said. "Like the play."

"That's one of those silly French farces, isn't it?" Elise said. "With slamming doors and love affairs and people who aren't who they say they are?"

"I am *not* calling her Tartuffe," Gillian said to no one in particular.

"We're leaving in the morning, right?" Francie asked, clapping her hands. "Should we pack?"

Stasia looked fierce. She hadn't been arguing but she clearly wanted to. Merle asked her, "Do you think we could delay one day? Just to make sure everything goes all right with the dog?"

"I can't believe you brought the dog back here." Stasia gave Gillian, then Merle the power of her disapproval. "She doesn't belong to you, to any of us. The vet could have found the owner. The *rightful* owner."

Merle bit down on her molars. She felt a headache coming on, one that had been building since breakfast when Gillian demanded that they go back to Bergerac. "Can we put it off for a day, Stace?"

"I'll have to change hotel reservations, the bag taxi, the restaurants."

"It's only two nights," Annie said.

Gillian cleared her throat. "I'm not going. Why can't we just stay here? We've got a dog and a teenager to look after. I don't need to walk around France anymore. It was fun but I'm done."

They stared at her for a moment, this stranger in their midst.

"Thank God, the voice of reason," said Francie.

"You don't have to look after me," Tristan protested. "I can take care of myself—and Tartuffe. And Albert is right here."

A jumble of voices rose then: outrage, shock, hurt, curses. Stasia got right in Gillian's face and told her she could just go home if she didn't want to walk through France, that nobody wanted her on this trip anyway. Gillian told her to go stuff herself, that she'd do *what* she wanted *when* she wanted. Then Francie got in Stasia's face and said that she had invited Gillian and to be nice to her friends for a change. Annie separated them and told them all to calm down. Elise stood by, shocked and a little teary. Merle buried her face in her hands.

"Enough already," Annie said. Francie opened her mouth to say something and Annie wagged a finger at her. "Stop. This stops now. I shouldn't have yelled at you guys yesterday. I think I may have opened the floodgates of bitching. I apologize for that. We were doing so well before that."

"No, we weren't," Elise said, pouting.

Annie glared at her. "Yes, we were. We were having a helluva good time."

"We just weren't talking about it. It's good to get things out in the open." A tear escaped Elise's eye.

"Is it?" Merle murmured.

"You guys go back to the other house." Annie shooed Francie, Elise, and Gillian out the door. "We'll see you at dinner. We're going to that truffle restaurant at eight—what's it called?"

"*Les Saveurs,*" Merle said.

"Meet us there. We'll talk about our plans then."

Merle retreated to the sunny garden and sat down in her favorite place on the wall under the acacia tree. She felt limp. Her worst nightmare come true, the sisters finally get to go on a grown-up trip together and find out they can't stand each other. Maybe they should all just go home and pretend this never happened.

Yesterday with Pascal drifted into her mind, how calm and peaceful it was with him again, as if they'd never been apart. He didn't tell her anything about his year, the wife he'd left years before, his elderly father, his work as a policeman. After recapping the criminal histories of the villagers, he was quiet. He was just there. The constant barrage of talking, feelings to be tiptoed around, the petty grievances of her sisters were wearing her down. It didn't feel like a vacation, it felt like one long Thanksgiving dinner.

Would Pascal come to dinner tonight? He said he would but now she wondered if she should put him off. No outsider deserved this family mess.

Annie joined her on the low, bumpy wall. "That damn Gillian. She started this."

"Stace and Francie gave it a good go."

"I shouldn't have lost it yesterday. I wanted all of us to have a good time on this trip, to really enjoy each other's company."

"We are, Annie." Merle took her hand. "We will."

"Gillian's attitude is poisonous. Like she enjoys pissing us off. What's her deal? Do you know anything about her besides she works with Francie?"

Merle frowned. "She's from Colorado, I think. Why?"

Annie looked up at the sky. It was impossibly blue. "You know how sometimes I get vibes about people? The ones I've been getting from Gillian worry me. Her aura is brownish, which means negativity, distractions. I heard at Ward and Baillie they call her 'The Girl in the Empty Dress.'"

"What does that mean?"

"She's there but not there. Secretive. What's she hiding?"

"Did you ask Francie about her?"

"That went nowhere." Annie got up and sighed. "Is it Oh-Wine-Thirty yet?"

Stasia stepped outside when Annie went in for refreshments. She hung onto the back of a metal patio chair, looking sheepish.

"Are you okay?"

Merle nodded. "Don't worry about me."

"I'm sorry I lost my temper. We can change the dates. It might cost some money but of course we can change the reservations."

"We should just go. Take the hell off."

"You mean it?" Stasia sat on the wall in Annie's spot. "I really want to get out of here. Your little town is sweet and all. Mostly." She laughed. "But I love walking through the countryside. I didn't think I'd love it but I do. It makes me feel like a kid, walking to school on trails through the woods, looking at the flowers, watching the birds. It's kinda magical."

Merle took her hand. "It is. Let's do it."

Stasia frowned. "You think it's okay to leave Tristan with those cows?"

"I think he's safe. Why? Did he say something?"

"I just don't like Gillian. She's such a—a beeatch, as my kids say."

"Do you know anything about her background?" Stasia shook her head. "Forget about her. She's not going to ruin our vacation. We won't let her." Merle put her arm around her shoulders, feeling the tension there. Odd, and so right, to be reassuring her older sisters.

Stasia relaxed. "Where's Pascal? He's coming to dinner, isn't he? And if I haven't said it already, what a hottie. I totally get your little thing last summer."

"He'll be over soon. Try not to drool." Merle squeezed her sister's shoulder and looked at her watch. "Come on. Time to change."

At six everything was peaceful in the garden. Merle had changed into a skirt and tank top, using the lavender pashmina she'd brought for the plane as a shawl as she read her novel. Annie was still getting ready after collapsing for a short nap. Stasia sat across the green metal table in her sun hat. She loved the countryside but was deathly afraid of wrinkles. "TBB" is what Elise called her: tall, blonde, and bossy. But right now, she sipped her Pinot Gris and stared wistfully at the sky.

Tristan poked his head out the back door. "Mom, Pascal's here. And guess who he brought with him?"

She swiveled to see Pascal in a black dress shirt and jeans, his hair damp, talking over his shoulder to someone. She set down her book, pulling the shawl tight. What was this? She barely had time to think and there he was.

James.

"Oh, crap," Stasia whispered. "I forgot about Jimmy Jay."

Pascal clapped the other man on the shoulder in a friendly way. Merle felt whiplashed. How did—? Why was—? James carried a small red backpack and wore wrinkled khakis and a blue polo shirt with heavy underarm stains. He was six inches shorter than Pascal, rosy from the heat and a little fleshy. Mostly bald, in wire-rim glasses, he was laughing at something Pascal was telling him when he stopped in his tracks, gazing at the garden the way everyone did the first time.

"Well, I'll be a monkey's patootie. Look at this marvelous place."

James—Jimmy Jay to her sisters—retained his South Carolina drawl even after twenty years in New York. He worked at one of the white shoe law firms Merle solicited for Legal Aid. His firm had been very generous to the pro bono program. They'd been dating, if that was still the word for middle-aged people who went to dinner and the theater together, for three months.

Merle kicked herself into action. "James. How good to see you." She gave him a quick hug, blinking at his body odor. "I thought you were coming on the 25th."

"I know. But here I am in all my James Jeremy Silvers the Third-ness!" He lifted both arms wide as if estimating the size of a very large fish.

Pascal stared at him, dumbstruck. Stasia snickered behind her hand. This was one of James's favorite lines, a way to introduce his proud name and lineage. He always laughed afterward, like he was awkwardly doing now, as if it were a joke. He seemed so childlike, an undersized backpack dangling on his finger.

"Here you are," Merle said.

"I found him wandering in the streets," Pascal explained. "No French so no one would help him."

"Such a friendly little village," Stasia said.

"I rescued him from the clutches of the new *gendarme* who either knows no English or pretends."

As they poured wine all around, James explained that he messed up his ticket dates. His ex-wife used to make all the travel arrangements and now that he was on his own, the Internet had tricked him. "I know I put in the right dates but—" He shrugged. "Oh well!"

"You can come hiking with us tomorrow, James," Stasia suggested. "We're off to the east to see the River Lot."

"Hiking?" He laughed nervously.

Merle shot Stasia a look. She only smiled. "Merle is going. First thing in the morning."

"You're leaving?" James looked actually frightened. His travel ordeal must have involved more screw-ups than ticket dates and getting lost in Malcouziac. Merle had an impulse to fling him over the back wall.

"We'll see. We weren't expecting you, James."

"And we have plans. Reservations," Stasia added.

"Oh, don't change what y'all are doin' for me," he said, still with the scared rabbit look.

Pascal, a step behind him, gave Merle a mischievous smile. "I don't want you to leave either," he said. He moved closer to her, draping his arm around her shoulders. His voice was low and full of heat. "We have so much to catch up on, blackbird."

Merle was reaching behind his back to pinch him when Annie arrived in the garden.

"Oh, *Laws*. It's James." Around James she spoke with a low-country accent she'd gotten from some Nicholas Sparks movie. He didn't seem to notice. Her sisters mocked James mercilessly behind his back and to his face. Merle had brought him to a Mother's Day brunch. Her mother thought he was just grand. Love those southern manners, she had cooed.

Annie threw her arms around him and welcomed him to the village. "What a surprise."

"I'm early," James squeaked. He seemed smaller, deflated from his grand "here I am." He eyed the Bennett girls with new skepticism. Maybe it had dawned on him that they were teasing him. He was so far out of his league.

He ran his hand over his lips. "Can a thirsty traveler get another drink?"

They were a large group at dinner, sitting in sections. The younger girls sat at the far end of the table from the older ones, placing the men between them as a buffer. Just as well, Merle thought, she wasn't done being mad at Francie and Gillian. Pascal sat next to Tristan, Albert next to James. On Albert's other side was another newcomer, a young priest in his roman collar who was visiting Malcouziac, tall and a bit scrawny. Father Cyril was a former student of Albert's who now did a circuit of villages without their own priests. He seemed to be charming Francie and Elise.

Everyone had something made from black Perigord truffles, the delicacy of the area. Truffles shaved onto pasta, omelets with truffles, an enormous single ravioli stuffed with truffles and mushrooms, some sort of mashed celery root with truffles and a poached egg, almost anything imaginable. *Très cher, bien sûr.* Merle didn't have it in her, none of them did, to think about the cost tonight. Despite all their squabbling, everyone looked happy, even Gillian. Maybe they were wrong about her. Maybe she just needed a good French meal.

The two priests got up when Albert saw someone across the room. He introduced Father Cyril to several people before they rejoined them at the table for coffee and dessert.

James drooped closer and closer to his plate through dinner, his eyelids heavy. Pascal offered to walk him back to his hotel. James struggled to his feet and waved. He didn't bother speaking to or kissing anyone. The mood lightened, the younger girls laughing at something. No doubt at the expense of ol' Jimmy Jay.

Merle didn't care. She liked James. He was kind and thoughtful, like a sweet uncle who gives you presents. She laughed into her napkin at that thought and sipped more wine. She was a little buzzed. Annie said something about jet lag, "that despicable Yankee invention" in her low-country accent; Merle almost spit out her wine.

"So, Merdle," Stasia said, leaning close so that only Annie and Merle could hear. "How is Jimmy Jay in the sack? We're all dying to know."

Merle swatted her. "None of your beeswax."

"Come on, spill. We've got bets on the size of his—what do they call it in the South?"

"His pecker," Annie offered. "I've got ten bucks on three inches." She looked at Merle thoughtfully. "You haven't done it, have you? I don't blame you. He's a pathetic little turd with no doubt a tiny little johnson."

"Annie!" Merle swatted her too.

"You haven't? Really?" Stasia threw up her hands. "My bad."

Annie said, "What is he doing here anyway? He got his dates mixed up? I've never heard such a crock of shit. His hotel too? I don't think so."

Merle felt her face burn. They were right of course. James was polite. He gave her cheek kisses and held her hand to help her out a taxi. And that's all. She didn't think of him that way. What *was* she thinking, all these months, that suddenly she'd be attracted to him and everything would be fabulous? What the hell was she going to do with him here in France?

"Look what you've done," Stasia whispered. "She's going to cry."

Annie set her hand on Merle's arm. "It's okay, honey. We'll get rid of Jimmy Jay."

Did she want to get rid of him? Or did she just want to get rid of all of them and have some peace and quiet? She smiled at her two favorite sisters. That wasn't it.

"It's not James. It's all this bickering," she said. "And I'm not going to cry. It takes more wine than this." She held up her tiny wine glass and downed the last of a decent rosé.

"Then let's get out of here," Stasia said. "First thing in the morning, like you said. Leave Gillian and Francie and James and the fucking dog and hit the road."

"I want to. But I can't now."

"Jimmy Jay," Annie said.

Merle nodded. "But you guys go. Have fun. Take Gillian and Francie if you can."

"That's not likely," Stasia said. "Are you sure? I hate to leave Gillian with you."

"Are you kidding? Merle's the only one who can handle her," Annie said. Merle began to protest when she saw Annie smiling. "Pascal's back."

Stasia squeezed Merle's hand. "There. Things aren't as bleak as all that. You've still got the hottie."

Lawyrr Grrl

Where a woman can grrowl about the legal profession

BLOG—*The Cluster F**k*
Tagged *EVERYTHING!*
Posted June 20

You've been there, I know you have. The lawsuit that winds into a sticky gob of legal mumbo-jumbo, the negotiation that lasts seven days and seven nights while you exist on bad coffee and stale Twinkies, the simple case that peels like an onion into layers of misdeeds, lies, and malfeasance.

Yes, womyn, we can call it the Cluster Fuck. No ** required.

And so our little vacation in paradise-land has come to this: sister against sister, boyfriend against boyfriend, guest against host.

And I'm having a teensy meltdown. I warned you, didn't I? But I didn't see it coming until this morning. It was a late, boozy night after a crazy, boozy day. But we were rolling with it, most of us. After a long, delicious dinner, we went back to our host's lovely abode. Her garden is the center of the universe as far as I'm concerned. It smells like heaven and actually glows in the moonlight. If you stay in it too long, sparkles fly out your ass.

Well, it would be fun to give it a try.

As I was saying, we gathered in the garden, sated and happy after a three-hour dinner. Two priests came with us. One is retired, a neighbor, the sweetest man in the world. The other is fortyish, hunched over with a bald spot, but warm and friendly in that weak-chinned way. The young padre had some of the sisters spinning with laughter. He was new to our circle but we welcomed him with all our platonic grrlish charm.

Another new man came along, one sister's boyfriend, a local guy. I should say, *one* of her boyfriends, because a paramour from back home showed up today too. Yes, three new men in our Sisterhood Circle! This boyfriend back home, let's call him Homer. He went to dinner with us but he left early. We thought he'd gone to bed, exhausted from his long trip. A collective sigh of relief. Two boyfriends at dinner is one too many as I'm sure you're aware from your own adventures in romance-land.

Anyway, we're hanging in the magical garden around midnight, and the boyfriend from back home suddenly re-appears. Homer is stumbling, unsteady from sleep or jet lag or wine, who knows how he found the house in the dark. He lurches over to my sister and puts his arms around her, smacks her hard on the lips, and declares, "I need you. I want you. Come back to the hotel with me. I don't know what I'll do without you."

Then he starts to cry.

My sister stands there frozen with embarrassment and shock. She obviously doesn't want to go back to his room. Not only is he acting weird, he's an ass-hat. (Also a lawyer—redundant?) Local beau stiffens up as if to fight for her honor. She says she'll handle it while trying to pry Homer off her neck.

Homer babbles like a four-year-old idiot. Somebody asks if he's sleepwalking, he's that crazy-talking. Plus he is wearing pajamas. Blue stripes. And grandpa slippers.

I may have looked away for a second in embarrassment because the next thing I know, the young padre has jumped into the fray. He's trying to pull Homer off my sister. Homer spins, takes a swing, punches the nice young priest in the nose. Blood flies. Padre windmills back, catching Homer under the chin and sending him flying.

It was all quite thrilling.

Until, of course, everyone had to be cleaned up, sent home, and given a talking-to.

And then the morning comes. As it always does, whether you've got too many boyfriends, gone to bed too late, had too much to drink, or want the world to go away.

I am going walking today. Snap decision. Some of the sisters want to stay behind, but this menagerie of boyfriends, priests, dogs, and sisters is over the line. I usually embrace chaos, you know? That's why I'm a lawyrr. I love a hot mess. Then I can create order, put all to rights, find a speck of common sense in Crazy Land and build a case for rationality. But I went to bed last night and pulled the sheet over my head. I've had enough.

I don't know what will happen here today, but I'll be in the woods, pulling ticks off my scalp.

Sayonara, bitches.

8

Merle woke with the sun already streaming around the shutters, making golden stars on the peach walls of her bedroom. Annie was gone, her pillow cold. Merle looked at her watch. Eight o'clock already. She groaned, the headache that was yesterday pounding in her skull. Had James really thrown his arms around her and cried? Had he slugged that nice priest, Father Cyril? Today was going to be awkward. Maybe she'd just go back to sleep.

But duty called. Merle was nothing if not practical. Slipping into a cotton skirt and T-shirt, she pulled her dark hair into a band and pushed open the bedroom door. Stasia and Tristan were up. Their twin beds in the loft room lay rumpled. She went to the back window and looked down on the garden. Quiet for a change with the wisteria dropping purple petals in drifts. A wine glass sat abandoned in the dirt, stem snapped.

Merle tiptoed down the stairs. Tristan sat cross-legged on the floor by the dog basket, talking to his new best friend. What were they going to do with this dog? She slipped by him into the kitchen for coffee and fooled with the stovetop espresso maker, cursing herself for not getting the fancy electric one she'd coveted. While the water boiled, she poked her head out and asked Tristan where his aunts were.

"Next door, I think. They said they'd say good-bye before they took off."

Merle poured her coffee into a demitasse cup, splashed in a little cream, sprinkled some cinnamon on top, and walked out the front door. Elise, Annie, and Stasia stood in front of Yves and Suzette's charming house with its lace curtains and burgundy shutters. Their backpacks were on their backs, hiking boots laced, hats on heads.

A pang of regret, then anger, coursed through her. They were going without her. It sparked a childhood memory, an early hurt, when they all took their father to the train station without her. She was late, or sick, somehow left behind. They were a gang; she was the outsider, the tent pole to their tent, solid, dependable, and alone.

"Morning, sunshine," Annie said brightly. She gave Merle a hug. "Don't look so sad. We'll be back in two days."

"I wish I was going."

"There's still time," Stasia said. "We can wait."

Elise straightened her hat. "Francie's not ready yet."

"She's going?" Merle looked from sister to sister. That meant she would have to deal with Gillian on her own. And James. And Pascal. And Father Cyril of the Broken Nose. The coffee churned in her stomach. She threw back the last sip. If the sun hadn't been gleaming off the stone of the houses on rue de Poitiers, she would have sworn she'd felt the hand of doom.

"She changed her mind," Annie said. "Something about a cluster fuck."

"No idea what she's talking about," Stasia said with an eye roll.

"At least Gillian's not coming," Elise said. "So it should be fun for a change."

Stasia frowned. "I thought you liked her. You said she was interesting."

"I was just trying to be nice. Something you could take a lesson in, Stace."

"Don't start, Elise," Annie warned. "Did you have coffee yet?"

"You said we'd get some at the bakery. Why, am I caffeine cranky?"

"Yes, you are," Stasia said.

Francie burst out of the house. She wore zippered hiking pants and a bright blue shirt covered with pockets. Her auburn hair was tucked into girlish pigtails. She slung her backpack over her shoulders. "Whew. Sorry I'm late. Am I late?"

"You're fine," Annie said. "We better go." She turned to Merle. "You and Tristan have some fun. See you day after tomorrow. You have your cell phone, right?"

"Right." Merle tried to look cheerful. "Have a great time."

They turned and walked away. Stasia held her touring map in its plastic sleeve, studying it. Francie laughed, a high, joyful sound. Elise skipped, a girlish hop. Merle watched until they got to the corner, arguing, pointing east then west. Just before they disappeared, Annie turned back and waved.

As Merle turned to go back inside, Gillian opened the burgundy door. She was dressed as she'd been for the walking tour: safari pants with voluminous pockets, khaki shirt, and Aussie hat. No backpack, just her fancy camera slung across her chest.

Merle nodded, unable to think of anything to say. Gillian had managed to alienate the entire Bennett clan, not a small feat. She returned the nod without a smile, adjusted the camera strap, and stepped into the cobblestone street.

"I'm off to do some shooting around the village." She set her quick pace, arms swinging, marching down the street as if she didn't have a care in the world.

Merle watched her turn the corner. "Knock yourself out, girlfriend."

Pascal arrived while Merle and Tristan were watching the dog walk around the garden. She limped still but seemed more alert, eating a little leftover chicken. Merle was so glad for a friendly face she pulled Pascal to her in the kitchen. He responded as best he could, which is to say, he kissed her hard.

"Where is everyone?" he whispered, peering out the garden door.

"It's just me and Tristan—and the dog." An idea popped into her head. "What about last night? Wasn't that crazy?"

"I have been to check on Father Cyril at Albert's. His nose is as big as my fist."

"I can't believe James—" She shook her head. *No James, not now.* She smiled at Pascal and took his hand. "Do you have a couple minutes?"

They tiptoed upstairs and were naked in the time you can say "espresso." It was comforting to realize she hadn't forgotten the contours of his hips or the small scar on his neck. And he hadn't forgotten how to make love to an ancient woman now fifty years old. They giggled and shushed each other and lay spent and happy in the shadows of the shutters that lined the snow white sheets.

"I am so glad your Charlie's Angels have gone, blackbird," he said, nuzzling her ear. "They scare me."

She turned toward him and hugged his neck. He smelled like oranges and cigarettes. If only this could last. If only—

A knock on the door downstairs. She looked at Pascal with rounded eyes. It would be James of course, with his impeccable timing. She was so mad at him, for last night, for showing up in France at all, and early! What a—

"Mom?" Tristan, from downstairs.

She scrambled out of bed and stuck her head out the bedroom door. "Yes? Who is it?"

"It's the police."

"Madame."

The *gendarme* stood in the parlor. He was new and very young. Blond and peach-faced, he looked stiff in his navy uniform, fingering his cap. He rattled off something in French. Merle caught only "questions."

Pascal was tucking in his shirt when he arrived behind her. She checked her own buttons, having dressed in record time. "He has questions about last night. The priest."

Merle invited the policeman inside. They stood holding the backs of the dining chairs. The *gendarme* had a strange accent and Merle had trouble following him. Thank god Pascal was there.

"He'd like your version of what happened." Pascal then spoke to the *gendarme*, introducing himself as a *Policier Nationale* and also a witness to the incident.

"Ah, *bon*." The *gendarme* then turned to Merle, waiting.

"Tell him my friend James Silvers came here and—" What could she say? He was acting strangely? "And he was distraught."

Pascal translated. "He asks, was there an altercation?"

"Do you think Father Cyril has reported this already?" she asked Pascal. He nodded solemnly.

"It was an accident," Merle explained. "James was, um, hugging me. Father Cyril thought I was in some sort of trouble. It was a misunderstanding."

As she spoke Merle had second thoughts. James was hardly an innocent in this matter. What did he mean, coming around in his pajamas and making an ass of himself? As she listened to Pascal translate her words, she tried to find some explanation for James's behavior. And failed.

The *gendarme* nodded for her to continue. "Well, Father Cyril pulled James away and James reacted. By striking out. Then the Father responded with a blow of his own."

The *gendarme* asked another question. Pascal translated, "He asks, did James strike first?" then answered it himself. "*Oui.*" He continued, in French. "I believe the American had woken from a deep sleep and was confused. He was in his pajamas, walking the streets. Perhaps jet lag or wine was a factor. This was not his usual behavior. He is a lawyer from New York City, a civilized man."

The *gendarme* straightened, defensive. He said he didn't care what a man did at home; it was how he behaved in his village that counted. How he conducted himself on French soil.

"Ah," Pascal said. "*Votre ville.*" *Your village.*

The cop squinted now, looking at Pascal from head to toe as if that would intimidate him. He thanked them for clarifying the event, and said he would return if he had more questions. He asked where James was staying. Merle replied, "Hotel Quimet."

"Thank you," Merle said to Pascal after the door closed. "For speaking up for James. I don't know if I would have."

"Have you seen him today?"

She shook her head. "I thought I better let him sleep."

"The *gendarme* is probably headed straight to the hotel."

"He's a self-important little twatwaffle."

Pascal let out a laugh. "*C'est typique.* The uniform, the authority, it is everything to them. Still he is better than Redier."

Jean-Pierre Redier was the corrupt local *gendarme* from last year. Merle had put the mess behind her but her eyes went involuntarily to the stairway where he'd locked his handcuffs to her wrists.

"I'm sorry," Pascal said, reaching for her. "I shouldn't bring up bad memories."

"I never thanked you properly for fixing the bannister."

He held her to his chest. "Yes, I believe you have, blackbird."

They joined Tristan in the garden. The dog was walking carefully in the sunshine, lapping water from a bowl. Her son was beaming. "Look at her!"

"I'm afraid we will have to take her home," Merle said to Pascal. "Is that difficult?"

He shrugged. "A crate, a plane ticket. No problem. He is in puppy love, is he not?" He crouched down and gave the dog a toss of the ears. "Skinny thing. Is she eating?"

"Better every day," Tristan said.

"And what about you? Do you eat lunch these days?"

Tris grinned. "I'm a growing boy."

"Then come with us. I am taking your mother to lunch."

Her son frowned at the dog, reluctant to leave her. Pascal clapped his hand on Tristan's shoulder. "Bring her basket outside. She will bask in the sunshine."

They walked to a café off Place de la Victoire where on market day the stalls lined the ancient arched colonnades. It was Pascal's favorite place, shaded from the afternoon sun, secluded from the hubbub on the plaza. Three or four restaurants served coffee and lunch outside in the summer months there, separated by only a jute rope. Over here you could eat in peace and still see most of what was coming on.

As they settled into their seats, Merle spotted Gillian striding across the ancient stones of the plaza. She stopped to take a photo of the soldier's memorial then turned to look at the lunch crowd in the plaza cafés. She picked a restaurant and sat down at a table near the edge, setting her camera on the table.

Merle raised her menu, hoping Gillian didn't spot her. After they ordered, she risked a glance around Tristan. Gillian had her camera to her eye, taking shots on either side of her.

Pascal observed all this. "She didn't go with the Charlie's Angels?"

"She said she was tired of walking."

"She came over to see Tartuffe early this morning," Tristan said after glancing over his shoulder. "She said she was sorry about yesterday. The stuff about who gives the dog her pills. I let her give the morning cheese pill."

"You're very nice to her, Tris," Merle said.

"She's not so bad, Mom. The aunties are pretty mean to her."

"Are they?"

"The way Aunt Stasia was yelling? You know how bossy she can get—all, 'Do this, do that?' Yeah, they were really mean. I don't blame her for not wanting to go walking with them."

Merle looked over his shoulder again. Gillian had disappeared.

After lunch Merle decided she should check on James. Fortified with rosé, goat cheese salad, and two big, strong men at her side, she felt up to it finally.

Hotel Quimet was where she'd stayed when she first came to Malcouziac. It was a musty, provincial inn with yellow trim and dark interiors. But it was large enough to have a nice restaurant, one of James's requirements. They took the stairs to the third floor. Pascal knew the room from the night before.

Merle knocked. "It's me. Just checking on you, James."

The door flew open. He stood there in Bermuda shorts and a golf shirt, his hair damp and glasses fogged. He looked stunned.

"Are you okay?" Merle asked.

"Ah. I don't know." He looked behind him. His room was a wreck, clothes everywhere, bedding rumpled. "I'd ask y'all in but—"

"Let's go downstairs for coffee," Pascal suggested.

James found his sandals and they trooped down the stairs with its worn carpet and cigarette burns. Their table near the window overlooked geraniums in boxes and a narrow street. They all ordered coffee except Tristan, who got a chocolate mousse.

"Have you eaten?" Merle asked. She sounded like his mother.

"I just woke up," James said. He looked around the table. "I have this bruise here." He tipped up his chin. "Did something—?"

Merle looked at Pascal. "You don't remember?"

He shook his head. "And there's this." He showed them his skinned, swollen knuckles and looked at them anxiously. "Did I—? What happened?"

"You punched the priest in the nose," Tristan said cheerfully. "Wham, bam, thank you, *monsieur.*"

Merle touched Tristan's hand. James was speechless, a look of horror on his face. She asked, "You remember that Pascal walked you back here after dinner?"

James covered his eyes with a hand. The coffee and mousse arrived. He sipped his coffee. "You brought me back, right. Then I went to bed."

"Did you have more to drink? Or take something?" Pascal asked.

James's eyes flew around the room. "I remember I was lying in bed, worn slap out but too tired to sleep. I'd been up for thirty-six hours. I had this buzz in my ears." He rubbed his eyes. "Then, yes, I took a sleeping pill. Christine gave me a couple of hers. My ex-wife."

"Have you taken them before?" Merle asked.

"Never needed them. I thought I would need one on the flight but I just drank the free vodka in business class." He sipped more coffee. "The pill, of course. That's why I feel so groggy."

Pascal fingered his cup. "And why you were in your pajamas in Merle's garden?"

"I..." His mouth stopped working.

"And threw your arms around Mom's neck and cried," Tristan added.

"Oh God." James blinked rapidly.

Pascal crossed his arms. "What do you remember?"

He didn't recall it all but bits and pieces stuck in his mind. Wine at dinner, walking home, Merle's garden, his arms on her neck. He was embarrassed—mortified. They told him Father Cyril's nose was broken and that the police had been round. He turned white.

"Should I flee the country?" he asked Pascal.

Pascal's lip twitched. He was enjoying this, Merle realized. Her boyfriend's antics, highly entertaining to the old boyfriend. She looked at one, then the other. Pascal was not so old, maybe forty, she'd never asked. His black hair had two or three silver strands. James was two years older than she was. And the physical comparison between lean, tall, and handsome, to short, bald, and pudgy? Lopsided.

Pascal said, "I don't think that will be necessary."

"I've heard terrible stories about French prisons."

"Croissants limited to three days a week. Yes, it's a scandal. Don't worry. We do not put the peculiar or unruly in prison in France. We save that privilege for the truly bad."

James looked affronted. "Are you calling me unruly?"

"You wander the streets in your night clothes, enter a house uninvited, and strike a priest who is only trying to help the situation. What would you call it?"

Pascal glanced at Merle. She raised her eyebrows. He was pretty harsh to James who no doubt deserved it. He'd made an ass of himself last night, and her for that matter. But had Pascal gone too far? Time to apologize?

"What would I call it?" James repeated, sputtering.

The Frenchman looked at him evenly. "Peculiar?"

They ordered lunch to be sent up to James's room and left him to his own devices. He was rattled by the revelations of last night. As anyone who sleepwalks should be. He vowed to never take a sleeping pill again.

As they walked home, Merle realized James hadn't apologized. He had embarrassed her last night in front of her friends and relatives. He had suggested an intimacy that didn't exist. He had slugged a priest. He had walked around in his pajamas, a fact that was probably all over the village by now, the butt of jokes in every restaurant. Everyone would know about the priest's broken nose by Sunday mass.

Tristan said he was going ahead and ran off. Pascal took Merle's hand as they turned toward rue de Poitiers, and stopped near the arched gate in the *bastide* wall.

"I came by this morning to say good-bye. I'm off to St. Remy-de-Provence again."

She took his other hand. "It's not really St. Remy, is it?"

He laughed, his face cracking into a grin. "You know me too well, blackbird." He gave her a quick kiss.

Not nearly well enough. "Will you be back? I'm here for two more weeks."

"I will try. You know these investigations take time." Pascal investigated wine fraud, sometimes undercover as a roofer. A rooftop was a perfect vantage point to spy on vineyards.

"Will you call? I might need some virtual hand-holding."

He pulled out his phone. She gave him her new French cell number and he immediately sent her a text. "There. Now you can call. And never come to France again without telling me, blackbird."

He gave her a final hug and turned back toward the center of the village. She watched him stride across the cobbles, strong and purposeful. Would she see him again? Her heart rose in her throat. She had to hang onto that. Yes, she told herself. She would see him again, and more.

But first she had to deal with All This.

When Merle reached her house, Tristan was standing on top of the broken wall, looking out over the vineyards. Despite standing for centuries, defending the city against the English in the Hundred Years War and possibly the Cathars too, this section had surrendered to the vagaries of weather. Wind, rain, and cannonballs had dislodged the top of the wall. The big stones lay where they fell, littering the cobblestones, or were thrown over the side.

Her son had his hands on hips, surveying his kingdom. His cargo pants were dirty and worn, his T-shirt was stained. But he looked so happy.

He jumped down. "I couldn't get in. You locked the door shutters."

Merle frowned at her front door. The ill-fitting shutters, replaced last summer after the originals were ruined, were closed. Did she lock them? Maybe Pascal had done it. He was adamant about locking up.

She fiddled with her keys, looking for right one. But when she found it, she couldn't quite reach through the crack to get to the padlock. "Did we leave through the back?"

"No. Wait—because of Tartuffe?"

They walked down the street and up the alley with its funky moss strip down the middle. Josephine lived behind this wall to the left, near the corner, a few houses down from Albert, a pretty vine covering her back wall. Merle didn't know most of the neighbors. But as they approached their garden gate, Albert opened his and threw a plastic trash bag into the alley. He saw them and paused, a grim smile on his face.

"You have come to see Cyril?" Merle looked at Tristan and gave him a signal to go along. They stepped into his garden. Albert's plum tree was heavy with ripening fruit. On his patio table sat a coffee cup, a spoon, and crumbs.

"How is he?" Merle asked. They should have come earlier. So many "should have's" today. She'd been too busy having her way with Pascal.

Albert shook his head. "He did not sleep. Now finally he has relief from the pills and he rests."

"I am so sorry about all this, Albert. We've just been to see Mr. Silvers. He took a sleeping pill last night and it made him walk in his sleep. Not that it's any excuse."

The old man listened, nodding. "I see."

He was really upset with James, and by association, all of them. "Is there anything I can do for Father Cyril? For you? Please, tell me."

"The damage is done, I'm afraid. We must accept and move on."

Merle glanced at Tristan, imploring him for help. "James is really sorry, Albert," he said.

"Is he?" Albert sighed.

"He'll be here soon, Albert," Merle promised. They made their excuses and turned to leave, closing his gate carefully.

"He's pissed, isn't he?" Tristan whispered.

"I guess I would be too. Cyril was just trying to help and all he got for it was a broken nose."

"That hurts. I know." Tristan had his share of fights after his father died. "Do you think he'll forgive James? Albert, I mean. Father Cyril too. Aren't priests supposed to be all kind and forgiving?"

"We'll see." Merle unlocked their gate and handed the key to Tristan. "Lock up, then open the front shutters."

The garden had its normal air of safety and calm. Sunshine streamed down on the pear tree, lighting up the still-green fruit. Merle opened the spigot on the cistern and filled the watering can. She was pouring water on the roots of the pear tree when Tristan burst back outside.

"She's gone. Mom! Tartuffe is gone!"

Merle helped him look through the house in every cupboard and cranny. They pulled up the floor trap and went into the musty cellar just for good measure. No dog to be found. Her basket lay in the garden in the shade of the *pissoir* (which she really should start calling something more refined). Her water dish was gone.

Tristan was frantic, running through the house, up the stairs, back down. "Where could she be?"

"Calm down." Merle felt her own heart rate rising. "She can't have gone far with that leg. We'll find her."

"But how did she get out?"

"Maybe the aunties came back."

"Then where are they? Is there a note?"

Another round of panicked searching for a note. Nothing. They unlocked the garden gate again and went down the alley, knocking on each alley entrance. No one answered. They went around to the front of the houses and repeated the knocking. A few old ladies were home but no one had seen a dog. Josephine tried to get them to come in for cake and tea but they declined.

Reluctantly Merle knocked on Albert's front door. He made no attempt to look happy to see her. "Sorry to bother you again. We're looking for the dog. She seems to have escaped."

He hadn't seen her. He wished them luck, a glimmer of sympathy in his eyes. Tristan groaned in frustration and announced he was going to run around the village. He took off, skidding around the corner, arms flailing. Merle walked back to the house. She stepped inside, trying to think what could have happened to the dog.

Then she remembered Gillian. She'd probably taken the dog over to Yves and Suzette's. A surge of hope. Merle went back outside and tried the deep red front door. She knocked hard and called to Gillian. Pounded again. She ran back inside her house and upstairs, leaning out her bedroom window that overlooked her neighbor's garden. A small tree blocked most of the view.

She called again, "Gillian?"

Back downstairs she checked the cupboard, locating Yves's house key. Did Gillian have one? Merle knocked again at the burgundy door then unlocked it.

"Hello? Gillian, are you here?"

The house was quiet. Again Merle was struck with how chic and comfortable it was in its warm grays and jewel tones. When all this was done, next year maybe, she would ask Suzette to help her with her house.

Concentrate. Where was the dog? Tristan was going to be crushed if she was lost. She called out again, and again no answer.

Out the back door into the garden. Merle was sure she'd find them there. But the garden was empty too, a minimalist Parisian sort of mini-Tuilleries with gravel and trimmed shrubs. No flowers, no grapevines, no dog.

She squeezed her eyes shut. Her pulse pounded in her ears. If the dog was here, where could she be? Just to be thorough—and because she couldn't think of anything else to do—she went upstairs, looked under the beds, in the bathroom, in the closet. Maybe Tristan had found her wandering the plaza. Downstairs again, she headed back through the sitting room. On the glass dining table a small sheet of yellow paper flipped up and floated to the floor.

Merle & all:

I've taken the dog somewhere safe. Don't worry about her. She's fine with me. I've got her medications and her favorite gruyère. She's happy and walking well. Don't try to find us. It's best you leave this to me.

Gillian

PS: Had to take the car.

10

Merle sat at the scratched wooden table in the café, watching Tristan shove pepperoni pizza into his mouth. She'd brought him here to cheer him up, but it didn't seem to be working. The seesaw of teen emotions was stuck in the down position. He had been over the moon about the dog. The plans he'd made for her, the bed in his room, the yard. And now that she was gone, he was inconsolable. He didn't cry. He'd figured out the priorities for tears this year.

So many losses, so many surprises. School had been a mixed bag academically, possibly because he knew he was going to leave his prep school and move home. He knew some kids who attended Country Day: his cousins and some neighbors. But it would be a difficult transition at sixteen. They both knew it. It would be wonderful to have him living at home again, but he'd been thirteen when he left. But she couldn't fool herself into thinking it would be easy.

He wiped his mouth and polished off his Coke. He looked marginally better, making eye contact at last.

"How could she do that? What gives her the right?" He'd asked this about ten times already. He got his weakness for righteous indignation naturally.

"I guess she thought she had as much right to the dog as you did."

"Well, she didn't. She didn't take care of her like I did."

"No, she didn't."

"And I was the only one who was nice to her. Let me see the note again."

Merle extracted it from her purse. They'd read it, cursed it, and read it again. But one more time wouldn't hurt. Tristan smoothed it with his large palm. He leaned close, moving his lips as he read.

"What does she mean here? 'I've taken her somewhere safe.' Did something happen?"

"I don't know."

"The shutters were locked from the inside." Tristan frowned at her. "You didn't lock them."

"She might have done that out of courtesy." Not that "courtesy" and "Gillian" ever popped up together in her mind.

He hunched over the note again, ignoring the waitress even though she was young and pretty and giving him the eye.

Her boy was all grown up, tall with muscles from dunking the basketball and running cross-country, smart too, entering the science fair with complicated experiments she couldn't understand. Things that Harry was missing. It still made her sad, and she'd come to think it always would. No point in trying to erase what had happened. Harry's heart attack, alone at his desk, was nobody's fault. And maybe he wasn't the world's best husband. But he would be proud of Tristan today, just as she was. So she would be doubly proud for both of them. That was easy.

"Do you think Pascal can find her?" Tris asked. "Where *is* Pascal? We need him to get on this." He stood up, ready for action, and charged into the street.

After paying for dinner, she followed him outside. He asked her again, "Where is Pascal anyhow?"

"He had to go work on some police business."

"This is police business. She stole our car and our dog."

"Technically, she borrowed the car."

"Not really. And she didn't borrow the dog. She never said she was coming back. It's not like she asked permission. When you don't ask first, that's stealing, Mom." He handed Merle the note. "You should turn her in to the cops."

She had thought about that. Maybe tomorrow or the next day. Give Gillian a little latitude to return the car. Maybe she'd turn it in somewhere—anywhere—and it wouldn't be an issue.

"She'll probably wreck it and you'll have to pay for it," Tristan said as they walked home. The sky turned to flame, orange and pink, above the city walls. Couples, locals, and tourists walked arm-in-arm through the plaza, smiling. Merle wondered what it would be like to come here on vacation and enjoy peaceful evenings and sunlit days and have absolutely no drama.

"Mom! Are you listening to me?"

"Sorry. I was thinking about having a glass of wine when we get home and wondering if we have any of that Côte du Rhône left."

"You should be thinking about Gillian. And Tartuffe! And that stupid Renault. That's the problem here." He turned to her, frustration darkening his handsome young face. "Jeez, Mom, really? Wine?" He picked up his pace, leaving her behind with a huff of disgust.

Later that evening Merle took her glass of wine (the last of the Côte du Rhône) outside into the garden, along with her phone. Tristan was reading upstairs. He'd forgiven her for her wine but was still all for turning in Gillian to the authorities. Merle debated calling her sisters. They were having a wonderful time, she was sure, walking through the hills and woods and vineyards, and eating exotic meals at elegant restaurants. She didn't want to put a crimp in their fun. But Annie would be upset if she didn't call. Besides she needed advice about the car.

But Annie didn't answer. They were probably still out eating a late dinner, enjoying themselves with cognac and *crème brulée*. She sent a quick text saying Gillian had scampered.

Just after midnight a reply came from Annie.

Tris must be upset. I'll call tomorrow. All good here.
Francie got drunk! Stasia got a blister! Elise got a sunburn!

When James showed up about 1 a.m., Merle was still dressed, puttering around the kitchen. She peeked through the crack in the door shutters, making sure he was also dressed—in street clothes—and unlocked the padlock.

"Sorry. I know it's late," he said, rubbing a hand over his scalp. "My sleep's all messed up. I saw your light was on and thought maybe you were still up."

"Come in." She waved him through the door. "Do you want something? A glass of wine?"

"Oh no. I guess I better not." He looked around. "Are your sisters around?"

"They went on the walking tour. They'll be back day after tomorrow."

"You didn't go." He nodded, relaxing a little. That made Merle nervous. She could still feel those clammy hands on her neck. She didn't really think he'd do that again. But was it some clue to his psyche? His deepest desires? Ugh.

She led him out into the garden. It was still warm enough and the stars were bright. And the window to Tristan's room overlooked it. The light cast a square of yellow on the stones of the back wall. Merle pulled her shawl around her shoulders and sat under the acacia. James settled uneasily on the edge of a metal chair.

"Look, I—I want to apologize. For—whatever it was. It's sorta come back to me and I am awfully embarrassed. I don't know how it happened. I mean I do, but—sorry. It must have seemed pretty ridiculous for you too."

"It was," she said, not feeling particularly forgiving. "But the person you need to apologize to is Father Cyril."

"I know." He hung his head. "He didn't deserve that. He did swat me a good one in return though." He pointed to his chin. "Did I show you that?"

"Yeah, you did." In the mayhem about the lost dog, Merle had forgotten about James. She was a terrible host. "Did you eat dinner?"

"Oh, yeah, the food here is incredible. Everything they say is true." He smiled, bruises forgotten. "I went back to that truffle place. I had the duck and mushrooms, to die for. I wanted to swoon. No wine though." He laughed as if his antics were as simple as over-indulging in the grape.

She watched him. They didn't know each other. She'd never met his children or gone to his apartment. His accent seemed so strong now, foreign. What they had was superficial. Business. Why had he come to France? She'd never invited him and couldn't honestly say she wanted him here. She stood up and hugged her arms, feeling a chill.

"Have some fun while you're here, James. See some sights. I'm sorry I can't be much of a tour guide for you. It's not a good time. There's a bunch of stuff going on, my sisters, my son." And Pascal, she thought. She looked at James, huddled there, a stranger in her garden. She was exhausted and completely done with him for today.

"It's late. We'll talk tomorrow."

Texts between Annie Bennett and her father Jack

Annie: *Anything new on Gillian? She's disappeared with our rental car & pet dog and upset Merle & Tris*

Jack: *Ward & Baillee contact faxed her law diploma. Gillian Elaine Sargent, CU, '98. Nothing else. Still debating background chk?*

Annie: *No more debate. Do it, full-on, & pronto*

.

11

They slept late the next morning. Tristan hid his head under his pillow, just like Harry used to do, keeping the world at bay. Merle saw him as she emerged around nine. Her bedroom had started its climb to furnace temperature. The thick walls and ancient shutters couldn't keep out that Mediterranean sunshine. By noon it would be ninety in there.

She decided to go out for coffee and a run. She hadn't really had a moment alone since she left home. Pulling on shorts, a tank top, and running shoes, she stuck her cell phone down her sports bra, and the house key into a pocket. She would get coffee first, she thought. But when she walked around the corner, she spied the gate in the bastide wall beckoning her into the countryside. With the day promising to be a scorcher, she turned right and took off.

Just like last year, she thought with a flash of *déjà vu*. Last summer when she jogged the roads to the top of any hill that would take her. When she reinvented herself as a single mother, a single woman, a fundraising lawyer, a winer-and-diner. When she made peace with her dead.

Maybe a hard run would help her make peace with the living. She'd tossed and turned over James last night. She didn't like to hurt people. She liked him; he was kind, attentive. But the last two days had done her in. She didn't even respect him. Panting and grunting and slapping her feet on the old country roads helped her realize that she should wait until they were both back home to tell him. He should have his vacation. It would be unkind to ruin that.

She was covered with healthy sweat when she turned back in through the arched gateway and slowed to a walk, hands on hips. The sky was gray this morning, but sun breaks were popping through. The humidity was already up. Her cell phone rang as she turned onto rue de Poitiers. She pulled it out of her cleavage.

"Merle? It's James Jeremy—James." He was whispering, his voice squeaky and anxious.

"What is it?" She stopped, staring at her shoes.

"The police are here. At the hotel. I'm in the bathroom. They weren't going to let me call anyone."

"What do they want?"

"Want?! They want to fuckin-a arrest me! That priest has pressed charges." Now he was worked up, trying not to raise his voice and failing.

Oh shit.

"I am going to end up in a French prison. Just like I told Pascal." He pronounced the name like it rhymed with "rascal," which made a chuckle escape from Merle.

"They're at the gall-durned door, Merle. This isn't funny."

She bit her lip. "I'm sorry. I don't know what to do."

"Do you know a lawyer?"

"Um, yes." Last summer had acquainted her with more than one French attorney. "But not here in town."

"Well, get them here! I can't even talk to these frogs. They don't speak English! It's the global business language, for pity sake."

"This is rural France, James." She sighed, rubbing her forehead. "I'll find somebody. Hang in there."

"Easy for you—" A crash, then shuffling. "Get your hands off me!"

And the phone went dead.

An hour later Merle stood in the small entry of the *gendarmerie*, the police station, a utilitarian cement block addition at the rear of the *Hotel de Ville*, the city hall. She'd showered and put on a skirt and blouse. As she'd predicted the day had warmed dangerously and she dabbed her face with a handkerchief as she pressed the buzzer and waited for someone to appear.

Finally the young, sour-faced policeman opened the door. He stepped up to the long, gray counter as Merle's cell phone rang. She let it go.

"*Monsieur le gendarme, bonjour,*" she said, remembering how Albert's token of respect had gone over so well. He nodded. She continued in French. "I have come to report that my rental car was stolen." Don't beat around the bush. Gillian stole it, as Tristan said. "One of my houseguests took the keys and left without permission. I have no way to find her and she doesn't seem to be coming back. I will have to file a report with Avis." She dreaded that. The Avis clerks would not be impressed.

He pulled a form from under the counter and even gave her a pen. Before he turned to go, she added, "*Pardon, monsieur.* You have a friend of mine here, I think. *Monsieur* Silvers, the American?"

This was the real reason she was here. The rental car could wait. But she wasn't sure how long James would tolerate lock-up, croissants or not. His screech rang in her ears.

"We are in process of charging him, *madame*," the policeman said.

"Can I see him?"

He squinted at her like she had some nefarious plan to spring James. "He can see a lawyer when we are finished with the charging."

"But as a friend." She put a hand to her chest and batted her eyelashes, taking a few lessons from Valerie. "*S'il vous plait, monsieur.* He is a stranger here and very afraid."

The *gendarme* curled his lip in disgust. To show fear was cause for shame, or maybe James had acted badly. His yelling and squealing, no doubt. The *gendarme* shook his head and retreated, disappearing into the back. She knew that space, the interrogation room, the smoke of a thousand *Gauloises.* It wasn't pretty but it wasn't terrible either. James would live.

She set her mind to translating the directions on the form and carefully filling out the report of the stolen car. She'd left the paperwork in the glove compartment. But the second key had the plate number, Avis identification, and relevant details on the plastic ring. Halfway down the long report, she was stumped and had to call Avis.

They asked her if she'd purchased travel insurance, something she rarely bothered with. But on this trip with unknowns like Gillian, James, trains, planes, and automobiles, she'd gone for it. And now she was glad. It would still be a lot of paperwork of course; this was France. But it allowed her to get a replacement, even though she'd been so careless with the first.

Another call to travel insurance. Complicated but ultimately successful.

Finally, she was done. She pressed the buzzer again. Another fifteen minutes passed then the *gendarme* came through, his face stoic.

"*Madame.*"

"Can you look this over and make sure I've gotten everything?" She pushed the report across.

He glanced at it then spun it back, his finger pointing at a line. "Initial here." She did as he said. "And sign here. Then I need a copy of your passport."

Finally, he was satisfied and told her it would go to the regional office of the *Policier Nationale.* "You don't expect to see the auto again?"

"It's a rental," she reminded him. "They're giving me another."

That was mildly disgusting.

"Can I see *Monsieur* Silvers now?"

"*Non, madame.*"

"What about a lawyer? Is there an attorney in town? For Mr. Silvers's sort of misunderstanding?"

He opened a drawer and pulled out a business card. "*Voilà, madame.*" He slapped the card on the counter with more force than necessary and quick-stepped it out the back.

Merle smiled, pleased with herself for getting under the *gendarme's* skin. That was always fun. She spun the card around.

Michel Redier

§

ADVOCAT

Criminel Immoblier Famille

Michel Redier. His haughty visage popped into her mind, the cold blue eyes, the nose like a hatchet blade. The former mayor, having lost his powerful position with only a slap on the hand, was back in business as a criminal lawyer, and the person she must ask for help.

Just perfect.

On the way back to the house, Merle detoured into the *Petit Casino*, a convenience store near the Place de la Victoire. She didn't usually get supplies here. It was touristy and overpriced. But she didn't care today, wanting only orange juice, lettuce, and, of course, cheese.

The aisles were crowded, stacked with crates of beer, beans, and mustard. She turned sideways to get to the refrigerated case and agonized over the highway robbery of orange juice. Maybe just get fresh oranges? *Oh, fuck it, don't be so tight, Merle.*

On her way past the beer and wine, which made up half the shop, an old woman with a cart made her press back into an alcove by the service entrance. It smelled of rancid produce but she smiled at the woman, trying to look friendly. To her left was a bulletin board full of local notices: babysitting, houses to let, *brocantes* selling antiques, dates of markets, services of plumbers. And a large, fresh white sheet stapled on the top with a photo of a dog.

She stepped closer. Photocopied and blurry, the photo showed a curly-haired mutt, ears blowing in the wind. It was hard to tell exactly what the dog looked like. The profile view was not great. A tuft of hair on the top of the head. She tore the paper off the bulletin board and, folding it into her purse, paid for her groceries and walked home.

As she slipped the carton of orange juice into the refrigerator, Tristan skipped down the stairs. If his skipping was any indication, a good night's sleep had helped his funk. She turned, making sure she was smiling.

"Where've you been?" he asked.

"Good morning to you too. Orange juice? I just got some." There were pleasantries for a moment while she fixed him breakfast. It was nearly noon but what the hell. The summer was here. As he sat chewing on a croissant, Merle drew the sheet from her bag. She took a breath and set it next to him.

He stopped eating. "Where'd you get this?"

"Posted in the store."

He picked up the sheet, smoothing it like he'd done Gillian's note with his large hand. "This says—"

"Reward. Stolen dog. 'Aurore.' That's her name."

Tristan looked up at her. "Aurore?"

"I can't tell for sure if that's your dog."

He studied the sheet for a moment. "It must be. It's Tartuffe. Who is, I guess, Aurore? The vet said she was stolen." He looked closer at the sheet. "Ten-thousand euros? That's the reward? Isn't that a lot for a dog?"

"She must be special in some way. To the owners."

"You mean they're rich?"

"Or something."

He stood up abruptly. "I need to get on the Internet. Find out why she's so expensive. Did she look expensive to you?"

"She just looked like a dog."

Merle wasn't sure she wanted Tristan to go down this path. She'd brought the reward poster home though, so what did she expect? He couldn't mope forever; he deserved some closure.

"I'll take the iPad to Albert's." He paused. "Is he still mad?"

And then she had to tell him about James's arrest. Not much choice. They were a team now, a team of two. Tristan rolled his head around, disgusted with adults. No argument there. Then he said he'd go down to the school.

"Poachable Wi-Fi," he said, smiling at last, a mission to accomplish.

LAWYRR GRRL

WHERE A WOMAN CAN GRROWL ABOUT THE LEGAL PROFESSION

BLOG—Paradisio Perdu
Tagged *Blissed out, Missed out*
Posted June 22

The walking vacation (sounds suspiciously walking pneumonia...) is down to four of us sisters, and I have to say, it's an improvement. The two oldest sisters are close in age, and the two youngest. Between us is the middle sister, who often, she tells us, feels the odd man out. I feel for her. But on this walking tour, it's nice to be an even number and only sibs. Kinda peaceful actually. Feeling a weird giddiness take over. Could this be what they mean by "chillaxing?"

We even talked/grumbled/moaned/exclaimed about Law as we trekked along. Youngest sister is only a year out of school and suffering the adjustment period. You know, when you realize nothing they told you in law school is remotely realistic? When your personal life is sucked so dry you can feel the sandpaper down in your panties?

Only one of us four is married. I've been there, done that, got the financial distress and emotional scars to prove it. Oldest sister is, I thought, confirmed in her feminist solo-hood. Then she reveals she's been dating this guy for eight months, keeping it a secret. Because he's— wait for it—*fourteen* years younger. She showed us a photo of him and he's srrrsly hot, Scottish, and rich. Jayzus H. She has all the luck.

So we're getting all close and bond-y—she even tells us he wants to get married but she isn't sure!—then she changes the plan. We are to march back to home base instead of going on to lovely tourist town with fabulous outdoor markets and Michelin-rated restaurants. All because of That Girl.

Damn that sister who brought her friend along. (This is probably where I should admit it was me. But just between us grrls.)

12

The house was quiet, empty. Tristan was off poaching the Internet. The dog who had brightened their lives for an instant was gone. Her sisters were off making merry. Merle stood, arms folded, listening to a moth somewhere between the windowpanes. She couldn't stand it, this dim and dingy house. She had to fix it up soon or live outside permanently like the previous tenant. She stared at the trap door in the living room floor. Did the dormouse—*le petit loir*—still live down there? Right now she might welcome the company.

She took her cheese and Perrier into the garden and sat with her back to the sun, feeling it warm her shoulders and leach out the anxiety. At least she'd had that run. At this rate she'd probably not get another one.

She closed her eyes and made a list in her mind as she'd done as long as she could remember.

Things to do. Things to keep life on the rails. Things to make everyone happy. Things to make Merle calm.

Call Michel Redier again after lunch.

Visit with, twist arm of, cajole, and ply with wine, Redier the bastard.

Do not call people "bastard."

Do not dwell on the past.

Call dog owner on poster and verify identification.

Let go of dream of Tristan + dog.
Plan apology dinner for Albert & Father Cyril.
Buy seriously good wine for apology dinner.
Do not lament lack of last year's fabulous wine.
Do not make Gillian voodoo doll and stick with pins.
Take Tristan out to new winery/restaurant for dinner
Do not obsess on Pascal's butt.
Do not make James voodoo doll and stick with pins.
Call Annie back.

She went inside and got her phone. Annie answered immediately. It sounded like they were walking: shuffling, laughter, trees in the wind, the brush of fabric, the clomp of boots.

"Where are you?"

"We're headed back. We're near—where are we, Stace?"

"Between *Castelnaud* and the middle of nowhere."

"On top of a flat ridge. It's gorgeous," Annie said. "Keeping up a good pace. We should be there by six."

"You don't have to come back," Merle protested. "Don't change your plans. There's nothing you can do."

"It didn't feel right leaving you with the Gillian mess. It's Francie's problem. She should deal with it."

Francie, in the background, let loose a round of lighthearted cursing.

"Okay. I appreciate it."

"We couldn't enjoy ourselves with you having all this junk. Wait, Stace wants to talk to you."

"Hey, Merdle, guess what we found out? Annie has a serious boyfriend and she's probably getting married!"

"To Callum?" Annie had told Merle about him in the spring.

"She told you?" Stasia said something to the others, muffled by her hand or the wind.

Annie came back on. "We'll see you soon, honey."

Merle arrived on the doorstep of the French attorney at precisely three. She took a deep, calming breath. Her fluency worried her. Redier wouldn't speak English out of pride and spite. She remembered how her own attorney had been disgusted with him last summer, how the mayor had asked for a bribe, stonewalled her plans, and conspired against her.

He's a bastard. Accept reality. Do not fight it. But do not dwell on the past.

She smoothed her hair for the tenth time.

Tristan had returned a half hour before with news. Aurore, formerly Tartuffe, was a famous truffle dog that had been written up in newspapers last winter. She belonged to an old man about twenty miles away. Someone must have seen the article and stolen her.

"But she's smart," Tristan told her. "She got away from those dirt bags."

What did Gillian know? She must have seen the flyer and wanted the reward. That was the only explanation that made sense. A bit callous, but not outside the bounds of what they knew about her. Yet, why did she say in her note that she was taking the dog somewhere safe? Was someone else after the dog? With a reward of that size? Of course they were.

Tristan had accepted the loss of his new best friend. He was still bitter at Gillian, but knew if he still had the dog, she would have to go home to the owner, reward or no reward. He'd moved on to his next goal: getting out of the village and back to the "real world" where dogs are just dogs as soon as possible.

The lawyer's office was an elegant *maison de ville*, a three-story limestone townhouse with fancy lintels on the windows, deep hunter green shutters, and a carved arch over the glossy black door. A small plaque in polished brass announced the man's name and profession. Merle had never thought of him as anything but the mayor of Malcouziac. By the looks of his digs, he'd been an attorney for years.

She pushed open the door and stepped into an empty reception area with an oriental rug, chrome-and-leather chairs, and vases of roses.

The tinkle of a bell attached to the door echoed briefly then a slender older woman appeared, dressed in a navy dress and high heels. Merle had spoken with her earlier.

The woman whisked her into the back and opened the door to a bright, book-lined office where Redier sat, rimless glasses perched on his nose, behind a large oak desk. A legal office anywhere in the world, she thought as he rose, removing the glasses and shaking her hand.

"*Madame Bennett, assayez-vous, s'il vous plait.*" He gestured to a gray velvet chair and she sat down.

In halting French she explained she was there for a friend who had been detained by the *gendarmes*. She wasn't sure of the charges as they wouldn't let her speak to him. Redier appeared sympathetic, nodding and bobbing his white eyebrows. He was thinner than she remembered, gaunt and bird-like, still with that haughty demeanor. But what choice did she have—what choice did James have? He needed a lawyer. And a lawyer who knew the local *gendarme* couldn't hurt.

When she finished explaining the situation, how James had taken a sleeping pill and didn't remember much, how Father Cyril tried to help, how James reacted blindly, after all that, she sat back and looked at him, trying to figure out how to establish a connection. Asking for help from an enemy was dicey.

"This won't be awkward," she asked as he rolled a Mont Blanc pen in his long fingers. "*Entre nous.* Between us, because of the past."

He froze for a second, as if she'd touched a nerve. Then the curtain of propriety and his eyelids descended again. "*Non, non, madame.* It is all forgotten."

She doubted that but nodded. "You'll see him this afternoon then?"

He promised to do so and to call her with a report on the charges and how to proceed. They shook hands again and said good day.

As she walked home, she felt she'd handled things well with Redier. Like professionals, lawyer to lawyer. James would be out of jail this evening or in the morning. After that he could deal with his own defense. There was no point trying to see him again, not with that *gendarme* in charge. Jimmy Jay would just have to wait. Not an easy thing, waiting for French bureaucracy to grind its way through.

Feeling efficient, she tackled another item on her list. With her sisters returning, she changed the reservation at the winery restaurant to six people, then stepped through the alley to knock on Albert's garden gate. Inside, she heard the groan of a metal chair and crunching of footsteps on gravel. The old man opened the gate, wearing his blue coveralls that pulled tight across his bulging midsection. He stepped back, sucking in his teeth.

"How are you today? And Father Cyril?"

"He's better." Albert relaxed a little. "Come in, come in."

They settled onto the metal chairs. Merle felt sad, wondering if this was the way it would be between them now: tense, hurt, careful. He had been such a good friend.

He cleared his throat. "An awful mess. I told him not to go to the police but he wouldn't listen. I said, these are my friends. No matter what you think of them, we don't do this. But—"

"It's all right, Albert. We can't control our friends." She smiled ruefully. "I'd like to have you both to dinner, tomorrow if that suits you. My sisters will be back."

Albert tipped his head. "Will *he* be there?"

"Oh, no, no, no." What was she going to do with James? She'd been shutting him out of her mind. "This is to apologize. Bring *Madame Azamar*. Will Father Cyril come?"

"I will ask him." Albert leaned forward and patted her arm. "Thank you. You are a good person. You are right, friends do what they do. We love them but we can't be responsible for every action." Her shame about James's behavior eased along with the tension between her and Albert. "What became of the dog? Did you find her?"

"It's a long story. But no, we didn't find her."

Merle excused herself, slipping back into her garden and hanging the key on the nail set in the stones of the outhouse. Albert seemed to have forgiven her. A weight lifted off her heart. He'd been there for her so solidly last year when they barely knew each other. He'd taken Tristan under his wing, taught him fencing, given his home over to him and Valerie. She couldn't imagine the village without her friend.

She checked her watch as she stepped into the kitchen. There was barely time for a small glass of rosé before Annie, Stasia, Elise, and Francie descended on the house, all talking at once, haranguing her for keeping Callum a secret, describing sunsets, demanding to see Gillian's note, showing her photos, cursing Gillian, popping corks, drinking wine, spilling wine, asking about Jimmy Jay, cursing Father Cyril and James, and asking when dinner was.

So good to have them back.

13

Dinner at the Chateau de Martinac winery that evening was amazing: six courses, wine pairings, three desserts, hundreds of cheeses. White tablecloths were scraped for crumbs by young maidens, the silver was exchanged dozens of times, and candlelight twinkled in cut-glass bowls.

Merle was quiet, absorbing the joys of her family together again, listening to their laughter and squabbles. The bickering seemed lighter now that Gillian was gone, more the playful ribbing they'd always done instead of mean-spirited digs from the walk. She was glad they'd had these two days. They seemed so relaxed and happy. And this dinner was a perfect way to cap the tour.

As they sipped coffee, Annie nudged her with her elbow. "What about Jimmy Jay? Are you worried?"

"They're not going to do anything to him. They just like to make foreigners sweat."

"And then what? You and him." Merle just shook her head. Annie said, "I wish he'd never come. Where's Pascal?"

"Gone off somewhere to work."

Annie drummed her fingers on the table. "This Gillian stuff is making me nuts."

"I've reported the car stolen. She left me no choice."

"Where do you think she went? Where is her 'someplace safe?'"

"No idea." Merle looked at her. "Did Francie say anything about her?"

Annie leaned closer. "No, but I asked Daddy to get a background check on her."

"And?"

"Gillian Sargent didn't exist before 1995. That was the year she entered law school. Before that, there's nothing."

Merle glanced at her sister to make sure she was serious. Annie wiggled her eyebrows. Intriguing but not very helpful.

"Was there anything else in the report?"

"Just a speeding ticket in Denver. Get this. She doesn't show up on the CU graduation rolls. If you look at the lists, she's not there. But if you ask specifically for her transcript or graduation record, she pops up."

"What does that mean?"

"I don't know. But I'm going to find out."

The next day Merle focused on getting the dinner together, assigning dishes to sisters, cleaning to Tristan, flowers to Elise, who wasn't allowed to cook for good reasons. Stasia was a big help, her Martha Stewart nature in the forefront. Merle sent Tristan to find out if Josephine and Father Cyril were coming. With them, it made dinner for nine. It was market day in the village. Merle, Elise, and Francie went out with their baskets and bought masses of vegetables: lettuce, carrots, peppers, potatoes, onions, leeks, garlic, herbs. And two plump chickens. Merle asked the poultry man to cut them up for her and by late afternoon the *coq au vin* was bubbling in the oven.

At five she sat down for a break outside with a cold glass of Perrier and checked her phone. No news from James or Michel Redier. What if James was released and showed up during dinner? He had to be warned.

He didn't answer his cell phone. Maybe he left it behind in his hotel room. He might come straight over without warning. Merle whipped off her apron and ran upstairs to change her shirt. When she came back downstairs the table was set, flowers in place, napkins just so. Everyone was off somewhere, escaping the afternoon heat. She poked her head into the garden. Tristan was curled into the shade under the cistern, reading. She told him she had to run an errand.

"Can I come?" he asked, crawling out.

In the plaza the market was winding down. Tristan saw some boys he knew from fencing club and stopped to talk. Merle told him to be back by six-thirty and headed for Hotel Quimet as heat radiated from the stone buildings.

The hotel lobby was warm and smelled of rancid grease as she approached the reception desk. The clerk from last summer was on duty, a tall, forty-ish man. The plaque reminded her: Guy Framboise, Manager. He smiled uncertainly.

"Bonjour, madame."

"Bonjour. Do you remember me? *Madame* Bennett, from last summer."

He exclaimed and shook her hand. "Yes, yes, your friend is staying with us. I am so grateful for your confidence after that little business last year." He frowned then turned it into a smile like a contortionist.

Do not dwell on the past: that one was coming in handy.

"Is my friend here? Mr. Silvers."

"Allow me to call upstairs." The manager dialed and waited while it rang. He held it out so she could hear the endless ringing. "I am sorry."

"Can you check his messages? He might have left something for me." Maybe a note saying *I'm outa here. Going home.* Her fondest hope.

The boxes for the rooms lined the wall behind the reception desk as they had done for centuries. Little cubbies for each room, a place to leave your key when you went out so that thieves had no trouble entering your room. James's key sat in the box for Room 314. The manager extracted a small note and stood reading it.

He looked up, dismay on his face. "There has been some trouble?" He pushed the note across. An official crest in navy ink at the top said Ville de Malcouziac. The rest was written in that perfect schoolhouse script the French used. "Request for belongings of James Silvers. Deliver to Gendarmerie." Dated today at 9 a.m.

"What shall I do, *Madame* Bennett? Shall I hold his room?"

"Has his luggage been taken over there?"

He pointed to tiny scratchings on the bottom. "The maid has packed them. They were delivered immediately." The manager wrung his hands. "A most unusual way to check out." He muttered something about James's American Express card as Merle turned to go.

The police station was cool inside thanks to a window air conditioner and thick block walls. She pressed the buzzer and fanned herself. Eventually the *gendarme* appeared, his step stuttering as he spied her.

They exchanged *bonjours* before the business at hand. "I've come to see *Monsieur* Silvers."

The *gendarme* smiled. "Ah, but he is no longer with us. He has been transferred to Bergerac according to the wishes of his attorney."

Merle startled. "*Monsieur* Redier requested the transfer?"

Oh, yes, the policeman said, pulling up to full height. The attorney was here this morning, first thing, to arrange everything.

"And what are the charges?"

"*Coups et blessures*: assault and battery. *En état d'ivresse sur la voie publique:* disorderly conduct, under the influence, resisting arrest. And several more." He crossed his arms and lowered his eyebrows. "He is a dangerous man, *madame*."

As she walked home, Merle tried to reach Redier. He didn't answer. She felt relieved that she wouldn't have to deal with James tonight during the dinner party and guilty for feeling relieved. He was locked up and alone in a foreign country where he couldn't understand what was happening. But he did have a lawyer, she told herself. Redier would look after James's rights. Last year she'd been suspected of murder and they'd only kept her locked up overnight. All James did was punch someone.

Why hadn't Redier called? Was he doing all he could? She checked her watch and hurried across the cobblestones to dinner.

Albert, Josephine, and Father Cyril made the long trek around to the front door just after seven. Elise greeted them, shaking hands and showing them through to the garden. Merle was in the kitchen working on a risotto with *cèpes*, the local mushroom. She wiped her hands and gave Albert and Josephine kisses on the cheeks. Father Cyril paused, hand extended. His light brown hair was combed forward and pasted to his forehead. He wore his all-black uniform, with the roman collar, jacket, and all in the heat of summer.

But his face, his poor, poor face. He looked like he'd been run over by a tractor. His entire face was one big bruise with nasty red lines running out from his nose to his cheekbones and down to his mouth. It was hard to remember what he looked like normally. He'd sat at the far end of the table that night then in the garden it was dark.

Merle felt her breath catch. She blinked, tried to smile. "Oh, Father. I am so sorry." He shook her hand solemnly. It probably hurt to smile. Both eyes were blackened, one just puffy but the other swollen nearly shut.

"*Merci beaucoup, madame*," he mumbled, "*de votre invitation.*"

Albert and Josephine had stepped outside, following Elise. Merle put down the wooden spoon and took the priest's arm. "Please, come outside and have some wine."

On the way to the table where the glasses were set out, Merle touched Stasia's arm and asked her to go stir the risotto. It was time to make amends with the priest. She told him she'd found a nice Sancerre and he didn't look displeased. She handed him a glass of the buttery white wine and poured herself one.

"*Santé,*" she said. *To your health*, wildly appropriate. He merely nodded, clinked her glass with his, and took a careful sip. "Good?" He looked at her blankly. "*Pardon. Parlez-vous anglais?*"

"Of course," he said stiffly. "I studied theology at the Sorbonne."

She tried to look impressed. "I'm sorry. How are you feeling? Have you seen a doctor about the, um, injuries?"

He touched the end of his nose gingerly. "It will require surgery. I cannot breathe properly."

Merle murmured words of sympathy, as many as she could think of, and took a gulp of wine. What could she say about James or his arrest? Nothing helpful came to mind. She looked around the garden for someone to take the priest off her hands. Tristan was on the iPad. Elise was talking to Josephine, Francie to Albert. She tried to get Annie's attention by scratching her head but she was busy slathering goat cheese on a cracker.

"I hope, Father, this doesn't sour you toward all Americans."

His blue eyes, bloodshot and swollen, fixed on her. "It is unfortunate."

"My friend is very, very sorry. He will tell you in person as soon as he can. He's embarrassed and ashamed about his behavior."

The priest was silent, sipping his wine. The sunset hit the neighbor's windows, bouncing orange flares of sunlight into the garden. One of them lit up the priest's shoulder and ear. His ruined face seemed to glow, the purple catching the light. Still, not a crack in his bitterness. What had become of forgiveness? Merle set her wine down on the table.

"Excuse me, I must see to dinner."

Everyone loved the *coq au vin*. Exclamations all around. The meal was pleasant enough, wine flowed and was praised, many toasts to health and France, but the evening never rose above a state dinner between enemy nations. Tristan was quiet, shoveling food into his mouth and drinking too much wine. Annie tried to keep things merry but even she gave up after dessert. It was a relief when the neighbors said good night.

The sisters cleaned up the dishes, washing in shifts, and finally, hands dried, went back into the garden with a last sip of Armagnac. Albert had brought a bottle as a gift. Josephine had brought a basket of bread. Father Cyril, contrary to custom, had come empty-handed.

"Can I have some?" Tristan asked.

"I think you had enough at dinner," Merle told him. He shrugged and went back to the iPad, playing some game with guns and zombies.

The sisters settled into seats. Merle was exhausted. The brandy was smooth and good though, and the evening stars shone down on them. It was too perfect to abandon for bed.

"That went well," Stasia said.

Somebody harrumphed.

"Except for Cyril's face," Francie said.

"He must have a glass nose," Elise said. "I've heard of that. People who just shatter on impact."

"Or Jimmy Jay gave the boy a wallop," Annie said. General agreement: a wallop.

Merle took a breath. "James got transferred to Bergerac, to another facility. He may not be out of jail for a while." That was the only conclusion she could come to: James was not a quick turnaround.

Annie swore. "Really? For one punch in the maw?"

"Assault and battery, public intoxication, resisting arrest. And so on." Merle rubbed her face. "But he has a lawyer."

"Who?" Annie asked.

"The mayor. Remember him?"

"Tall, butter-won't-melt-in-my-mouth dude? Doesn't he hate you or something?"

"I didn't have a choice," Merle said, defensive now. "He seemed reasonable. I talked to him. He said all was forgotten."

"And you believed him?"

I wanted to. Merle downed her brandy, feeling it burn her throat and work its way to her fingertips. She hoped she hadn't made a mistake with Redier.

Francie cleared her throat. "I finally got hold of the secretary at Ward and Baillee. She's looking for some relatives of Gillian's, somebody we can call."

"To report her missing?" Stasia asked.

"Or give her a piece of my mind."

"As if she cares," Elise said.

"Well, I care," Francie said, getting worked up. "She's stolen the car for one thing. She's upset the entire vacation."

"She's not alone on that one," Annie added. "But I agree. We can't just leave her twisting in the wind. Who knows, maybe she was kidnapped or something."

"You don't think that," Stasia said. "She wrote a note."

"It's unlikely. But maybe she was coerced."

Elise laughed. "Can you imagine anybody getting Gillian to do something against her will?"

Annie said, "Francie, you're staying until when?"

"Saturday. I was going to go to Paris for a few days, but now I'll stay here and help look for Gillian. When do you leave?"

"We take the train to Paris tomorrow. Stasia and me," Annie said.

"I'll help you, Francie," Elise said. "We fly back together, right?"

"Can I go with you, Aunt Annie?" Tristan asked. "Valerie's parents said I could visit for a few days in Paris before I go home. Can I, Mom?"

Merle was too tired to think about travel logistics. "We'll talk about it in the morning."

"Mom, look at this."

Tristan stood beside her with the iPad. A photo filled the screen, glowing in the darkness. Father Cyril's multi-colored face stared back at her, the black eyes and the nose like a plump apple. Tristan had added a funhouse mirror effect that made the priest's face look twisted and grotesque, his swollen eyes huge, his nose jack-knifed.

"Cool, huh?"

14

Merle drove the old *Deux Chevaux* up to the train station in Bergerac with a half-hour to spare. She'd borrowed Albert's old car, a classic Citroën with eyeball headlights, fold-down windows, and a canvas roof. Annie, Stasia, and Tristan had crammed themselves and their luggage into it early this morning. When Merle got up, Tristan was packed and ready to go. He had Valerie's parents on the telephone before she could say "no."

Tristan and Annie stood in line to get him a ticket while Merle parked. By the time she returned, the departure and arrival board said the train was just five minutes out. They found their places on the platform—train travel was very organized in France. You were expected to immediately get into the proper car, find your seat, haul your luggage, and behave yourself. Tristan by this time was an old pro, lining them up at the assigned post.

"Did they say they'd get you to the airport on Friday?" Merle asked, suddenly aware she hadn't planned every detail of her son's new itinerary.

"Valerie's older brother is going to be there. He'll drive me." Tristan wrapped his arms around her. "He's twenty. Don't worry, Mom. I made it home last year all by myself, remember?"

She squeezed him tight. "Stay away from gypsies." A family joke. As a child Tristan was fascinated with street people.

"What if they want to give me their baby?"

"No gypsy babies." She gave him a pinch. She would miss him but he had computer camp next week and a basketball camp the week after. Stasia would make sure he toed the line.

"You can go to the Louvre with me and Annie tomorrow," Stasia told him as the train pulled around the corner, screeching into the station.

Tristan nodded to his aunt, rolled his eyes to his mother, and in a flurry of last-minute hugs, they boarded the train and were gone. Merle felt the lump in her throat she always felt when he left but tried to smile and wave in case they were watching.

Inside the station she spent a confusing hour at the Avis desk, explaining the stolen vehicle and arranging a replacement. She wanted it delivered to Malcouziac, something the clerk declared "absolutely impossible." Merle refused to take no for an answer. In the end they agreed. Her car would arrive tomorrow. It cost her but it was worth it.

Back in the little Citroën, Merle took a moment to regroup. She was here in Bergerac; she should check on James. She called Michel Redier's office.

"*Bonjour, monsieur.* I heard you got *Monsieur* Silvers transferred to Bergerac."

"*Oui, madame.* It was necessary because of the charges. My hands were tied."

"Why are there so many charges? It seems excessive."

He clucked. "It is the way it is done."

So very French. A convenient excuse for not trying very hard is what it sounded like.

"I'm in Bergerac. I'd like to see James. Can you make that happen?"

He stammered a little as if shocked then said he would try. He gave her the address of the *Police Municipale.* "I do not guarantee you can see him," the lawyer warned her. "It is, ah, an unusual situation."

"Why is that?"

"*Madame,* he could not stay in the *gendarmerie.* They are not equipped for that. I will call the *Municipale* for you. Wait one hour."

An hour? Merle started up the little beast of a car and muscled it into gear. She would do some shopping then. She found a large supermarket and parked where she wouldn't have to put the 2CV into reverse. Her arms were already tired.

An hour later she stepped into the utilitarian, blocky building that housed the *Police Municipale.* Bergerac was not large, it just seemed that way compared to the tiny Malcouziac where the population had been on a downhill slide for over a hundred years and now numbered about 300 souls. By comparison Bergerac was a metropolis. Posters in the lobby of the station announced new security measures and surveillance cameras, as well as youth fairs with events like "*skate, rap, danse, graff.*" Trying to engage their rowdy youth, it seemed.

The young receptionist with black hair and very red lips frowned at her accent and kept saying, "*Quoi?*" Merle repeated everything three times. Finally, she took a slip of note paper from the desk and wrote, "*James Jeremy Silvers III, American. Je demande une visite.*" *I request a visit*: that was civil enough. The woman's kohl-rimmed eyes widened with comprehension. She took the note through a door, leaving Merle in the lobby with a nervous couple whispering to themselves. Ten minutes passed slowly then a uniformed officer appeared.

He was a large man, broad in the shoulder, wearing a crisp, militaristic navy uniform with patches and medals. His hair was gray at the temples, dark and slicked back on top. He carried the note and nodded solemnly to her.

"*Parlez-vous français, madame?*" She nodded. He continued in slow French, which she appreciated. "The American arrived here last night. We kept him one night only then transferred him to the Provincial Guard in Périgueux. The court is there, *madame.* We are only a municipal service for Bergerac."

Merle listened hard and frowned. "Why is he being held on these charges? It was one blow, a very small fight, really just a misunderstanding."

The officer glared down his nose. "That is not our business, *madame.* We only transported the prisoner." He handed her the slip of paper and dismissed himself.

Back in the car Merle got out her map. Why was the French state taking such a hard line on James? Was it something he'd done back home? She didn't know much about his past, except his divorce. She couldn't imagine he'd ever gotten into trouble, then wondered about the sleeping pill defense. Maybe he was prone to angry outbursts. She'd make sure he was well-rested when she told him they were finished.

Périgueux was almost due north, some twenty-five kilometers. Not far in a modern auto. She'd never been to the capital of the Dordogne. It was the opposite direction from Malcouziac. In the back seat, her groceries began a fragrant decline. She pictured James in a chic French prison jumpsuit, eating croissants. Was he angry? Frightened? She would give Redier a piece of her mind.

She wrangled the ungainly map back into shape then put the car in gear and headed home.

On rue de Poitiers, Francie and Elise had moved out of Yves and Suzette's house and into the loft room upstairs in Chez Merle. They had stripped the sheets on Tristan and Stasia's beds, washed them in the tub outside and hung them to dry on the line in the garden. When Merle returned with the groceries, they both pitched in, hauling in bags, putting things away. They seemed diligent and serious, and it made Merle suspicious.

"The cleaner came next door," Francie said. "About eleven. We were out already."

"And we've been to the edge of the schoolyard to get Wi-Fi," Elise added.

"Any news from home?" Merle said, cutting into a new block of sheep cheese. Francie plucked a piece and moaned with pleasure. They waited for her cheesegasm to subside.

Francie licked her lips. "Not from home. That cop came over, the blond, unpleasant one. He said—I think, my French is not great, as you know—that the rental car has been found in a parking lot by a train station on the outskirts of Toulouse."

Merle frowned. "She got on the train?"

"Or got another rental car."

Elise said, "Why can't they just run her name on the rental car agencies?"

"They who?" Merle asked. "Nobody's looking for her."

"Do people take dogs on trains here?" Francie asked.

"Service dogs mostly. Do you think she'd pretend to be blind?"

Francie laughed. "What a picture."

"We didn't see any dogs coming down from Paris. Not even little frou-frou ones," Elise said. "She would stick out with a dog on the train. She's on the run. My bet is she rented another car."

"To go where?" Merle asked. "We need to find out more about her. Maybe she has friends in France. Did you get any info from the law firm?"

"I talked to Sandy, the secretary. She talked to Gillian's assistant, Jonathan. He said her family was all dead and she was secretive about her friends. He thought she had a boyfriend, or maybe a girlfriend, but he didn't know who they were."

"Girlfriend like *friend* or like *girlfriend*?" Elise asked.

Francie shrugged. "Does it matter? We just want to find somebody she might reach out to while she's running around France."

"Call Jonathan and see if he'll snoop in her office," Merle said, handing Francie her cell phone. "It's for her own good. She could be in serious trouble for stealing a car."

"It's too early there. Speaking of trouble, did you see Jimmy Jay?"

"He's been transferred to Périgueux, to the Provincial jail or something. He'd already been shipped north."

Merle put together a late lunch for them and they sat in the shade of the acacia tree, sipping Perrier and eating salads. Elise complained that she had thought she would lose weight doing all this walking around. Francie pointed to the cheese as the culprit.

"When will you get such a fabulous variety of cheese again?" she declared. She pulled out her iPad and began typing. Keeping a record of cheeses, she explained.

When lunch was finished, Francie called Jonathan at Ward and Baillee. Elise took the sheets off the line, folding as she listened. Merle carried the dishes into the kitchen, put away the cheese and bottled water. She stared at the bottle of Sancerre in the refrigerator and pulled it out, pouring herself what she considered a very small glass of wine. Strictly medicinal, as her father would say. Tristan was gone, her favorite sisters had left, James was who knows where, his lawyer was inept or conniving, Pascal had quit her bed, and their houseguest was on the lam with a stolen dog. And the day was still young.

Francie was talking loudly in the garden. Taking her wine outside, Merle settled into her spot on the low wall and listened.

"I know she's a private person, Jonathan. You're not telling me anything new. She went on this trip with me, didn't she? I thought she was my friend. Now she's disappeared. I'm worried about her." Francie rolled her lovely blue eyes at Merle. "Think about this, Jonathan. She may never come back. Yes, I do mean it. She is going to be charged with grand theft auto in France if we don't help her. We had to report the car stolen. It was a rental and it was gone. We didn't have a choice. The only way we can help her is to find her."

Francie began pacing around the table, gesturing like she was trying to convince a jury, or strangle someone. "Right. It's for her own good. You understand that. Excellent." She flashed a smile. "If we don't help her, who will? Well, I'd like to find that out. Does she have a sister or brother somewhere? A cousin? Aunt or uncle?"

Another round in the gravel. "You have her email password? Why didn't you say so? No, no, I won't tell Mr. Baillee. This is just between us."

Francie made typing gestures with her free hand. "Go to her inbox. Tell me what you see in the last week or so." She shook her head. "Go farther back. Look for anybody named Sargent."

"Contacts," Merle said.

"Look in her contacts." Francie waited. "Nobody named Sargent?" She shook her head. "Okay, check her mail, in and out. Anything that isn't firm business." She listened then spoke to Merle and Elise. "She ordered a European cell phone." To Jonathan she said, "Did she get it? Did she leave you a number?" Francie went back to her iPad on the metal table, tapping in numbers. She read them back to the assistant.

"Have you called her? Did she call you? No, we never saw her use a phone here. She didn't give us the number." Merle shook her head.

Francie threw one hand up to the heavens. "That is super helpful, Jonathan. Now, can you forward any personal stuff in her email to me? Go back as far as you can. Anybody who emailed her, or vice versa, anybody who seems like a social connection, friend or relative. Great. My Ward & Baillee address is fine. I can access it here. You're a trooper, Jonathan. Thanks a million."

Elise stood with a pile of folded white sheets in her arms, frowning. "She had a phone all this time?"

"Apparently." Francie set the phone on the table. "He said she ordered it back in April."

"Was she planning something back then?" Merle said. "And why didn't she use it while she was here?"

"Maybe she did," Elise said. "Maybe she was making phone calls on the sly."

"How would we know?" Francie agreed.

"Call her," Merle said.

Francie picked up the phone again and consulted her iPad for the number. She wasn't on long. "Clicked off after half a ring. No voicemail."

"She's got it turned off," Merle said. "So the cops can't track her."

"Are the cops after her? You said nobody was looking for her," Elise said. "That cop seemed more concerned about the rental car."

"With the property returned, they aren't going to mount a manhunt."

"But she's still got stolen property," Francie said. "A very expensive dog. Probably worth more than that Renault."

Merle hadn't called the dog's owner. She went in the house and found the reward poster on a side table in the living room, splashed with red wine. Back in the garden she punched the number into her phone.

It rang three times then a weak woman's voice answered. "*Allo?*"

"*Allo.*" She spoke in her slow French. "I am calling about the dog. You posted a reward?"

A rustling, a clunk as the phone was set or thrown down. Voices, hushed, rising, down again. Merle waited. "*Allo? Quelqu'un est là?*"

More voices, a squeak from—a woman? Then a low, raspy voice in response, pleading? Finally someone picked up the phone.

"*Allo.* Who is this?" A younger man, odd accent.

"I am calling about the stolen dog. Are you the owner?"

"*Oui.* You have the dog?"

Something was off. She had expected relief, excitement, even tears, and had been worried that she couldn't tell them where the dog was. But this she hadn't expected, a hard voice, uncaring. He didn't call the dog by her name.

"No, I'm sorry. We saw her. We found her on the edge of the road while we were out walking."

"Where?"

"Near Loiverre. But that was several days ago. We took her to the veterinarian. She was very sick."

"The veterinarian. Where was that?"

She hesitated. So many questions. "Can I speak to the owner please?"

"I am the owner! I told you!" He was shouting. "Who are you? Have you stolen my dog?"

"I told you," she said, worried where this was going. This was not the owner; she was sure of that. Possibly a relative or someone helping the owner. "We found her by the side of a road. But now she's gone. I just wanted to tell you that we think we saw her and she was okay."

"Where has she gone? She ran away?"

Or something. Merle looked at the top of the tree. "Yes."

"When?"

"Three days ago. We didn't see the poster until after she disappeared. I'm sorry."

"Where do you live? By your accent, you are an American?"

"We're, ah." She paused. They probably just wanted to know where to look. "We're in Malcouziac."

"And the dog was with you before she so expertly slipped away?"

This was getting seriously weird. "I'm sorry. I hope you find her. Good-bye."

Francie and Elise were standing there, watching her.

Merle set the phone down. "Well, that was strange."

"What's going on?" Francie asked.

"The article Tristan found about the truffle dog said that an old man near here owned her. That he was in his eighties."

"So?"

"That wasn't an eighty-year-old on the phone. He spoke French with a strange accent. And he was very suspicious. Lots of questions." Merle looked at them, a sinking feeling settling hard in her stomach. "Like he was out looking for the dog or somebody who took her."

"Maybe it was his son. They're probably scouring the countryside," Elise said. "They don't *want* to pay that huge reward. They just want the dog back."

"You look worried," Francie said to Merle. "Do you think they're going to come over here and shake us down? We don't have the stupid dog and you told them everything."

"Not about Gillian."

"We need to find her before they do," Elise said.

"They don't even know she has the dog," Francie said. "They don't know she exists. Let's just find Gillian so she can avoid getting thrown into the Bastille."

As they went back into the house, Elise said, "At least we know one good thing about Gillian. She didn't take the dog to get the reward. She just loves her. She really does want her to be safe. If she was after the reward, she would have turned the dog in by now, right?"

Francie sighed. "Then what the hell is she doing with the thing?"

15

Hector and Milo got tired of stealing eggs. Milo quickly bored with early morning raids on Jean Poutou's hen house, and Hector grew weary of cooking them on the tiny camp stove. It was a relief the morning the old man confronted them in the barn and they were given no choice but to give up their hay berths for soft beds in the farmhouse, strong-arming the old man and confiscating his shotgun.

The old woman was a problem. She didn't want to cook for them and Milo was worried she would poison them. But food was food, as long as it wasn't eggs. The truffle business had given the old couple a comfortable living, it appeared, a full larder and overflowing freezer, and Hector felt it was his right to have a part of it.

But not the reward. They'd given up that idea when Signora Dellapiane had called them and offered the same amount, the ten-thousand euros. But locating the dog was proving difficult. In the end, waiting for someone else to turn in the dog for the reward seemed the best plan.

The signora hadn't been all generosity. There was anger in her voice, and if he wasn't mistaken, desperation. She needed this dog. And if they didn't bring it to her, she threatened to call the authorities in Italy and France and tell them that Hector and Milo stole the dog, that she'd heard them planning it. Give up their identities. Make them live on the run at best, or in jail at worst.

And no money. That was what Hector thought the most about. He had decided he would give some to his sister. Her little Angelina was so sick. Something the local doctors could not cure. They needed money to go to Rome for hospitals. Without his share of the signora's payment, Angelina might die. He thought of the little girl at night before sleep. He had no wife. No children. Angelina was all he had.

Hector enjoyed the Poutou's modern bathroom and took long baths, stretched in the clawfoot tub. He strutted through the Poutou farmhouse, picking up china trinkets to get a rise out of the old woman. He demanded she wash their clothes after she turned up her nose at their odor. She was plump and hysterical, making her face turn red with anger was amusing. It broke the boredom of waiting for a call.

And finally, just as hope slipped away, a call. He slammed down the ancient telephone receiver. The old woman (he couldn't be bothered to remember her name) trembled in her apron, shrinking into a worn armchair covered with flowered fabric. Her gray hair had come loose from its pins, floating around her fat face. Milo was outside with the old man while he did his chores. Feeding the chickens, watering the vegetables: such an exciting life.

"Never answer the telephone. Did I not tell you?" Hector stood over the woman menacingly. He raised his hand to slap her. Mostly to make her quake in fear. "If you answer it again, I kill your old man. Do you hear me?"

She bobbed her head, chin quivering.

"Go finish the dinner. And remember you will taste it before you serve it."

She scuttled into the kitchen. Hector tried to think. He pulled out his map book, fingered through to the Dordogne. Where was Loiverre? Had the American lied about that? At least at the start she believed he was the owner. He hadn't played it well. He should have squeezed out a few tears.

He and Milo had been in Malcouziac just a few days ago. All the villages ran together in his mind, a mishmash of half-timbers, cobbles, and stone. He was sure they had been there, the bastide town with the broken wall on one side. Asking around about the dog, trying not to attract attention. Listening to other diners at cafés. Reading lost and found posters. It hadn't been much, but it was all they had. To think they had been so close.

He wanted to leave. But what about the farmer and his fat missus? Would they call the police? Thinking was his specialty as he told Milo often. But now the facts seem to leak out his ears. What would they say? That they were forced to cook for guests? Held captive by olive pickers? Would the cops laugh at the old people or hunt them down like dogs?

He would have to take that chance. This lead, this phone call, was the first thing in days. He had been worried the dog had been stolen by truffle hunters who recognized her from the newspaper. But now it appeared she was just on the loose, running around the countryside. They must find her, and fast before someone else recognized her from the reward poster.

The old woman was in the kitchen. Hector stepped up beside her at the stove and looked into the pot of boiling chicken. The herbs were fragrant. He would miss the old woman's cooking, he had to say. He opened the refrigerator and stuffed cheese into the pockets of his jacket. She was watching him. He squinted at her, daring her to speak. She turned back to her pot.

Two apples from the bowl on the table went in with the cheese. Hector stuck the book of maps in his back pocket. He would look up these tiny villages later. He went to the front window and looked for Milo. He trailed after the old man coming out of the barn. Poutou limped along, not so fat as his wife, but with one bad leg and terrible eyesight. His thick glasses glinted in the sunshine.

Hector picked up the shotgun and a box of shells from the table by the door. He could hear the old woman in the kitchen, the clink of plates and silver. Time to go. His fingers twitched on the gunstock.

At last the latch lifted and Poutou and Milo stepped into the front parlor, bringing in a gust of wind full of fresh-cut hay and chicken guano. Milo turned to shut the door and saw Hector standing there. Hector shook his head. *Quiet, you filthy son of a bitch.* Poutou didn't notice him, pausing by the pegs to struggle out of his jacket.

Hector took his chance, stepping up behind Poutou, raising the stock of the shotgun above his head. Bringing it down hard on the skull with a *thunk*. The recoil of the blow surprised Hector and he stumbled backward into a tray of cut glass dishes, sending them crashing to the floor.

The old woman rushed into the room. When she saw Poutou lying there, bleeding, out cold—not dead, Hector hoped—she rattled off some patois neither of the Italians understood. Hector regained his footing, the shotgun half-hidden behind his leg.

"He must have lost his balance. Fallen into the table," he said, pointing to the broken glass and upturned tray. "I will get my truck. We can take him to the doctor, *madame*."

She continued to make a fuss on her knees by the old man. Blood reddened her hands, making her squeak like a pig. Hector motioned Milo out the door. On the threshold Hector spoke in a kindly voice to the old woman: "Be patient, *madame*. I will return."

Hector shut the door behind them and turned to Milo. He pointed with the shotgun. "Run."

Lawyrr Grrl

Where a woman can grrowl about the legal profession

BLOG—Cherchez la femme
Tagged *Some Serious Shit*
Posted June 25

Drama ensues, lawyrr grrls. That Girl has flown the coop. And I wouldn't really care, except that I brought her on this adventure and she is my law colleague. She's as close to a friend as I have at the firm. I'm not sure she has any other friends. Can I just go home without trying to figure out why she took off with a rather expensive mutt in tow? Not in good conscience, which is something I'm trying to improve in myself. Lawyrrs need a good conscience, even when—especially when—things get hinky.

So I've spent the morning working my plan. How to find, track, *cherchez* this here *femme*. The last we heard, she was in Toulouse, so that's where I pick up the trail. I have to take my baby sister along because her French is much better than mine, and God knows we're going to be dealing with people who won't speak English if their lives depended on it. *Oops*. I just told you where I am, didn't I? Yes, in *la belle France*.

I've found out two things about my disappearing colleague: 1) she has a European cell phone that she never told us about, and 2) she called in to the firm two days ago and cleared her calendar for an extra week, telling them she was having a wonderful time and wanted to extend her vacation. No one thought much of it. It's coming up on fourth of July holidays; everyone who can is taking time off. I'll be back next week, of course, picking up everyone's slack. As is my joy in life.

I'm going through her correspondence, trying to figure out where she'd go. A diligent lass, she rarely used her work email for anything else. But my source inside the firm discovered a hidden digital folder inside the mail server (I told you not to ask) that includes cryptic messages from accounts with names like XK3#% and 99b@*Z= — obviously not their real names. The messages themselves seem coded, and fascinating as hell: "The bottles on the lake twinkle in the moonlight" and "Once a barfly, always a marigold."

But I don't have time for coded messages. I have to find That Girl and help her clear her name (another don't ask moment) so we can all go home and resume our thrilling Lawyrr Grrl Lives. We may be whiners, but we get the job done.

As baby sister says: we will be sleuths!

16

Merle waited all morning for a call from James or his lawyer. The house was empty again, and too quiet. Francie had snatched the keys to the new rental car as soon as it was delivered early in the morning. She and Elise packed their bags and took off on the trail of Gillian. They headed south toward Toulouse, they said, where she'd last been spotted.

Standing in the living room gloom, Merle made an addition to her to-do list: *Scrub the wax off the wood floor.* She pushed the table against the fireplace, stacked the chairs on top of it, and wedged the little sofa under it. The small tables and lamps she took upstairs, then filled her bucket with soapy water, found the big brush, and set to work.

An hour later it was clear elbow grease and dish soap weren't going to cut it. She traipsed over to the hardware store to ask about a wax removal product. They sold her something, who knows what, plus pink rubber gloves. The product was smelly and she dug out her bandanna to cover her nose and mouth like a bandit.

At noon there was still no word from Redier. Stretching her back in the garden, she stripped off her gloves and called him. The receptionist said he had gone to Périgueux. Yes, to see about *Monsieur* Silvers. No, she didn't give out his mobile number, that was not done. But she would mention that Merle had called.

The scrubbing was therapeutic. Her shoulders burned, back and forth, in and out. It was like walking: repetitive, slightly boring, but meditative and progress was made. Hard work at times, easier at others.

Concentration on the work at hand. Merle had never really been one of those women who clean when they're anxious. But she could see how it worked, the fixing of the immediate when the other was out of control. She switched hands, worked on, tied towels around her knees for pads, then switched hands again.

Still, she couldn't get Gillian out of her mind.

Where would she go? Who was she keeping the dog safe from? Was she in danger herself since she had the dog? Francie thought so. The redhead was prone to the fanciful, that was true. She should have been an actress. Merle smiled, picturing Francie pace in the garden as she charmed information out of Gillian's assistant. Francie was good. She could talk a turnip into soup as their mother used to say. But her French was bad. Despite being named Francine, she had taken Spanish in school. Elise's was decent but she hadn't practiced it much on the tour, letting her older sisters do the talking. Merle hoped they didn't get into any trouble. The new rental, a Peugeot, was spotless and had less than 200 kilometers on it. At least that would be functional.

Stop worrying, Merle told herself, attacking the wax with renewed force. Francie and Elise would poke around Toulouse for a couple days, eat some great French food, and come back. They'd take the train to Paris on Saturday and fly out on Sunday as planned.

She sat back on her heels, feeling the ache in her arms. The voice of the man on the phone, the one who said he was the owner of the dog, played in her head. *Where do you live? Your accent. American?* Why had she told him about Malcouziac? But the dog was gone. She couldn't help him now.

At three o'clock Michel Redier called, finally. He had miraculously recovered his English fluency. "I have seen your friend, *Monsieur* Silvers, *madame*. He is well and sends his regards."

His regards? "Tell me how he is doing, really." Merle walked into the sunshine and pulled the bandanna away from her chin. "Is he in good spirits? Is he being treated well? Is the food okay?"

"Yes, yes, *madame*. Be assured we treat everyone fairly in this country. With human decency, no torture."

"Okay." It was hard being American sometimes. "What's going on with his case?"

"He will be presented with his charges in court tomorrow afternoon. Then we will see what happens next."

"What do you think will happen next?"

"He may have to stand trial, *madame*. The charges are very serious. The judge in his case has seen many *futbol* riots. He does not tolerate hooliganism. But these are things that are yet to be decided. There is no point speculating. The facts will speak for themselves."

He rang off, excusing himself as he was driving. Merle stared at the phone. Would Father Cyril be in court with his messed up face? Unbelievable. James might actually be headed for a French prison for throwing a single punch. And what could she do about it? She had no standing in France. She wasn't his relative or his lawyer. Should she call his ex-wife? His children? His parents? She didn't know any of them or their telephone numbers. Who else? Father Albert? Cyril was his pupil, his fellow priest, his friend. The American consulate? They were in Nice, hundreds of miles away.

She sat under the acacia tree and pulled off her other rubber glove, throwing them both on the ground. She could think of only one person who could help. It was time.

It was seven before Pascal returned the call. Merle had stripped three-quarters of the living room floor. The stairs were looking bad now. They were next. But first a quiet evening in the garden, goat cheese salad, wine, and a little freaking out over her wayward American friends.

"You sound worried, blackbird," Pascal purred.

"James is going to be arraigned in court tomorrow. Should I go?"

A pause then, "Are you serious? On what charges?"

"Assault and battery, resisting arrest, public intoxication. I wonder if Redier even mentioned that he'd taken a sleeping pill."

"Michel Redier? *Le Maire*?"

"The very one. He might be the only lawyer in town. The *gendarme* gave me his card. Believe me, if there had been anyone else." She sighed. "What should I do? Can we get him out of this?"

"Where is this arraignment then?"

"Périgueux. They transferred him there. I haven't seen him since he was arrested."

"What time is the court?"

"Afternoon. That's all I know."

"I will meet you there. Text me as soon as you know the time."

Merle let out a long breath as she rang off. She looked at the sky, the blue fading into twilight. She wasn't alone. Pascal would be there.

Then she remembered she didn't have a car—again. She could borrow the Deux Chevaux from Albert again. But she'd borrowed it so often and it was unfair to presume that it would always be available.

She dialed Michel Redier's office. It was late but possibly he would be there. It rang and rang; he was gone. But he had called her from his car. She scrolled back through the call log, hoping he didn't block his cell number. There it was: the three o'clock call.

"*Oui. Allo.*" He sounded gruff, annoyed.

"*Monsieur* Redier, it's Merle Bennett. I'm calling to find out the time for Mr. Silvers' arraignment tomorrow."

"Sixteen, uh, four o'clock." It sounded like he was at dinner. She better make this quick.

"And you'll be going to court, I assume?"

"*Oui. Bien sûr.*" Of course.

"If you don't mind, I'd like to ride along with you. To Périgueux."

"It will be very brief, *madame*. A matter of minutes."

"I understand. But I'd still like to go."

Voices in the background, chatter, forks, laughter. Then a terse "If you wish. I will leave at eleven."

Merle put out her navy dress for court and tried on the only dressy shoes she'd brought, red ballet flats. Without hose they were sticky and uncomfortable, but she didn't have anything else. If she had time in the morning she would check out the women's shop in the village. Most of the clothing fit only tiny French women.

She stood at her upstairs window watching the garden in the

moonlight, feeling a slight movement of air, too light to be called a breeze, flowing up from the vineyards below. The rows of grapevines hugged the hillsides, undulating like a snake. What had this land been like before wine? Grass? Rock? There were still some hills like that, untouched pastures full of piles of native stone thrown around like giants' toys. Despite James, or maybe because of him, she felt the incredible chance events that led her here. She was grateful to have lived this long, to have had these moments. Fifty years, she thought with a shiver. What would the rest bring? Would there be someone to love, grandchildren, a man in her bed and in her heart?

Stop now. She heard Annie's voice. *Right here, right now.* Merle closed her eyes to listen to the village going to sleep, the yip of a dog, the snap of a rug, the flat pop of a door slam. Far away, a cow complained. Closer, a car door *thunked.* It was like an incantation, a spell that put the village to bed each night, softly, willingly.

The night air blew a little more, ruffling the lace curtain. She was trying to decide if she would leave the window open despite the occasional bat that flew in when the knocking came from downstairs. She startled, the magic of the evening gone. Were Francie and Elise back already?

Tiptoeing down the stairs, Merle edged around the pile of furniture. The shutters on the front window and door were both closed and locked. Being here alone she wasn't taking any chances. Moonlight shone through the side window. Her shadow stretched across the stripped planks. She stepped quietly up to the side of the glass-paned door.

Someone was out there, pounding.

Merle leaned in front of the door to see through the inch-wide crack between the ill-fitting shutters. By the size, a man.

"Madame? Madame! Êtes-vous là?"

Definitely a man, one who didn't know her name. Not her sisters, someone they sent, or even the *gendarme.*

There was whispering, low and conspiratorial. Two men. Merle moved over to the window. But the shutters were the originals there with a tight fit.

"Madame?" He continued in odd, unsophisticated French. "We

spoke on the phone earlier. About the dog. My Aurore. I am so worried. Please, *madame*. Can we talk please?"

Merle froze. He had found her. She pressed her back into the wall, a chill down her arms. They had tracked her from her information and her accent. Easy enough since she was the only American woman who lived in Malcouziac.

"You know about the reward, *madame*. It is very large. Ten-thousand euros, a small fortune for some. I can give it to you if you tell me where the dog is." A pause, more pounding. "I know you are there, *madame*," he said menacingly. "I can see you." Then the hissing of the other person, an argument, words jumbled and strange.

Then, finally, "*Zut alors,* it is late. I will come back in the morning, *madame*, and we can talk. *Bon soir!*"

17

Michel Redier slipped his silver Mercedes neatly into a parking slot behind the Greek Revival courthouse in Périgueux, the *Palais de Justice*. The sedan was big and powerful, taking the winding back roads through the Dordogne with ease. Redier obviously enjoyed his car. Or he enjoyed making Merle cling to the door handle.

But you wouldn't know that by looking at him. He had the face of an ice block hardened by many winters. No smiles as his vehicle hugged the turns. The only expression he made was clenching his teeth as he powered along at high speed.

He gathered his briefcase and files from the back seat and looked over the roof of the Mercedes at Merle. He wore a black suit with a dark green tie and a white shirt, all very severe. "I will see you at four then."

He'd barely spoken after ushering her into his beloved car. He explained he needed quiet to think while he drove. She respected that, the trial preparation mode. But she now had no idea what was to take place at the arraignment, what defense he was preparing for James, or what charges carried what penalties.

And she was tired. She'd barely slept last night, hearing bumps in the dark, startling her awake. The house on rue de Poitiers was meant for company. She didn't like staying there alone. She'd slipped out through the garden gate before nine, before the men returned to pound on her shutters again. What would they attempt in daylight? She didn't want to speculate. She'd made sure the house was locked tight, plus the garden gate. She couldn't do more. With two hours to kill before meeting the lawyer, she sat in the bakery with a croissant and a café au lait, reading the *International Herald Tribune* she'd bought at the *tabac*. She wrote a postcard to her parents and another to her friend Betsy, in which everything was golden and lovely, and fixed the postage. She was getting to be quite the accomplished liar. Her coffee was almost done, the paper perused front to back, when Father Cyril entered the *patisserie*.

His face looked better. Both eyes looked usable now, though still discolored. The swelling of his nose had gone down and his upper lip appeared normal. His right hand was wrapped in a bandage, something she didn't notice the other day. He wore the usual all black with the roman collar, and his mousy brown hair was brushed forward. It gave the impression of a gladiator after tangling with the lions.

Cyril and his companion, a stoop-shouldered young man with spiked hair bleached platinum, ordered coffees then turned to sit down in the bakery. Father Cyril saw Merle and nodded, then as if suddenly remembering who she was, stiffened.

She stood up and offered her hand. "Father Cyril, good morning."

He shook her hand with his left, unbandaged one. "*Madame,* I am sorry. I have forgotten your name."

"Bennett," she said. "Merle Bennett."

"Yes. The friend of *Monsieur* Silvers."

Was that a sneer? Difficult to tell with all the bruising. "How are you feeling, Father?"

"Somewhat better, thank you. The surgery will take place soon." He glanced back at his friend who was sipping his espresso. "In the meantime I have services to perform here and in several other villages. I am very busy." He nodded and almost clicked his heels together. "Good day, *madame.*"

So he wasn't attending the arraignment, it appeared. That would be a plus for James. Now, abandoned by Redier in the midday sun in Périgueux, she took out her phone and texted Pascal.

Arrived Pgx with Redier. Need ride home. Call when you get here

Then she wove through the parking lot and around to the front of the elegant building, through a square with a statue of Montaigne in search of the tourist office and a restaurant recommendation. It was after noon. All the stores were closed anyway, might as well do as the French do and eat lunch.

Map in hand, she followed the directions to a restaurant called *Hercule Poireau*. It made her smile. Whose Agatha Christie joke was that? Her phone pinged.

Give me an hour, blackbird

Her *rossini de canard* had just arrived at the table when she spotted him coming through the door. He wore a sports jacket, blue shirt, and a tie of all things. Still in black jeans though. He wove his way through the red checked tablecloths and slipped into the chair opposite, next to the window. Before he sat down he leaned in and kissed both her cheeks.

"What is that lovely aroma?"

"Duck with *foie gras* in a truffle sauce. It smells heavenly, doesn't it? I wasn't even hungry."

With quick work Pascal ordered a *rossini de canard* for himself, plus wine and coffee. He looked at his watch. "We don't have much time. No leisure for me."

"The arraignment isn't until four." They had nearly two hours.

"I've been to the *Palais de Justice*. Two cases were dismissed in the morning. The judge comes back from lunch in one-half hour and he will move things up."

Merle dug into her food, wishing she had more time to enjoy it. Her nerves suddenly buzzed. What was Redier's plan?

"Did you see the mayor over there?"

"Going to lunch with the judge."

She swallowed some *foie gras* and set down her fork. "What?"

Pascal nodded. "He is not to be trusted, blackbird."

They arrived in the ornate nineteenth-century courtroom forty-five minutes later as James was being led through a doorway and into his seat.

Wood panels lined the walls halfway up to the soaring ceiling where ornate chandeliers hung. Wooden pews stretched across the gallery like a church. A platform rose in the front of the room, where a long desk with three microphones waited for judges. Only one appeared, a balding man in his sixties who looked like he enjoyed a good meal. His frameless glasses sat on a bulbous red nose. He wore a black robe with a large white cravat, sweeping up his skirts as he sat behind the middle microphone.

Pascal and Merle slid into the second row behind James. He wasn't handcuffed and wore one of his own suits, gray with pinstripes, a bit rumpled. He glanced at Merle nervously then turned away.

Michel Redier and James sat at one side of the courtroom while the government prosecutors occupied a place of honor near the middle. There were two of them wearing plain black suits, one short, one tall, their backs to the gallery, standing before the judge.

"Is that him?" Merle asked, looking at the judge. Pascal nodded. Then the proceedings began at a pace she couldn't follow. She wondered what James thought, sitting so still, hunched over in his chair as to make himself a smaller target.

Pascal seemed to be following just fine but there was no opportunity to ask what was happening. Merle pulled a notebook and pen from her purse and wrote "?"

He scribbled on it and passed it back. "Making case for *juge d'instruction*. Unusual." He listened some more as the prosecutors continued their argument. Then Merle wrote, "Why is Redier not speaking?" Pascal returned: "*Juge d'instruction* usually limited to major crimes. Murder, rape."

Merle turned the page. "Can you say something?" He shook his head. Merle felt her blood pressure rise. James had no idea what was going on. They weren't translating for him, and his attorney appeared to be taking a nap.

She scribbled, "Translator?" Pascal raised a finger and nodded. The droning of legal voices went on, and then finally there was a pause. Pascal rose and buttoned his coat.

He cleared his throat and begged the pardon of the judge. In a clear voice, to a rather startled row of attorneys, he said he was a friend of the defendant and wanted the court to be aware that *Monsieur* Silvers was an American and had no French. He understood nothing that was being said in the proceedings and thus could not participate in his own defense.

The judge, clearly put out by the interruption, asked Pascal for his name. "Pascal d'Onson, *Capitain, Police Nationale, Monsieur.*" He added that he was also a witness in the case so had grounds for the interest of justice.

The judge wavered between glowering at Pascal and at James. And back to Redier. *"Monsieur Redier? C'est vrai? Il ne parle pas français?"*

The former mayor stood slowly, half bowing as he nodded in deep respect. He said, yes, it was true. James spoke no French. He would, of course, appreciate a translator if the court saw fit.

A general commotion then, as orders to find a translator were given to a bailiff-type person and the judge announced a short break. He stood, saying they would reconvene in half an hour. Pascal and Merle stayed in the courtroom, as did James and his lawyer. The judge and prosecutors disappeared.

"What's going on?" Merle whispered. "What is *juge d'instruction?*"

"It means examining judge. He can do his own investigation." Pascal shook his head. "It is not done in these minor crimes. I don't know what the prosecutors are thinking. Maybe the judge is about to retire and wants to go out in a blaze of glory."

"Do you think the judge and Redier concocted some plan over lunch?"

"I cannot imagine what." Pascal glanced at her. "I think Redier has not forgotten the past."

Merle felt a chill. "Will they let me speak?"

"Possibly. It is not so formal at this point."

A translator was rustled up, a blonde woman in a navy suit, glasses, and sensible shoes. The prosecutors then the judge returned. The translator sat next to James and, as soon as they reconvened, began whispering in his ear. Merle wished she could listen in.

As best she could figure, evidence began to be presented. Photographs of Father Cyril's face. Medical records. Other documents, testimony from police officers. Merle heard Albert's name.

Merle scribbled on the pad. "Why didn't they get statements from you or me?" Pascal shrugged. "Tell me when to speak. I'm getting up," she wrote.

Another half hour went by, slowly, with long pauses for reading documents, looking at photographs. Pascal put his hand on Merle's knee: *not yet*. Then, after Redier stood and made some sort of statement and he was sitting down, Pascal waved her up.

"*Excusez-moi, Monsieur le juge. Je voudrais de mettre une déclaration. Je demande le traducteur.*"

The judge huffed, annoyed again. This time a female was asking to make a statement, *how rude*. He waved the translator over to the center of the room. The young woman started with the judge's question. "Please speak in English. Your name is?"

"Merle Bennett. The incident in question was at my home. I was a witness. I talked to the *gendarme* but no one asked me for my statement, so in the pursuit of truth and justice, I came here today."

The judge listened to the translation, pursed his lips, and told her to proceed.

"James Silvers is my friend and has been a guest in my home," she said, speaking slowly, pausing for translating. "He is a lawyer in the U.S. and a father of three children. He had just arrived from a long day of travel from New York City and was very tired the night of the incident. He may have been walking in his sleep. He acted strangely, yes, but no one was in any danger. I did not feel threatened. None of my other guests felt they were in danger from Mr. Silvers.

"Then Father Cyril, who I had only met that night, jumped into the situation. He didn't know any of the Americans. He was under the misconception that I needed his help. I did not. Mr. Silvers reacted rashly, but it wasn't personal. It was a misunderstanding. I beg the court to have pity on Mr. Silvers as he is not the sort of man who hits people. He is kind and gentle."

After the translation she turned to Pascal. "Agent d'Onscon was also a witness to the events and he can corroborate my statement."

The judge listened to the translator then cocked an eyebrow at Pascal. *"C'est vrai?" Is that true?* Pascal rose and said, yes, it was true. He added that *Monsieur* Silvers may have been affected by a sleeping pill he took that night.

The judge waved to the translator. She resumed her seat by James. Pascal sat down, staring straight ahead. Merle also sat, unable to tell if she had made any dent in the proceedings.

The prosecutor made another statement; the translation was whispered to James. The judge said something to Redier who nodded, then the hearing was over. The prosecutors and Redier rose as the judge swished out in his black satin.

Merle sat stunned. "What happened?"

Pascal turned to her. "I'm sorry, Merle. James will stand trial in two weeks. But they are letting him out until then under Michel Redier's supervision."

18

They waited in the courthouse lobby for over an hour for James and his attorney to appear. Merle and Pascal sat on a hard bench, paced, used a drinking fountain, worked their phones. The marble floors caught every whisper, sending them bouncing to the soaring roof. Better to keep to oneself here.

Courtrooms didn't scare Merle anymore. Starting when she was seven, she went with her father to court, watching from the last row in the balcony, playing with her shoestrings and occasionally thrilled by her father's oration. By the time she got through law school, the magic of the courtroom had dimmed. Stuffy, formal, and care-worn, it was a place of business like any other. Business that decided people's fates, their futures, their fortunes, yes. But to look at it with any sort of mystery would be a mistake. Only go in with the "knowns," the professors said. Never with the "unknowns." There were no Perry Masons in real life.

French court was an alien world. She couldn't understand what was going on. Procedure was a blur. The conventions and rituals were superficially similar but underneath lay philosophies, tradition, and values she didn't know. She made a note to herself to study French law and its foundations. Some fun winter reading.

Finally James appeared through a side door, blinking in the sunshine streaming through high windows. He was pale, shaken. He carried his suitcase in one hand and his briefcase in the other. Redier followed him, giving a uniformed officer some paperwork as they departed.

"James." Merle walked up to him, uncertain if she should give him a hug. He looked like he needed one though so she made it quick. "How are you?"

"Been better," he wheezed, glancing up at Redier who stood almost a foot taller. "At least you got me a lawyer."

She turned to Redier. "I don't understand why you couldn't plea bargain. Drop some of the charges for a guilty plea. Get James out of this."

Redier looked down his long nose. "That is not done in France, *madame*. The charges stand."

"But why go to trial for one punch? Isn't that a waste of everyone's time?"

Pascal said, "Unless the whole thing is dropped, they go to trial, Merle."

"This is not America, *madame*," Redier said haughtily.

"So I've noticed," James said. "I have to go home with him." He nodded toward his lawyer.

"Is he to be your houseguest?" Merle smiled, hoping Redier would be whipping up cappuccinos for James.

"His room at the Hotel Quimet waits for him," Redier said. "He will be safe there and check in with me twice a day."

"He's got my passport, my driver's license, my credit cards and my phone," James said. "Are you giving me back my phone? I need to call my wife."

"Ex-wife," Pascal corrected. James squinted at him then turned to his lawyer.

"Under supervision," Redier said. James rolled his eyes. "We must go. Come, *Monsieur* Silvers."

Merle and Pascal walked outside with them, down the wide steps to the street. The afternoon heat lay thick on the stone, radiating through the soles of their shoes. It was only as Redier, with James tagging along, disappeared around the corner that Merle remembered she needed a ride home. She turned to Pascal. "Are you driving me back?"

"The car's this way." He led her into the square. A bench under a tree was dirty with bird droppings but he brushed it off and they sat on one end. They were quiet for a moment then Pascal said, "You need to go home then? There are chores waiting for you there? Things on your endless, poorly written list of *choses à faire?*"

Merle smiled. "What do you have in mind?"

"Same as always." He slid a hand around her waist and pulled her close. "I hear of a hotel near here with a river and a lovely restaurant. Very secluded, very romantic. We could pretend we were at the beach again."

"And this hotel, they have a room?"

"By chance, *oui.* A delightful room, *chérie*, with a big soft bed and no view at all."

The drive north to Brantôme from Périgueux wound along riverbanks and cliffs, by Renaissance turrets and wooded hills. Merle sat back in the car, watching the countryside and Pascal. He owned an old green BMW sedan with tan leather seats, and he drove fast like Michel Redier. He had to slow as they reached the village as it was built on an island surrounded by a canal.

"*Les moulins*," he explained. Old mills with water wheels and many canals made Brantôme the Venice of Perigord. It was beautiful—all this water, cascading here and there, the bridges, the orange tile roofs, the square towers. They wound through the town, around the pedestrian center, and out of town toward the north.

"Just a bit more." He turned into an unassuming drive with a large house with a green mansard roof. Pink roses climbed the front walls. It didn't look large enough to be a hotel. Pascal parked by the front door and told her to wait.

Merle sat back on the warm leather seat and smiled to herself. For a second she thought of James and his predicament then banished him from her mind. She'd gone into a small store in Périgueux and bought a toothbrush, a hairbrush, and some moisturizer. Otherwise she had no luggage. She looked into the back seat and saw Pascal had a small overnight bag. He'd planned ahead, the scamp.

Within minutes they were ushered into a room at the top of the property to a separate building connected to the main house by winding gravel paths. A large water wheel plied the stream, cascading cups of water as it made its lazy rounds. The stream itself was fairly wide, some ten feet, with two arched bridges over it. The mill the water wheel serviced was an ancient stone building that now housed the dining room, the young man showing them their room told them. He gave Pascal a knowing smile as he bowed out.

Merle stood at the windows that overlooked the stream, bridges, and water wheel. Roses bloomed on both sides of the stream, and other flowers, foxglove, daisies, and lavender. Sunlight filtered through the leaves, sparkling on the water. It was like a fairy tale, this view. An old painting. A dream. Then some very real arms circled her from behind and a convincing set of lips touched her neck. She turned away from the landscape. *If this is dreaming, let's sleep awhile.*

As they kissed she slipped her hand down the back of his pants. That caused a whole series of clothes-rending events, bouncing-on-bed situations, and thrashing-on-sheets scenarios.

She'd never been so comfortable with a man. He made her laugh and made her wet at the same time, something she once thought impossible. She used to be so serious. Everything was proper and planned. Her sexual experience wasn't extensive, being married for twenty years to a man who had other interests. Before her marriage she had three or four boyfriends, none very serious and at least two whose technique in the bedroom failed to impress. Pascal, in contrast, had numerous tricks up his sleeves—or would if he were wearing anything.

His tongue explored her breasts, down her stomach, and between her legs with enthusiasm. He stretched her arms above her head and held them there with one hand while he rocked her gently under him, slowly bring her to climax. Only then did he move hard and fast for his own enjoyment.

They lay on the scented sheets, examining the glazed ceiling, watching the play of light reflecting off the water skip across the plaster.

A clock ticked in the bathroom and she tried to block the sound. How she had needed this, needed him, a man who saw her only as a woman. No games, no intrigues. Last summer there were moments when he had tricked her, led her on, yes, even lied to her. But this summer, all was forgiven. She had learned to take Annie's advice and be right here, right now. The past didn't matter; neither did the future.

She took his large hand in hers and examined his palm. The scars on his fingertips, the thick calluses of hard work, the muscled wrist, the curls of black hair, it all fascinated her. He was a *wunderbeast*, strong, fierce, full of secrets. If only she could read palms, find out if his lifeline intersected hers for more than a few nights, a few summers. But that wasn't very "right now," was it? She let a long, satisfied breath escape her mouth. She wasn't the Calendar Girl, obsessed with time anymore. She would let it have its way with her.

No more lifelines and to-do lists, no more rigid Merle. She laid his hand on her stomach, spreading his fingers wide. This is what she wanted, what she craved. A life full of love and acceptance, warmth and . . . maybe some wine.

Pascal rolled toward her and nuzzled her ear. "This is mine," he whispered, moving his hand lower, roaming over her hipbones, hair, thighs, claiming it all.

He was ready for another go. Oh to be young. She pulled her fingers through his hair and kissed him long and hard. The afternoon sun lit up the windows, languid and golden, bright with promise. There was nowhere else to be, nothing else to do.

She could hear her sisters now. *Carpe diem, Merdle.*

After a late, leisurely dinner where Merle was too blissed out to eat (the only explanation for picking at truffled pasta), she and Pascal strolled back to the room, pausing on the bridge to gaze at the water. The moon wasn't up yet. The stars were bright, leading the way. She was just about to point out Cassiopeia when a shooting star blazed across the sky.

"Make a wish," she said.

Pascal squinted. "Got it."

"What did you wish? You can tell me."

He took her hand and led her over to the gravel path and the steps. "Then it won't come true. The best secrets are those kept in your heart."

"Next to me? Am I there in your heart?"

"*Bien sûr, chérie.*"

As he turned on lights in the room, Merle closed the drapes. She heard a beeping. In her sex-and-wine haze, it took a second to recognize it as her cell phone.

Francie: Elise took off. Put her on a plane in Toulouse. I'm back to Malcouz tomorrow. No joy re Gillian.

Merle: No problems for Elise, I hope?

Francie: New case she wanted in on. Work, honestly!
Hope you're not too lonely. See you in the a.m.

She debated telling Francie she wasn't actually at home, wasn't missing her sisters, and wasn't the least bit lonely. But wasn't that the beauty of the cell phone? You could pretend to be anywhere, in church or court or on the moon, when you were actually rolling in the lavender with your French *amour.* Let them think she was pining away. There was a crazy sort of satisfaction in being underestimated.

Pascal called her name. He was stretched out on the bed, naked, sheets thrown in a pile. He patted the empty spot on the bed next to him.

"Come sing to me, blackbird."

LAWYRR GRRL

WHERE A WOMAN CAN GRROWL ABOUT THE LEGAL PROFESSION

BLOG—*Cherchez my French ass*
Tagged *Cheese, Brie, Fromage, diet, Camembert, Delices de France, weight loss, Chevre, French Kiss, and more cheese*
Posted June 28

Remember that scene in *French Kiss* when Meg Ryan pigs out on cheese on the train and then realizes she has lactose intolerance? Well, that, my friend, is me—except for the gas. Just the piggie part. Oh lord, *c'est* totally *moi*. One of these days I will turn into a big old wheel of cheddar and be rolled away to the Mold People's Home.

But enough about my addiction. The Sisterhood of the Traveling France winds down. We're three down, two to go, it's the fourth quarter or ninth inning or something. No sixth wheel found, no dog recovered.

That Girl is officially on her own. I have no idea where she went, why she left, or what she's thinking. She may have relatives in Italy, according to a sleuth back home but time's up. Without more to go on, I have to throw in the towel.

Come home, girlfriend! We need you to second on the Morrison lawsuit!

Ta ta.

19

It was well past noon by the time Pascal pulled his BMW up to the bastide stones at the dead end of rue de Poitiers. He parked behind the new rental car, the gray Peugeot. The drive home was bittersweet for Merle. It felt in a way like an end and a beginning, holding hands in the car like teenagers. He had to go south again for his work at some undisclosed gorgeous location. And she would go home soon too, although she might have to extend her vacation to attend James's trial. Maybe some relatives will come over for support, Pascal said. Work on that, he recommended.

Pascal was jealous, she realized with a smile. She could hardly ignore his comment about claiming her nether regions as his property. And today at breakfast he had made more disparaging comments about James's behavior. Merle could only agree. Slugging a priest on your first day in a foreign country? Not the best *entrée* into a society that prided itself on civility. And that was, despite several revolutions and beheadings of monarchs, mostly Catholic.

"Pranking the Pope would have been better," Pascal said. "Cyril is a holy man, a Frenchman. That will not go down well in court."

Pascal called James "your little friend" or "King James the Third." Merle knew she should tell Pascal that she and James were finished. That she was going to break it off, whatever "it" was, as soon as they got back to the U.S. But she should tell James first. It was only fair. And what if she was wrong? What if Pascal wasn't jealous of James and was only helping her and, well, fucking her for old times' sake?

As Pascal opened the car door for her and walked her to the house, she felt a little lost. "When will I see you again?"

"Very soon, *chérie*. Very soon."

He gave her a quick kiss and turned back to his car. She stood there stupidly, holding her keys and her heart in her hands, until he roared down the street and was gone. For a second she tried to will him to turn around, to come back to her. Then she came to her senses—*stop it, Merdle. Be practical. You live an ocean apart*—and unlocked the door.

Her sister's roller bag sat inside the door with her briefcase on the edge of the table. "Francie? I'm back." The house was quiet as a dormouse.

Merle unlocked the back door and poked her head into the garden, calling again. Then she went upstairs, a knot of worry in her gut. Her sister was at the market, that was it, or running some errand in the village. On one of the beds in the loft lay Francie's purse and her iPad. Would she go out without her purse? Maybe she just stuck some money in her pocket.

Merle tried to relax, slipping out of her dress and the stupid red shoes and into shorts and a T-shirt. Maybe she'd go on a run while Francie was out. Maybe Francie was on a run. Who was she kidding? Francie didn't exercise, that was clear to everyone on the walking tour.

Back downstairs, Merle got the cheese plate out of the fridge. Francie must have been cheese shopping because there were some new and different ones. Merle cut off a wedge of Delices de Pommard and washed it down with Perrier. She located her running shoes with the socks still stuck inside and pulled them on. After locking the back door, she pocketed her key and opened the front door. A slip of paper lay on the threshold. She'd missed it somehow on her way in.

Francie left a note. "Good girl," Merle whispered.

It was a cheap sheet of lined notebook paper, written in French. But Francie didn't know French and why would she—? Merle read the words, covering her mouth with her hand.

We have the American. If you want to see her again, give up the dog. We will contact you tonight.

Frozen in place, Merle tried to comprehend what had happened. The night before she left, those men, pounding on the door, asking about the dog. Had they come back? Why would they take Francie? Who were they?

This had to lead back to her call to the dog owner. Where was that phone number? She spun around, searching the room, still a mess from her scrubbing. She ran into the kitchen, frantic. Where was the reward poster? Then she remembered the number would be on her phone.

In the living room, she dug her phone out of her purse. She wound back through the calls, trying to remember when she'd contacted the dog's owner. She tried one. Michel Redier answered. She hung up.

She tried another. It rang a long time then finally a man answered in a gruff voice.

"*Allo, bonjour, monsieur*," she began in French. "I am looking for the owner of the dog, Aurore. I spoke to him several days ago."

"He is indisposed. Who is calling?"

"I talked to someone there about finding the dog and taking it to the veterinarian."

"You have the dog?"

"No, I'm sorry. She ran away again. May I ask who this is?"

"Claude LaFleur, *Gendarmerie*. The owner of the dog has been attacked, *madame*. He is in the hospital. We are investigating. If you can help, if you know anything about the situation, we would appreciate it."

She tried not to gasp, to control her emotions. The thought of Francie with such men made her throat catch. "I—I talked with a younger man. I don't know who he was. He seemed a little suspicious. I told him we found the dog, that we took her to an animal clinic, then helped her heal for a few days before she ran away again. I told him I lived in Malcouziac. He showed up here night before last, very late. I heard them outside but I didn't let them in."

"What happened, *madame*? *Continuez, s'il vous plait*."

Merle shut her eyes. "It's my sister. I-I got a note. She's been kidnapped. They want the dog in exchange for her."

The *gendarme* was very calm and made her repeat what happened when the men came to the door, everything that was said on the phone.

"Are these the same men who attacked the dog's owner?" she asked, her heart pounding. Just saying the word *kidnapped* was too much. And *attacked*. It was unreal. *Breathe, Merle.*

"Possibly. It appears the owner and his wife were held captive in their home by two criminals who wanted the dog. The reward is very high. It attracted attention."

"I saw the poster. But what should I do? My sister, she—" Merle gulped, trying to slow her breathing, to remember Annie's advice for not hyperventilating in court. *Hold your breath, let it out slowly.* "She's with them. And I don't have the dog to exchange."

LaFleur took down all her information and said someone would be by the house to talk to her shortly. The local *gendarme*, she expected. What help could they expect from him? She had to call Pascal. He would know who to bring in. Someone experienced.

Oh my god. Poor Francie. Was she hurt? Afraid? Merle bent over, a visceral pain in her gut from imagining her sister in distress, tied up, bleeding. No. She couldn't believe it. Francie was strong and smart and beautiful. She would talk her way out of it. Wouldn't she?

How could this have happened? If only Merle had come home last night instead of letting Pascal lick her from head to toe. It was her fault. She should have been here. But last night couldn't have been a mistake, could it? It was too flat-out wonderful. She didn't know what was happening here last night. So whose fault was it? Was that important? She wasn't above putting blame on Gillian. If she hadn't run off with that stupid dog, none of this would have happened. If she hadn't stopped to pick up the dog by the side of the road and hadn't insisted on rescuing her from the vet.

Where the hell are you, Gillian?

The dog. Merle pictured the little thing, sweet and timid, limping around the garden. If she could find the dog and give it to these miscreants, then Francie would be safe.

The dog was the ticket. She had to find the dog.

20

Annie wasn't answering her cell phone. Merle tried to remember her schedule, where she was today. Annie worked in Pittsburgh for a non-profit environmental group. She was often on the road, lobbying or arm-twisting or filing briefs in various courts. She'd flown home several days before. Merle frowned; she'd forgotten what day it was. Saturday. Right. Maybe it was today Annie flew home? Merle was losing her internal calendar just when she needed it, and it freaked her out for a second.

She paced in the garden, mentally listing all the things she could do to find Gillian and the dog. Calling Pascal was on the list, on the top actually. But she balked at involving him without getting her head around what was going on here, getting a strategic plan in place. She'd just asked him for a favor, and he'd come through with flying colors. And she'd repaid that favor, she thought, smiling to herself. But no. Must not think about Pascal's butt. Must find the dog. To find Aurore she had to find Gillian. To find Gillian—

What did Francie know about her? She'd talked to Gillian's assistant in the law firm. The emails. Merle rushed inside, up the stairs. There was Francie's purse and iPad on the bed. Merle turned the tablet on. A blogging site popped up, a control dashboard for a blog called *Lawyrr Grrls*. Merle stared at it. Did Francie write this blog? *Without telling us?*

An internet connection box popped up. Francie had cell service on her iPad and never told them, making them run around town to poach Wi-Fi. Merle tapped on the latest blog post at the top of the list and read it quickly. Yes, Francie was writing this, about their trip, about Gillian. Merle went back to the list of posts and read each one, back to the beginning of the tour.

Initially pissed off because Francie was baring family details, Merle had to smile at her sister's style. She was funny and sarcastic and right on about practicing law. And she concealed enough details that it would be hard to make an identification. Merle re-read the last few posts about Gillian's disappearance, and a draft that Francie had saved but not posted. It chronicled her time in Toulouse with Elise. Merle skimmed it, looking for Gillian details. They had tried to investigate at the train station and came away empty-handed. They asked at Avis and EuropCar rental agencies and were turned away. They used a photo of Gillian to show around. Merle pawed through Francie's purse and found a wrinkled 8-by-11 sheet, printed with a photo from the trip, Gillian holding Aurore, on the square in Loiverre the day they found her.

Setting aside the tablet, Merle went methodically through Francie's purse. Her wallet, camera, pens, tickets, receipts, gum, mints, granola bar, a tourist brochure of Toulouse, a pamphlet of a cathedral. Merle set them all out on the bed, then picked up the camera and turned it on. She flicked through the photos. Francie had taken hundreds on the trip; at least fifty in Toulouse. There was Elise by a fountain, pigeons on a lawn, a bridge and river, a church steeple, a sunset, lots of food on plates, wine bottles, sexy men. Then, one of the train station from the outside, from inside the lobby, a woman behind glass at a ticket window, a sour-faced Avis agent with her mouth open, a man at EuropCar with his hand up, shielding his face from the photographer. Making friends near and far, that was the Bennett girls.

Merle clicked forward through the photos. She stopped on one she couldn't see very well, a white rectangle of something. Taking the camera into her bedroom, Merle downloaded all Francie's photos to her laptop then searched through them. There, on a table with a fork.

A wine list. Merle's shoulders sagged. Two wines were underlined, a Sancerre and a Provence rosé, presumably what they'd drunk that evening.

How was she going to find the dog? The trail was cold now. Gillian could be anywhere. All they knew was that she'd left the rental car at the Toulouse rail station. And that her assistant said, according to Francie's latest blog post, she possibly had relatives in Italy.

Merle returned to Francie's iPad. A notice popped up: new mail. Merle found her mail box (password saved thank goodness) and opened it.

The first email was from Elise, a short note asking about her arrival time. Elise was apparently picking up Francie at the airport tomorrow. Merle closed her eyes, thinking hard what to say to Elise, to their parents, about Francie's kidnapping.

She could imagine the outcry and distress the information would cause. Somebody would fly over at great expense just to hold Merle's hand—because there was little else to do. Somebody would call the authorities. Merle had already decided to delay that while she tried her own tactics. She'd told that *gendarme* at Aurore's house so her duty was done. The police were not her friends these days, not in France. Somebody at home would make a stink in the newspapers or on Twitter or something. It would make things worse. No, she had to try to keep the cops out of it for a few days. Try to make some headway.

Merle opened her eyes and re-read Elise's email. There were two ways to go: pretend to be Francie or write as herself. She chose the second option and tapped out a note. "Merle here. Francie decided to stay on for a few more days. Will let you know her ETA as soon as possible."

Why Francie wouldn't write herself went unanswered. Merle opened the next email. It was from Gillian's assistant, Jonathan Greil.

I stayed late at the office last night to dig around. I'm really worried that Gillian isn't answering my emails. But she did return one phone call yesterday, cryptically as usual. It was on voicemail when I got into the office in the morning. She said she was staying in Europe for a few more weeks and that she would call Mr. Ward directly to explain. That everything was fine.

When I ran into Mr. Ward in the break room, he asked me if I'd talked to Gillian, and I said no, just the voicemail. He frowned like he was angry. Later in the day he made a point to come up to me in the hall all smiles, clapped me on the back, to tell me everything was fine with Gillian, that he'd talked to her and her position would be waiting when she got back. I asked when that would be, on account of being her assistant. He said he wasn't sure but if I wanted to take some vacation that would be fine. Can you believe that? He basically told me to get lost for a couple weeks, all paid. I don't know what to think. Old Ward never takes a day off unless somebody dies. I'm going to work next week but then, what the hell. Off to the Hamptons. Jonathan.

No real news there, except that Gillian was staying in Europe for a while. The next email was also from inside the law firm. But before she could open it, Merle heard someone knocking downstairs. She'd wondered how long it would be until James made himself known. She'd been dreading seeing him again, especially now with much bigger problems than his.

But it wasn't James. The blue jumpsuit tugged across Albert's ample girth as he waved at her through the glass. She unlocked the door. "*Bonjour,* Albert."

He wasn't smiling as he stepped inside. "You are all right, Merle?" He looked her up and down as if checking for injuries. "You are back and everything is fine?"

"Yes." She frowned. "Why do you ask?"

He wiped his brow, visibly relieved. "I found this letter under my door." He pulled a sheet of notebook paper from a pocket of his jumpsuit and handed it to her. "I came right over. I was so worried."

Merle recognized the handwriting immediately.

We have the American woman. You will cooperate or we will kill her. Say nothing to les flics *or you will be next. More tonight.*

Merle stared at the words in French, uncomprehending for a moment: *Nous allons tuer.* This was harsher than her note. She extracted it from her back pocket, smoothing them side by side on the table.

"Does it say, *we will kill her?*" Her voice broke.

"But it is all fine, Merle. You are home, you are safe."

She wondered what she should tell him, looking at his kind, blue eyes. Why had the kidnappers sent him a note? Albert followed her glance toward Francie's suitcase. He blinked nervously. "And your sisters? They are fine too?"

Merle couldn't lie to him. After she told him what had happened and they exclaimed and hugged and worried aloud, she poured them both a medicinal glass of wine. They sat in the darkened parlor on the lumpy horsehair settee and stared at the floor.

Albert downed the last drops in his glass. "I heard two men were in town, asking about Americans. The girl at the *tabac*, the one with the fancy eyebrows, she tells me this yesterday. They asked about American women."

Merle struggled to process this. "Did you meet them?"

He shook his head. "I forgot about it until this morning when this note showed up at my door."

The kidnappers must have thought she lived alone, in which case no one would get the ransom note left in her door. Albert's note was to get the ball rolling, get somebody to look for the dog. "Did she say what they looked like?"

"Let's go ask her."

Aude of the fancy eyebrows would be called a Goth in the States. She had several pierced rings in both dark eyebrows and wore heavy black eyeliner with lipstick the color of dusk. Merle had wondered why she lived in this small, conventional village, how she put up with some of them, but was afraid to ask. It didn't pay to be nosy, even with French Goth girls.

Aude and Albert were old friends. She smiled at him and immediately turned for a newspaper. He shook his head, explaining they had some questions. He introduced Merle.

"*Bien sûr*. I know *madame*." Her English was good.

"These two men who came in, the out-of-towners," Merle began.

"*Les inconnus*," Albert said.

"Yes? What about them?" Aude asked, snapping her gum. She wore all black, down to her fingernails.

"Can you describe them?" Merle asked.

"One tall, one short. Only one talked. The other I keep an eye on for the stealing. He may have slipped some cigarettes into his pocket."

"How were they dressed?"

She shrugged. "Normal. Dirty."

"What did they look like, their hair, noses, scars, anything?"

"Brown hair. Or black. Unshaven. Ugly. They talk a little funny. An accent."

"What kind of accent?"

"I don't know. Funny."

Merle squinted at her. "Have you seen them since?"

"No. Just the one time. I tell them don't come back."

"What exactly did you say?"

"They ask if I know an American woman who lives here. I say no. *Pardon, madame*, I did not want to give them your information. You never know."

"Thank you, Aude, I appreciate that. What did you tell them about Albert?"

"I say, somebody who lives at his address might know an American. No names, *Père*."

"*Merci*," Albert mumbled, looking a bit rattled.

"Why would you do that?" Merle asked, crossing her own arms.

"They would not leave the *tabac*. They stay and talk, push away the customers, read the magazines, never buying. They smell bad. Finally, I tell them your address, *Père*, just so they will go."

They thanked the clerk and stepped back into the small plaza. The metal tables and chairs outside the *tabac* were deserted. Here was where Merle first met Albert, where he took her under his wing, became her friend. Here he was, helping her again.

"I wish she hadn't done that. I think you should leave town for a while, Albert. Go visit that brother of yours in the Languedoc. Work on your tan."

The old priest was startled, then shook his head. "No, no, no. I will stay with you in case they come back."

"Visit your brother, Albert. See how his grandchildren have grown."

"I could not leave. I would not enjoy myself." He took her arm, leading her through the streets. "I will stay with you tonight. We will face whatever comes together."

21

Merle bought two *jambon* sandwiches at the *boulangerie* and she and Albert walked back to her house. They ate their very late lunch tensely in the garden. Merle thought about last summer when Albert had been badly injured because of her. She couldn't allow him to get hurt again, no matter what happened to Francie. She had to talk him into leaving the village. Maybe after tonight. Because she felt marginally better having him with her.

Albert had a fencing class in the early evening. He went home to prepare. Merle retrieved Francie's iPad from upstairs and sat in the shade of the acacia tree, reading the last email. It was from Gillian's assistant, Jonathan, again.

Ms. Bennett. Is everything okay over there? I haven't heard from you in awhile. I've been looking through G's emails because I don't have much else to do. Take a look at the one from May 8 marked 'Legal,' and again, more recent, June 25. These are not law-related as far as I can tell. J.

Merle went back to the file marked "Gillian mail" and scrolled through to May 8. The email was from someplace called Net Buddy.

Ms. Sergeant,

Once you are done with the paperwork for the lawsuit can we meet at the usual place.

S.

Not much to go on. Her name was misspelled. Why had he thought that was not law-related?

Merle found the email from June 25. It had a subject line of "when" with "xxx" in the "from" box and was from another Internet café, this one called Webi.

'Buono. Saturday. Pastis.'

Italian, English, French. What did it mean? An assignation for Saturday? Where? And who was she meeting? Merle went back through the emails. None of Gillian's outgoing emails since she left for France were saved at the firm. Either she wasn't using that email address or she wasn't sending emails. This lone email from the 25th was important, cryptic as it was. It had slipped through the cracks, maybe sent by mistake to the law firm.

Merle went back into the house and poured water into a glass. If only she knew more about computers, about the Internet, about how to trace an email. Pascal would know or know who to ask. She paused, staring again at the iPad. She opened her phone, scanned her contacts. She'd sent him email before but not from her phone. She sent him a text asking for his email address to send him something.

Then a short note to Jonathan. This time she did pretend to be Francie; it was just easier. She told him she was fine, staying in Europe for a few extra days. And to please continue to send anything fishy on Gillian's account.

Then another email to Francie's boss, Mr. Baillee, asking his forbearance for another week of vacation, that she'd caught a bug and didn't want to spread it to the entire East Coast and didn't she have some sick days coming? Merle tried not to beg too much; it was so un-Francine.

As she clicked "send," a knock on the front door rattled through to the kitchen. Merle poked her head out and saw it was James. Gulping down the water, she straightened, girding her loins for manfriend drama.

"You're back," he said, stepping inside. "I came by last night but no one was here."

Merle waved him back into the garden. "I decided to stay over up there."

He nodded, too preoccupied with his own problems to get the message. "I hit the sack early. Didn't get much rest in the slammer."

She folded her arms and feigned concern. "What does Redier say?"

"Not much. He didn't do much in court, did he? I'd get another lawyer if I could. Do you think I should? What happened to you last summer? Wasn't there somebody else involved, a real lawyer?"

Merle bit her lip. She had told James all about last summer, several times, and didn't want to do it again. "I can give you a name. If you aren't satisfied with Redier."

"How would I know? The whole justice system is completely different over here. No plea deals? What the hell is that about?" He was wound up, jittery.

"Can I get you something? Water? Wine?"

He agreed to a glass of white wine. She poured two glasses of wine and put some of Francie's cheese on a plate with some grapes. *Semblance of normality.* Francie should be eating her special cheese. Merle set the tray down on the green metal table. James waited to be served, biting his nails in the shade of the west wall. Merle handed him a glass.

"You have the guy's name? The other lawyer?" James gulped wine. "Where's he located? Nearby? Somebody in that town, what is it, Perigoo?"

"He's in Bordeaux."

"Is that close?"

"Not particularly. But it's the capital of this region. You want me to get it right now?"

"The sooner the better. This Redier is jerking me around. I have vibes about people. You know that about me, Merle. I get a bad one off that frog."

Back in the house Merle did a search on Francie's iPad for her criminal attorney from last summer, scribbled down his information on the back of an envelope, and once back outside, handed it over.

James stared at the number. "He's good, you say? He got you off?"

"It didn't come to that."

He had finished his wine. "Can you—?" He held out his glass. Merle bit down on her molars. For somebody who loved French wine, he sure hated France.

Refill in hand, he started up again like a machine wound too tight. She'd seldom glimpsed this aspect of James Jeremy the Third, the steel-trap mind of the lawyer, the questions shotgunned out without a pause for answers. He questioned Redier's record, his cronyism with the judge and various people in court, on and on. He circled back to Father Cyril.

"What does he hope to gain from filing charges? Is his job in danger? Is he a pedophile? Will his face heal faster? Will he regain his dignity?"

"He did look pretty bad."

"Like somebody who fell down the stairs? Worse than a fist to the schnozz? Right. Looked pretty suspish to me. Maybe he did a little extra work to make it look worse? Do you think after the criminal case he files civil charges against me? Tries to get some money? Is that his angle?"

"Maybe. I don't know how that works in France."

The questions rolled on. Could Cyril claim loss of wages? Medical bills if he has socialized medicine? Loss of dignity? Loss of complexion? Did he lose eyesight? Where was he from? Why was he here?

"Did you bring a laptop with you?" Merle asked.

"Of course. Plenty of correspondence to keep up on, especially with them holding me over."

"Does your family know?"

He sagged, his manic energy flagging. "I had to tell the ex. My youngest was expecting me back for her birthday party. That's not happening, at least for old pops. The ex gets all up in arms, says she's coming over to help lead the cavalry. I told her, help with what, buying shoes? 'Because that's all you're good for.' Not true, not true, I didn't say that. But she's bleeding me dry with child support."

"Is she coming over?"

"Tuesday. Is that tomorrow? What's today? Whenever Tuesday is. Couldn't stop her. Never could. So I'll have that hot mess on top of my other troubles."

Merle felt herself smile. His ex would keep him busy and distracted. "Why don't you try to find something out about Father Cyril? Google him."

James whipped his head toward her. "They have Google here?"

"They do. It'll be in French, but you can tell it to translate for you."

He stood up suddenly, poured the rest of his wine down his throat. "God love Goo—" Rapping on the front door. James froze. "You expecting somebody?"

Merle stood slowly, trying to stay calm. "Maybe." She looked at her watch. Could it be Albert returning? Or was it the men who had Francie? She turned toward the kitchen door.

James took her arm roughly. "Wait. Don't answer it. It could be for me." He pulled up his pant leg and showed her his electronic ankle bracelet, glowing green. "They made me wear this. Can you believe it? Bastards."

"But you're allowed to roam around the village, aren't you?"

"They didn't say exactly. Or I didn't understand it."

They walked on tiptoe over the crunchy gravel and up to the side of the kitchen door. From there you could see straight through to the front door. The shutters were open. She peeked around the edge of the doorframe.

"It's the *gendarme*," she whispered, feeling strangely like a child playing cops and robbers.

"He's a double bastard." James took her arm, holding her against the house. The leaves from the pear tree poked at her neck. "Stay here. He'll go away."

More knocking. They waited a few minutes until it stopped for a good stretch. Merle chanced another look. "He's gone."

"He'll be back."

Was the *gendarme* there about Francie or James? She hadn't told him Francie was missing. She didn't want to tell him. Not because it sounded so awful, though it did, but because James was really only capable of one full-blown incident at a time. He had his hands full with himself.

"You should go," she whispered. "Slip out the back."

Merle watched him skip sideways down the alley, trying to make himself small against the back walls of her neighbor's gardens. In his cargo pants and Jets T-shirt, he wasn't exactly inconspicuous but he'd probably get back to the hotel all right. He paused at the street, gave her a thumbs-up, and darted out.

Albert should be back from fencing practice soon. She knocked on his back gate but there was no answer. Retreating into her own yard, she locked the garden gate, hung the key inside the kitchen, and sat down at the table to worry.

After five minutes she got annoyed with herself. Francie was out there somewhere, scared, vulnerable, maybe hurt. Something had to be done.

22

Pascal had sent a text with his official police email address. Merle turned on Francie's iPad and forwarded the two strange emails on to Pascal with a note asking if he could trace them. She poured herself another glass of wine and found his reply when she got back.

"What's this about, blackbird? Your boyfriend's business?" She texted instead.

MBennett: *Can you talk?*

He replied to the affirmative and she dialed. His voice warmed her. "What are we drinking, *chérie?* Is this—what do they call it—the drunk dial?"

Merle set down her wine glass. "No. This is serious, Pascal."

"King James the Third?"

"No, it's Francie. My sister. The one with the—" *Big tits.*

"Red hair. I remember, blackbird."

"Someone left a note under the door. She's been kidnapped by the men who want the dog." Merle gulped a breath, then a slug of wine.

"Slow down, *chérie.*"

"They were here Thursday night. I didn't tell you. I didn't open the door, but the lights were on. They knew I was in here. They wanted to know about the dog. Then when you dropped me off, all of Francie's stuff was here but no Francie."

"She didn't just go for a walk?"

"It's been hours. Everything is here, Pascal. Her purse, her camera, her suitcase, everything. The only thing I can figure is they thought she was me."

"What does the note say?"

She read it to him, the words no more enlightening the tenth time than the first. Francie was gone, captive by thugs.

"And have you called the police?"

"I called the dog's owner. To find out who they were. I talked to them on the phone before, that's how they found me. I told them I lived in Malcouziac. Anyway, a cop was there. He said the owner had been held by two men, then attacked. They wanted the dog."

"They were waiting for someone to call with information for the reward," Pascal said. "And you did."

"But I told them I didn't have the dog! Why would they take Francie?"

"The criminal mind isn't logical, *chérie*. So they will come back tonight?"

"I guess. Albert is going to stay with me. They gave him a note too, with even stronger language. Now he's in danger because he's my friend. Just like Francie, because of me."

"Keep things locked tight. I will send the *gendarme* over to keep an eye on you." He paused. "What are these emails you send me?"

"Sent to Gillian. I have to find her. She has the dog."

He told her he would call later and make sure she was all right. She wanted to ask him where he was, was he close enough to come here, but she bit her tongue. She would have to make it through the night with only an old priest at her side.

An hour later, as purple light crept over the bastide wall, Albert arrived at the front door, a bottle of wine and a baguette in hand. He wore khaki trousers and a white shirt, part of his fencing uniform. Giving her *bisous* on both cheeks, he set the food on the table. Merle locked the shutters behind him, double-checking the padlock.

The evening stretched out in front of them. Albert had brought a book and settled in to read on the horsehair settee. Merle went through Gillian's emails, searching for something, anything, to lead them to her. Night fell and she locked the kitchen door. Albert dozed, his book slipping to his round belly. Merle looked at the sky out the window in the kitchen, the stars shining in the velvet night. Shadows crept across the garden.

Pascal called at eleven. Assured that everything was calm, he told her the two emails had been sent from different places. Net Buddy was in Florida, outside of Tampa. There were several on the Gulf coast. That was the email in May with the "meet at the usual place" message.

The other address was more intriguing, from inside France, a village near the Italian border, north of Nice. It was remote up there, full of hermits and smugglers. The Internet café was a single terminal in the back of a convenience store, known to authorities as a useful spot for criminal activity.

"What about the message itself? Any ideas?" she asked.

"Pastis? The drink of course but also the name of bistros, hotels, and cafés."

"Is there one near there?"

"In fact, in Nice there are three. Café Pastis, Bistro Pastis, and outside, in an old chateau in the hillside, Hotel Pastis."

"So they met in Nice. Maybe."

"Could be. But not much of a trail there."

"If Gillian is in Nice. . ."

"Maybe. For one day. Could have been a week ago."

Merle sighed. "I have to find her, Pascal."

"Does she use a credit card?"

"Maybe. But I—wait, I have her cell number." She searched through her phone and found Gillian's number that Francie had called. "She didn't answer and it sounded like she may have it turned off."

"We will track her. She will turn it on." His voice lowered. "I don't like you there alone, blackbird."

"Albert is here."

"Very comforting. He can poke them with his *epée*." He sighed. "I cannot leave here now. Maybe in one day, or two. Come to me, *chéie*. You should not be alone."

"I'm all right, Pascal. I saw the *gendarme* on the street earlier."

"And your boyfriend? Is he with you?"

"No. He has an ankle bracelet so he doesn't wander."

"Perfect. Come to me and he cannot follow."

She promised to think about it. She couldn't really plan anything, could she? Not with Francie's fate in the balance. She set down her phone and watched Albert snore. When the knock came on the door, she almost jumped out of the chair. Albert woke with a start, his book dropping to the floor.

"*Quoi? Qui est là?*"

Merle put a finger to her lips. Another knock. Then the scratch of wood. She saw the paper being pushed through the crack in the shutters. Merle realized they could see her easily in the light, though she couldn't see them. She ran up the stairs, opening the window over the door. As she eased the shutters open, she saw the top of a head, a man in a dark cap. His face was hidden by the brim. He stood at the shutters, peering inside, then looked around, dried his palms on his pants, and ran down rue de Poitiers into the darkness. No sign of the *gendarme* in any direction.

Downstairs, Albert stood unsteadily in front of the settee, his glasses askew. Merle went to the door. She scooped up the note and relocked the door. Under the floor lamp by the settee, she smoothed the paper against the cushion.

"What does it say? Is your sister all right?" Albert whispered.

Bring the dog to Montpellier in two days.
We will tell you where tomorrow.

"Montpellier?" Merle repeated.

"It is to the south some ways. On the Mediterranean."

"Yes, I—Where is Francie?" She wrapped her arms around her sides, tightening against her ribs. She felt in danger of flying into pieces. "Why haven't they said anything about her?"

"We should talk to *Monsieur le Gendarme*. He will know what to do." Albert had more faith in *gendarmes* than anyone.

Merle grabbed her phone. "I'll call Pascal." She stopped. "Wait. Did they leave you a note?" They hurried out through the garden, the alley, both gates. Inside Albert's yard the sweet smell of ripening plums was thick on the night air. He opened his back door and led her through to the front, where he'd found the other note.

Unlike hers, his door shutters fit perfectly together with no cracks. "It wasn't until I unlocked the shutters that I found it on the street." He fiddled with his padlock and there it was, wedged by a hinge.

"Lock up," Merle reminded him. They walked back to his kitchen table and examined the note under the light.

"It's the same," Merle said. At least they didn't mention killing anyone.

"They must know we don't have the dog," Albert said, frowning at the scribbles.

"They're counting on us to find her." She turned to the priest. "And we will."

Albert let Merle out his back gate, watching the alley as she went through into her garden. "*Bon soir*, Albert," she called over the wall.

"*Bon soir*, Merle." His gentle voice floated on the breeze. She locked the doors tight and stood in the silent house. Again she thought she didn't like being alone here. She wanted to go to Pascal. But Francie. Where were they holding her? Was it close by? They were here in Malcouziac. Why make the exchange in Montpellier?

Two men, the *gendarme* LaFleur had said, held the dog owner and his wife at their farmhouse. These guys must be scary in some way, threatening, violent. They had weapons or were cruel with their fists. By their notes though, not educated. Some kind of demands must be on them. Why else would they kidnap a woman just to get a dog? A very expensive dog but still, not worth a human life. Maybe that wasn't the way they looked at it. The dog owner may recover or not.

Merle sat down at the table, stared at the cold fireplace, and tried to reason like the kidnappers. They want the reward money. They needed the dog. They go to the owner's house, hold him against his will, waiting for a call about the dog's whereabouts—so they can return the dog to the owner for the reward? That made no sense. They are burned at the owner now. He knows who they are. Unless they got a third party to return the dog, get the reward, and give it to them. Would the third party be Francie?

There had to be something simpler than this. Was money not their object at all? If they didn't want the reward, they must be selling the dog to someone. Maybe Aurore was worth much more to a truffle hunter.

Merle sighed, glancing at her watch. It was nearly one but Pascal answered. "They were here. One guy, with a note. Same note at my house and at Albert's. The *gendarme* disappeared."

"Did you get a look at him?"

"It was too dark."

"Read it to me."

She read the short sentences. "Why Montpellier?"

"It is a city. Easier to approach unseen in a crowd. Maybe they plan an escape by sea." He paused. "I am near there. Come, blackbird."

"I have to wait for instructions. I have to be here tomorrow night."

"Albert will get a note. He will call you. *Chérie*, these are criminals. Stupid, dumb dog thieves perhaps, but without a conscience or they wouldn't have beaten that old man and taken your sister. I have called the *gendarmerie* in St. Paul, where the dog owner lives. The old man is still unconscious. But the wife has given them good descriptions and an artist is working on sketches."

"And then what?"

"Then the heat comes down on them. The sketches go out to every village, every city. All the *gendarmes* in the area will be watching for them. Police will be looking for them. And they become much more desperate."

"Jesus Mary," Merle whispered.

"Come here, blackbird. Pack your suitcase right now and get in the car."

Merle sank to a chair, her head in her hands. "It's so late, Pascal."

"You are right, you need a clear head. Get up with the birds. I will text you directions. Promise me, blackbird. Promise you will come in the morning."

23

The route Pascal had chosen through the hills of southwest France, stony and barren and sometimes impenetrable, could best be described as "scenic." Avoiding Toulouse and the highways, he'd mapped a back roads trail. Across into the Quercy and through many Cahors roundabouts, it wound along the Lot River. Slow going, with tiny villages, but picturesque with arched bridges and crumbling yellow stone and mossy tile. From there, she plunged away from civilization into a *Parc Naturel* full of pine trees and a place for "Le Camping." There was plenty of time to worry as the morning sun glinted off the lazy river and shot through the pines.

She slept for three hours. After Pascal hung up, Merle found Jonathan had sent Francie another email. No news to report, just a friendly missive. Something about it, about the Francie everyone liked, the one admired for her beauty and wit, almost broke Merle's heart. She'd too often dismissed Francie because she was pretty and flaunted it. She was more than pretty, she was a knock-out. Was she jealous of Francie? She was much younger and always would be, and it was hard to hold her beauty against her. It was amazing she hadn't remarried after the airline pilot fiasco. Men swarmed around her but no one was special enough to snag her. That model from last year, the pretty boy—she'd tossed him aside after a few months.

At two a.m., Merle realized she hadn't found Francie's cell phone. Did she still have it? Merle pawed frantically through her sister's suitcase.

The phone was tucked into a side pocket. Three new text messages: a general hello from their mother, one from the law firm okaying her for sick leave, and one from somebody named Jason: *hey, babe, what's shaking, sweet cheeks?* Francie's text from Toulouse was her last.

At three, Merle wrote Albert a note, explaining she was going to find her sister. She asked him to get help from the *gendarme* if he felt anxious and to please consider going to his brother's house. Before she left, she would slip it into his door. Then she'd climbed the stairs and attempted sleep. She lay on the bed, watching the moonlight on the bedroom ceiling, every muscle tense, her head pounding. An owl in a faraway tree hooted.

What the hell was she doing here in France? This was supposed to be a fun sister trip. It was, for a while, before it all came crashing down.

She got up and called Annie again. Still no answer. She left a message this time. "Call me."

Now, on the road, driving was at least action, forward movement. The landscape flattened out east of the pine forests heading into Rodez. Cow pastures, horses, and vineyards filled the fertile land between the hills. She stopped for gas and coffee in Rodez on Avenue de Montpellier, overlooking the river. She drove southeast through another forest, a park, then more hills. The Peugeot chugged along as she merged onto the toll road near Millau, the espresso keeping her awake.

She reached the outskirts of Montpellier and pulled over to call Pascal. She could hear the relief in his voice as he gave her directions to a hotel near the center of town.

The moist Mediterranean air warmed her face. Montpellier was a big city, almost as large as Toulouse but prettier with palm trees and the smell of the sea. She got lost inside the city twice then there was Pascal, waiting on the sidewalk.

"What does this dog look like?" Pascal asked as they settled in their chairs for lunch. The bistro was in the old part of Montpellier near a large, open plaza. Merle felt the coffee buzz drain away and munched on her third piece of bread. He said, "Maybe we can find a similar one."

He hadn't been able to get any more information about Gillian's whereabouts or the kidnappers from the various agencies. The sketches hadn't come in yet.

"A wavy coat like a poodle. Smallish, maybe eighteen or twenty inches. A little curly hair on the face and head. Brown and white," Merle said.

"Have they seen it, these thieves?"

"The photograph in the newspaper and on the reward poster."

Pascal sat back in his chair. "I wonder."

"What?"

"Someone snatched the dog, right? Took it from its cage. Who do you suppose did that?"

She squinted, putting it together. "Same two?"

He shrugged and drank some wine. He wore an actual white dress shirt with his collar open, with black slacks, a black leather sports jacket, and cowboy boots. This was as dressed up as she'd seen him. He must have some high-level official business here. And yet he was at lunch, with her.

He twirled his fork. "I'm thinking they are clowns, right? But they manage to get the dog from the owner's kennel. Put it in their car or whatever. Then, somehow, the dog escapes."

"After they take out the ID chip. Did I tell you that? The vet thinks that's what her injury was."

"Okay. Then the dog runs off and they are in big trouble with whoever they are stealing the dog for. If that is right, they have seen this dog. They know the dog. It would be hard to fool them with another."

"You think it was a contract thing?"

"Without a doubt. Some *trufflier* saw that article and needed a new dog. The truffle business is very—" He made a slashing motion across his neck.

"Cut-throat." Merle shivered, thinking of Francie. Their lunch came, chicken with *haricots verts* for him and steak *frites* for her. Despite her nerves, Merle attacked her meal, ravenous. Even Pascal was impressed. "Poor starving American. It is good you have someone to buy you meals, penniless gypsy."

He had to go to work. He gave her his hotel key, told her to make herself at home. It was a small family-run hotel on a narrow side street in the *Vieux Ville*. The old town was all walking streets, cobblestones wheeling out from the plaza. She carried her small bag from a community parking lot three blocks away and slipped up the stairs to the third floor of the hotel.

Pascal's room was utilitarian and plain, a threadbare blue spread over the blankets on the small double bed, a cramped bathroom, and a table with one chair in the corner. Merle spread out her laptop, the iPad, and her notes on the table. She took out her phone and called Albert.

"*Mon Dieu, je suis très inquiet!*" His English was failing him, that's how upset she'd made him. "I do not see the note until after I am at your house for long minutes, knocking, thinking you too have been taken by the bad men."

"I'm sorry to worry you, Albert. I had to leave very early or I would have called. I'm safe, and I want you to be extra careful. Can you please consider going to visit your brother tomorrow?"

"I am just an old man. I know nothing about this business."

"But these men don't know that, so be careful. They should leave you another note tonight. Call me when you get it, all right?"

He agreed, calm now. He had fencing practice with his summer club again—all week. He couldn't leave. She gave him the hotel's phone number in case her cell phone didn't work. He muttered a little, scolding her again for frightening him, and hung up.

Pascal had told her they would need to involve the *Policier Nationale* very soon. A kidnapping was serious business and they couldn't handle it themselves. As an officer, he had some discretion but the time would probably come as soon as they found out the rendezvous point.

Merle stared at the cobweb in the corner of the ceiling. She didn't want to involve the police. She couldn't explain it really, just that her experiences in that department didn't inspire confidence. The longer Francie was held, the less the chance they would find her, or find her in good shape. If the police got involved, everything would slow down. It just made sense to Merle: leave the cops out of it. One more day and they'd know where the exchange point was. Francie would be there and Merle would get her sister back. She had to.

In the meantime she would search for Gillian. She opened Francie's email again. Jonathan had written again.

Ms. Bennett. I heard you're sick. I hope it's just that "French Flu" you hear about when people go to Paris and don't want to come home. I found one more email. It was in Gillian's spam folder.

Merle downloaded it. It was again from a strange IP address and in French.

'Votre reservation est confirmée. Nous vous accueillerons le jeudi 27 Juin, pour deux nuits. Merci de votre visite.'

Gillian had made a reservation somewhere in France for two nights, last week. Merle read it over three times, wondering why the hotel name wasn't listed. Had Gillian scrubbed it somehow? Had she meant to delete it and it ended up in spam? Merle forwarded it to Pascal, asking for another Internet Provider search.

This was the first solid lead since Gillian turned in the rental car in Toulouse. Someone had written to her from near Nice, but had she actually gone there? Merle did a Google search for "hotel pastis" and up came dozens of hits, chief among them the Peter Mayle novel and a ritzy joint in St. Tropez. She searched for "café pastis" and again, hundreds of mentions of the concoction on menus popped up.

Maybe it was a clue, not a place. Somewhere they'd met for a pastis, that foul-tasting anise drink, milky green and only palatable when watered down massively. Merle had one, and only one, years before. But the French loved them, especially in the south.

If it was a clue, it was useless to her. Merle stared at her notes then dialed the Hotel Pastis in St. Tropez. Putting on her best sweet-sounding voice, she tried to wrangle some information out of a clerk who sounded like she was born with a posh spoon up her ass. Client visits are "utterly" confidential.

Merle kept at it, searching the Internet and Gillian's emails until exhaustion and the sun in the west window warming the room caught up with her and she curled into a dead sleep on the bed.

Dinner was late at an inexpensive bistro. Merle insisted on paying, she told Pascal upfront. He was offended, she could tell. But she wasn't a penniless gypsy or a kept woman. She squeezed his knee between courses, making him forget to be angry. She kept her phone on the table until Pascal recommended putting it in her pocket. The waiter was disapproving. But Albert didn't call before they walked back to the hotel through narrow streets in the glow of streetlights.

In the room she turned to Pascal. "I'm sorry this isn't Périgueux again," she said. "Not as much fun."

He kissed her and said, "We will always have Périgueux."

She smiled. "Such a romantic."

"I am French. We invented it."

He was back in his uniform, black T-shirt, jeans, and motorcycle jacket. She buried her nose in the leather of the collar, smelling him, memorizing it for the long winter ahead. She didn't want to think about winter or home. But she was practical. It would come; she would go home. With Francie. Definitely with Francie.

They were standing there, arms around each other, nuzzling and making wishes, when the call came. Merle jumped, pulled her phone from her pocket. "Albert?"

"*Oui, c'est moi.* I am okay." His voice was shaky.

"Did something happen?"

"I must tell you, *c'est vrai? D'accord.* I am walking home from dinner with Father Cyril. He has a room in the back of the church now." There was the sound of a cork popping and the glug of liquid being poured.

"Albert? What happened?"

"*Pardon.* I need some wine to calm down. So, I am walking by your *rue* and a man runs around the corner and knocks me down. *L'heurt. Boom.* He spins away, disappears down the street."

"Oh my god. Are you all right?" Last year's attack, the gash on his head, came flashing back.

"*Oui, oui.* I land on my derriere. Quite a large target. No harm done. Just the pride."

"I'm glad you're okay." Merle raised her eyebrows at Pascal. "Did you find a note in your door?"

"I dust myself off and walk home. And *voilà*, in the crack of the shutters, the letter. I will read it to you. 'Meet at the center of the Polygone, 1800 hours, tomorrow. Bring the dog.'"

"I need to get a pen, Albert." Pascal handed her a pen as she grabbed her notebook on the table. "Can you read it again please? Slowly. And spell that place."

She wrote it carefully, then read it back to him. She spelled back "Polygone," pronounced like "polygon" but French: *po-lee-gawn*. Albert added, "I am now thinking it is a good idea to visit my brother, Jean-Paul."

"Yes, Albert, please go. Fencing can wait. Be safe." She thanked him and turned off the phone.

Pascal was frowning at her notebook. "The Polygone is a *grand* hall for shopping. What do you call them in America?"

"Shopping mall?"

"Yes. Very busy that time of day."

"Where is it?"

"About five blocks from here in the center of town." He looked very serious. "It is time, *chérie*. We must bring in the troops."

24

From the first meeting early the next morning in the *Police Nationale* offices in a large, government complex on *rue de la Vielle Poste*, Merle felt a sense of foreboding. This would not end well. Pascal, a loner, was now a cog in a task force for major crimes. He had come here to investigate some huge winery in the Languedoc that was suspected of mixing cheap Chilean wine in its Vin du Pays d'Oc, the usual scam. Now he was reassigned temporarily to the task force but in an adjunct capacity, translating when necessary, a minion. A burly man in a navy uniform with a chest full of medals asked her for all the ransom notes, the details of the dog, her sisters' information, Gillian's information, her disappearance with the dog. Everything she had, which wasn't that much.

There were sour faces all around the table in the lofty conference room when they realized that days had passed since the first ransom note. A curse, a brisk rebuke. She told them about the call to the *gendarme* at the dog owner's home. This caused a riffle of excitement and indignation, running around, phone calls. It was a long day. By three in the afternoon, she was dismissed, told to stay in her hotel room. Grave and silent, Pascal found her a taxi. In the cab she texted him.

I will be at the Polygone when it goes down.
You don't have to tell them but I will be there

She shut off her phone angrily. This was her *sister*. How dare they shuffle her off with a pat on the head? The cab let her off near the hotel. She found a café and ordered a coffee and a salad. Visions of a SWAT team and very large weapons swam in her head. How were they going to trick them? No one knew what the men looked like unless those sketches had finally arrived. Would a rough sketch be enough to recognize someone in a large, moving crowd? They could have changed their appearances, cut their hair, shaved mustaches. They could use a third party; who knew how many were in the gang. Pascal doubted they would bring Francie to the shopping mall. It was too risky. So how would they find her? He guessed there would be another note, directions to where she was hidden after they took off with the dog. They would get instructions when they passed off the dog.

But there was no dog. Merle's stomach hurt. She had told the police that the thieves knew this dog, that no substitute would work. She ate quickly and went back to the hotel, staring at the ceiling from the bed, checking her watch. The limbo was excruciating. Being swept aside from her own sister's fate made her feel helpless and sad. *Where are you, Francie?* Balling her fists against her eyes, trying to block the visions she kept seeing, she felt so frustrated. She lay there trying to force out a few tears for the entire situation.

But this wasn't the time for crying.

The Polygone was huge, an American-style indoor mall, unlike any she'd seen in France. One end was modern, with an arched glass roof, not far from the Old Town. At five-thirty Merle watched people stream in and out then headed around the building to find another entrance. The opposite side was built with Greek touches, a pediment, arched windows, trailing vines, very dramatic.

The effect was a massive pagan temple for the worship of perfume and haute couture if a look inside the Galeries Lafayette was a clue. Bustling with clerks and shoppers, it smelled like a field of sweet flowers. Merle's eyes burned a little as she wound through the sample counters of the huge department store to the mall entrance.

Where was the center of this monstrosity? A *polygone* had many sides, right? If this was one end then the center would be forward.

The mall had several levels of shops like any self-respecting suburban American mall. Lines of boutiques, some brands she recognized, others new to her, strung along the balconies as she peered up. Escalators connected the floors at intervals down the shiny hallways.

Merle checked her watch. She expected to see cops by now. She stopped at a jewelry store window to watch the traffic for single men. Most young men had their arms around women, or traveled in packs. Solitary men were rare. One passed with a small red shopping bag. Would the kidnappers use a bag like that to hand over the directions to Francie? He kept moving into the crowd. Another man dressed in a smart suit walked by, heels tapping on the marble floor. Too spiff to be a cop.

She continued down the ground level of the mall, pretending to window shop. At the far end, escalators brought shoppers down from the other entrance, the one with the glass roof. She dawdled down the opposite side. The grocery market was there, the Monoprix. It was stuffed with people, coming and going, with string bags full of dinner ingredients, wine, towels, plants, bread, shirts, cakes. She watched the action for a minute, fascinated, then pushed through the throng.

On the other side of the crowd she paused, trying to gauge where the center of the mall would be, when she saw Pascal on a top balcony with cell phone to his ear. She stepped out of his line of sight, behind a large potted tree.

This must be the center. Behind her was a clothing store for teenagers, bright colors, T-shirts. She eased into their doorway but immediately had to move to let a group of girls inside. She walked on to the next boutique, a men's store full of ties and shirts. She looked back, trying to spot the police. Where were they? A man in a baseball cap leaned out from behind the escalator, talking on his phone: definitely a cop. In the corner of her eye she saw a women's store directly across the hall. Turning on her heel, she made a beeline for it like a woman on a mission.

The windows of the shop were full of mannequins in various stages of undress, in panties and bras, slacks halfway down, breasts exposed. The reflection in the windows served as a mirror. Five minutes until six.

Her pulse quickened. She pulled out her cell phone and checked for a message from Pascal. Nothing.

A yipping sound, a dog barking, came from somewhere behind her. She turned, looking for a dog. Just shoppers, feet shuffling, bags rubbing, laughter, far away music. She looked right, down the row of storefronts. Several stores down a woman stood alone. She wore a long blue skirt that hit her shins, a baggy, beige sweater, and red tennis shoes with anklets. Her hair was an unnatural shade of honey in a straight, blunt cut. She was thin, mousy, the kind of woman who didn't want to attract attention, nervous, eyes darting around. She spotted Merle and looked away. Merle put her eyes forward, into the store. When she looked back, the woman was gone.

Merle followed two women into the store. They were chatting in French. She gave her standard *"bonjour"* to a clerk then positioned herself behind a rack of blouses where she had a good view of the central walkway.

Her phone rang. It was 5:59. She considered ignoring it, but a woman next to her smiled and said something. Merle pulled it from her pocket. It was James.

She hadn't told him she was leaving town. If there was one thing she would change about this trip, it would be a toss-up between leaving Gillian or James at home. No, that couldn't be true. No Gillian would mean Francie wouldn't have been kidnapped. James was just a pest.

"James, how are you?"

The French woman's eyebrows went up: *Ah, American.* Merle shrugged: *sorry.*

"Where are you, Merle? I've been over to your house twice."

"Something came up. What's going on?" The clerk gave her a dirty look. Merle stepped out into the hall, phone to her ear.

"I called that criminal attorney you recommended and he's going to take my case."

"Well, that's good news. You can get rid of Redier."

Something was happening under the escalators. Merle could see several sets of legs. But the center was still vacant, the occasional solitary shopper intent on getting home to dinner. A glow from the late afternoon sun hit the high windows, setting them aflame.

James was talking about his case, his prospects, his witnesses. Merle half-listened. "Uh-huh. Right." Then, there was the dog yipping again. She whipped her head right, then left. "Can I call you later? Bye, James." Where was that dog?

Out of the crowd the mousy woman in the long skirt strolled toward a metal bench in the center, a bundle now under her arm. Covered with a dark brown towel or blanket, it was roundish and oblong. Was this part of the game plan? In her other arm she held a large market basket which she set down on the bench. Gently she transferred her bundle into the basket and bent down to talk to it. She patted it. After a moment there was the barking again and the woman patted the bundle once more. She straightened and looked around, clutching a small purse strapped to her shoulder.

Minutes passed. The woman soothed her bundle multiple times, the barking came and went. If she had to guess, Merle would say it was a recording; it had a repetitive, mechanical sound—great if the kidnappers are idiots and they don't actually check if that's a real dog in there. Merle covered her mouth to keep from groaning. This was idiocy.

She wandered down the storefronts, feeling the weight of waiting. Awful thing, time. Why had she ever thought she could tame it? When things were going well, it went too fast, like when children were growing, or vacation days, nights with Pascal. She felt a visceral ache, a longing. *Pascal.* She took a breath and let it out. Not now. Francie was the one she was searching for, the one who was lost. The one she waited for in this temple of consumption.

Across from the Monoprix again, Merle decided to mingle in the crowds outside the big green doors. As she walked toward the doors, an older couple was exiting. He had the groceries, she had the dog, a little purse dog, white and fluffy. It wriggled in her arms and she was scolding it. *"Tranquille, mon trésor!"*

They were a good distraction. Merle turned and stepped in behind them. Over their shoulders she could see the woman with the bundle and beyond her the men under the escalators. She glanced up to see two other cops trying to act nonchalant one level up. She craned her neck, looking for Pascal and walked smack into the woman, startling everyone including the little dog, who started to yap wildly at her. The man with the bags began to shout at the woman and the dog, perhaps at Merle, obviously losing all patience. The woman, who had that fake orange hair the French love and wore an expensive cream-colored suit, tried to calm her pet. She succeeded in getting hysterical herself.

In the commotion the dog leapt from her arms, landing with a smack and a squeak on the marble, skittering with sharp nails as he got his footing. A blue rhinestone leash trailed as he barked madly, celebrating his freedom, heading south.

The woman began to squeal. The man, dressed in a suit and tie, threw down his groceries and took off after the beast. Merle stood there stunned, trying to think of something to say in French that would be helpful. Was this part of the police charade? If so it was spectacular. The man skidded as he turned and fell to his knees, cursing.

The little dog emerged on the opposite side of the center court, stopping to pant and look around, his little pink tongue hanging out. The bundle on the metal bench began to bark as if on cue. The white dog perked up his ears and took up the call, yapping as he scurried toward the bench. In a gymnastic leap into the air that caused the woman with the honey-colored hair to jump backward in fright, the dog pounced on the market basket. They rolled sideways off the bench onto the floor, the white dog on attack. Into the basket he went, pawing, snarling, biting at the bundle, barking like the little mad thing he was. He pulled the bundle out with his teeth, whipping it back and forth, then tossed it aside and went back into the basket for more.

Merle put a hand over her mouth. Laughing or crying, both were out of the question. She glanced under the escalator—empty. Likewise the balcony. The man arrived, red in the face, and pulled the dog out of the basket. It twisted and snapped as he handed the animal to his wife. On the floor by the basket lay an orange stuffed rabbit, some wiring and electronics, and a brown blanket. The woman had vanished.

Merle backed away from the scene, now circled by shoppers shaking their heads. She stepped behind the first row of onlookers, hoping the cops hadn't seen her. Did she cause the exchange to fail by bumping into the old couple? Had the kidnappers even showed? Were they here right now? She looked at the shoppers frantically. They all seemed to be carrying bags of groceries or clothes or toiletries, smiling and congenial, enjoying the show.

Inside the Monoprix she tried to calm down. She bought a bottle of white wine, some goat cheese with a blue rind, the kind Francie liked, some hummus and raw carrots, and a baguette. Her hands shook as she got money out of her purse. She dropped some coins and said she was sorry once too often.

In the mall again, the crowd was gone, as was the basket and toy rabbit. Merle sighed. *Don't give up, Francie. Never give up.*

25

Gianluca Gribaudi had hoped it wouldn't come to this. The Italian *trufflier* had made up his mind that day when Bettina refused to accept his help with the dog. He had been so kind, so generous, and she disrespected him yet again. She was an old woman; she had no business hanging onto her land and distribution connections. If she had been nicer to him, had told him the truth, he could have helped her. But now, it was all for his own *famiglia*.

One of his own workers had told him about Hector and Milo. There are no secrets in the Piedmont. At first Gianluca thought he might dispatch his son to bring the dog back, but the boy was busy in the city. The young people rarely wanted to help with the business any more. So off he went. It didn't take long to find two idiot Italians looking for a dog, not with the reward posted everywhere.

But now, in the stone barn high in the hills overlooking Montpellier, he listened to Hector's excuses and grew angrier by the minute. Milo came out of the back room once used for hay storage where the girl was confined. He had taken her some dinner: sausage and bread. And wine, Gianluca saw, frowning. The man made himself ridiculous, the way he fawned over the pretty American.

But now Hector was finishing his sorry tale. "The police were everywhere. I could see them, talking on their phones, all over the shopping center. They think I am stupid but I see them. I have a nose for *polizia*. The old man, that priest, must have called them. I told him no *flics* but he must have called."

"And the dog? Was the dog there?"

"There was a dog all right. But not our dog. They tried to trick me. Then another dog ran up and upset the basket with the animal sounds. No, no truffle dog. No Aurore." He sobered, seeing the scowl on Gianluca's face. "I am sorry, *signore*."

Gianluca's temper was rising to a boil. He lashed out, smacking Hector hard across the face. "Idiot. You are worthless!" Hector took a step back and opened his mouth to speak but Gianluca slapped him again. "You will get the priest and bring him here. He has ruined everything for us. We will make him pay."

"*Sì, signore.*" Hector fished the keys to the truck out of his pocket. His cheeks glowed.

Milo stood hunched in a corner, trying to be inconspicuous. Gianluca glared at him through slitted eyes. "Are you giving her a five course meal?"

"No, *signore*, only sausage and roll." He still held the unlabeled wine bottle by the neck. "And a small sip of wine so she can sleep. She says she is awake all night on the straw mattress."

"It will not kill her to stay awake," Gianluca growled. Hector remained frozen in place. "What are you waiting for? Go get the priest."

Hector shuffled out the door. They heard the truck's engine turn over. Gianluca pulled out a wooden chair and sat down. He wore peasant clothes and they itched, the baggy pants now dirty. The woman called out and Milo straightened, at the ready. He glanced at Gianluca. "Go see what she wants."

Taking the woman was a mistake, he saw that now. It seemed simple at first, based on Hector's tale. He couldn't put his finger on what went wrong except the American was not what he expected. She was pretty with large bosoms and a mouth that wouldn't stop. His wife was the same way, talk, talk. Luckily, he couldn't understand the American. If she would just be quiet, he could show her some of his special Italian hospitality. The thought was there but he wasn't sure the will was. Slapping her was easier than fighting her with his cock. It would be nice to put her in her place, but he had bigger problems. He had to figure this out or lose his land. He didn't need distractions like that.

Milo came out of the room with the empty plate, poured a glass of water, and went back. The woman was tied to the bed, she wasn't going anywhere. It had been four days with her. Too long. Gianluca was tired and surrounded by *stupidos*.

He went to the doorway. Milo stood next to the bed, watching her drink the water, a simple-minded pleasure on his face. The woman was disheveled, her hair tangled. She stared at Gianluca as she sipped slowly. As she handed the empty glass to Milo, she smiled at him. "*Grazie*, Milo." She looked at Gianluca in the doorway. "And fuck you, *signore*." She smiled sweetly as she said it.

His English was bad but he knew what she said. His temper spiked again. He took a step toward her. He needed his anger now, he was so tired. He hadn't slept either. But she couldn't speak to him that way. He raised a hand and she scuttled back onto the bed as far as she could with her ankle rope. He roared at her, raised his hand higher, just to see her cower and shiver. He wanted her to beg forgiveness, to take back what she said. But there was defiance in her eye.

He slapped her, not as hard as he'd slapped Hector, but enough to make her cry out in pain. Milo squirmed, backing away. The woman began to speak then closed her mouth, her lips tight against her teeth. A spot of blood formed on her bottom lip.

Gianluca felt his anger dim. He had hurt her, frightened her. This was good. But it would not help find the dog. He hoped that she would know where the dog was hidden, but so far they'd gotten nothing from her. He told Milo to get out, backed away himself, giving her one last disdainful glare before locking her in for the night. He had made up his mind.

He must call for an enforcer from home.

26

Pascal didn't return to the hotel that night. Merle stayed up until one, watching the moon shadows creep down the street. At ten he had texted a cryptic "working late" but nothing more. He didn't owe her an explanation. He didn't owe her anything. She had eaten the food from the grocery store and worked on the iPad for hours, then crawled under the covers, defeated.

She was packed, standing at the door at seven-thirty when it opened. Pascal looked tired, drawn, and a bit surprised to see a woman in his room.

"I was just going," she said.

"To breakfast? Wait for me to shower." He looked at her bag. "Can you wait?"

She nodded and sat down again at the table. There were things she couldn't do, like trace IP addresses and phone numbers. Otherwise, the police were bungling it, in her opinion. That mechanical barking and bunny rabbit? It was so stupid it infuriated her. But she would keep her opinions to herself for now.

Pascal came out of the bath and dressed quickly. He towel-dried his hair and was ready in ten minutes, waving her out the door and down the stairs. At the same café where she'd had lunch the day before, he ordered them coffees and omelets. Merle set her bag on the floor under her chair, waiting for him to speak.

The coffees arrived, café au lait for her and a double espresso for him. He tested it then downed it in one gulp.

"We have been out all night, looking for her," he said, his voice raw. "We got a hit on a traffic camera but only a partial number."

"What kind of car?"

"A *camionette*, a small farm truck."

"Where did it go?"

He shrugged. "We lost it. They must be somewhere close by. We looked in the hills. Everywhere within a fifty-kilometer radius."

She sighed. It wasn't his fault the brass pinned their hopes on a mechanical rabbit. "What now?"

"Keep searching. Have they contacted you again?"

"Albert hasn't called."

"You should go home then. Wait for them to contact you again."

She frowned at her omelet. She wasn't hungry enough for a five-egger, today or ever. Hadn't he begged her to come here? Said it was dangerous at home by herself? But she wouldn't argue. She pulled out Francie's iPad. "I sent you this email yesterday. It's another IP address we could trace. From Gillian's email."

He pulled out his phone. "I sent it in." He scrolled through messages. "It is a small hotel, a *gîte*, outside of St-Émilion. Close to Bordeaux."

"I know it. Famous wine."

"It's called La Rosette." He looked up. "You will call there?"

"Or you can."

"I will do it. Please, the best thing is to go home and wait for communication from the kidnappers." She nodded, biting her lips. He pushed away his plate and wiped his mouth. "I must go. We will find her, Merle."

She blinked then, feeling the emotion, the strain of the last few days, rise to her cheeks. He stood up and touched her shoulder. "Go home, blackbird. I will call you."

She retraced her route across the hills and mountains to the Dordogne, wondering at every turn if Francie was somewhere nearby. It was an awful feeling, this helplessness, this knowing that someone you love is possibly hurt and afraid and you aren't there. The omelet churned in her stomach, and high on a mountain, Merle got out of the car and tried to vomit. Instead the pine scent cleared her head. Anxiety would not help her find Francie.

Soldier on, Merdle. If only her brave sisters were here to help.

She reached Malcouziac by one in the afternoon and unlocked the house, looking for notes. The one with the instructions for the exchange at the shopping mall was the only one on her doorstep. Upstairs she packed more clothes into her case, throwing the dirty ones on the bed, and grabbed water and cheese and grapes from the refrigerator. Her car packed again, she drove around the block to Albert's.

He didn't answer the knock. She walked down to Josephine's. The old woman came to the door dressed to the nines as usual: white hair coiffed, necklace sparkling, in a melon-colored skirt and blouse. "*Madame* Bennett, *bonjour, bonjour*," she said, smiling.

Merle gave a hasty greeting. "I'm sorry, I'm in a rush. Have you seen *Père* Albert?"

"*Oui.* He gave me some plums. He said he was leaving for some days to visit his brother."

Merle gave a sigh of relief and thanked her, excusing herself for not coming in. She backed the Peugeot down to the main street and headed west, toward St-Émilion.

La Rosette was a small bed-and-breakfast with four rooms in a renovated stable. It sat on a winding country road surrounded by vineyards. St-Émilion was clustered on a hill and famously picturesque but Merle had no desire to see it. She pulled off the lane, blocking the driveway, and knocked on the green door of the one-story stucco house. A boy of ten or so answered the door, looked at her, and called for his mother.

Maman was a plump, cheerful blonde, wiping her hands on a towel. "*Bonjour.*"

Merle pulled the photo of Gillian out of her bag and explained she was looking for this woman. "She has this dog with her. I believe she stayed here last week."

The woman frowned at the photo then her face cleared. "*Ah, oui, bien sûr.* The police have just called about her. You are police?"

"No. I'm working with them to find this woman."

"I tell the police she is here just one night. She pays for two but *pfft*. Gone."

"Did she say where she was going?"

"She speaks no French." The woman rubbed her dish towel on her chin. "She is American, yes? Like you? She is your friend?"

"She was staying at my house in Malcouziac when she disappeared. We're worried about her."

"The little dog was *adorable*. My son, Paul, he wanted to keep it." She called to the boy. He reappeared. Tousling his brown hair, she asked him if he remembered the dog from last week and the woman, the dog's owner. He nodded. *Maman* asked him if the woman said where she was going.

"*L'Italienne?*" he asked.

"No, Paul, the American," his mother said. "With the dog."

His small brown eyebrows crimped. "She was Italian. I heard her talking on the phone."

Merle showed him the photo. "This woman?" He nodded. The mother asked him again about the Italian. He was adamant.

Merle spoke in English then, "You know English?"

"And a little Italian," Paul said in English. "I am eleven years old." His accent was strong but he knew the language. "*Elle parlait l'italien.*"

His mother shrugged. "He is a smart boy, my Paul. He knows a little German too."

"Did you understand what she said, Paul?" Merle asked.

He shook his head. Merle asked if anyone else who worked there might have overheard Gillian. *Maman* said they were a small operation, no one besides the family, and her husband worked in town. Paul wriggled away. "Do you have a registration book?"

The woman waved her into the foyer. She opened a drawer in a buffet cabinet and pulled out a red notebook. "Here: Florence Jersey. *États-Unis*. She paid for two nights, in euros."

A scrabbly signature. Someone had printed the name next to it, presumably when Gillian made the reservation. She had used a false name. Merle shouldn't have been surprised. Hotels might require a look at your passport in Europe, but these small family-run businesses probably didn't.

"Did she show you identification?" Merle asked.

"I think so." She squinted at the writing. "Paul might have checked her in."

Back in her car, Merle jotted down the name: Florence Jersey. Did it have any significance or was it just something Gillian made up? Was she from New Jersey? Was that going to help find her?

Merle spent the night in an over-priced room in a one-star hotel on the outskirts of St-Émilion with hard beds and scratchy towels. She sent emails to Elise and Annie, asking if they had any more information on Gillian. She said she wasn't ready to give up.

Her sisters were uncharacteristically silent.

27

Silent, that is, until 5 a.m.

Merle's cell phone rang, waking her from a restless sleep on the uncomfortable mattress, dreaming of horrible things being done to Francie. She sat up, glad to be awake. "Annie."

"Sorry to call so early. What time is it there?"

"You know perfectly well." Annie never set her watch to local time when she traveled, thinking it would somehow make reentry easier.

She chuckled. "You're right. Is it light over the rolling hills of the Dordogne?"

"I'm not in Malcouziac. I'm trying to find Gillian. She stayed in a little bed-and-breakfast place near St-Émilion."

"Interesting. How'd you find that out?" Merle told her about Pascal tracing the IP address. "Wow. Nice to have those resources at your fingertips, so to speak. Is he there?"

"Working in the south, gossip girl. A couple other things have come up. Gillian apparently speaks fluent Italian. Not sure what that means."

"She does look a little Italian. That thick, dark hair."

"Sargent isn't an Italian name, is it?"

"Could have been Anglicized. Sargento?"

"Yeah, okay. That's probably nothing. She used another name when she checked in. Florence Jersey. Do you think there's any significance to that?"

"Let me Google it." A few taps later, she said, "There's a town called Florence in New Jersey. I thought Gillian was from Colorado. That's what she told them at the law firm."

"I don't believe anything she's said. Why is there no record of her existence before law school?"

"I wondered that too. I have a friend in Colorado and I pulled a few favors. He called the law school for her background information, said they were considering her for a position. He's an assistant DA. But they told him it was sealed."

"What does that mean?"

"A few things spring to mind, he said. She might have a juvenile criminal record and those documents are usually sealed."

"In her law school application?"

"She might have felt it was necessary to divulge that information. Sometimes they ask. Then she got them to seal it again. So that's one. The other one is a little hinky but that's how I roll. What if she's in witness protection or was before law school?"

Merle blinked, processing that. "Probably a dead end then."

"Not necessarily. But, yes, difficult. How hard do we want to push this? Talk to Francie about it. Is she still with you?"

"Asleep," Merle lied. "She agrees with me. Push it all the way. We need to find her. Maybe she's got some relatives or friends in Europe from her childhood. We can contact them, make sure she's safe. At least see if she has a connection to this town in New Jersey."

"What's she going to do with that damn dog?" Annie asked. "Such a bizarre thing, kidnapping a dog in a foreign country."

Annie still didn't know that the dog was a truffle hunter, and very expensive. Merle hesitated, wondering how much she should say. "Listen, I found out that dog is special. There was a reward posted in town for ten-thousand euros for it. It's apparently sort of famous for truffle hunting."

"Truffles? That little bitch, no pun intended. She took off with the dog to claim the reward?"

"If she did, she didn't get it. The dog hasn't been returned to the owners. Maybe she's just a dog lover."

"This is getting too weird." *If she only knew.* "Let me look around this New Jersey connection. I'll call you this evening."

Merle lay back on the pillow, feeling the soreness of her neck from driving yesterday. She hated lying to Annie. She hated lying in general, but being a lawyer had made her all too practiced at it. She justified it by telling herself that she was saving her sisters—and parents—from undue stress. They would find out about Francie's ordeal, but only after it was over and from Francie herself, safe and sound at home. They were thousands of miles away. The middle sister was on the ground. The tent pole would take care of this.

The light was creeping around the curtains. Merle opened them then jumped back into bed. A row of geraniums bloomed across the way, blood red in the dawn. She opened her email. Elise had written to ask about Francie.

I hope I don't get it, whatever it is. There was some jack wagon hacking on my flight, spreading germs near and far.

I did a Google search on Gillian and deep inside was a Flickr account, you know, photos. It's password protected. Jonathan doesn't have a password. But I know a guy who knows a guy... anyway I will crack into it tomorrow, for sure. A longshot probably. More tomorrow. E.

Merle wrote a quick note back to Elise assuring her Francie was fine. More lies, or as they say, well-intentioned pseudo-factoids. But the photos sounded promising. Merle closed her eyes for a minute but her mind was whirling with anxiety. Every day, every night, that Francie wasn't found was another drop of hope leaking out of the bucket. How did people do this? How did a parent remain sane when their child was kidnapped?

Tristan. Her boy. Merle wrote him a short email, saying she was thinking of him and loved him. She didn't say she was glad he was safe at home but she was. Yesterday Stasia had written saying all was well and that Tristan and his cousin started computer camp.

Sleep was impossible. The sun crept over the tile roofs, slanting across plazas and whitewashed walls and down the endless rows of grapevines surrounding St-Émilion. Birds swooped, garbage cans rattled.

Merle showered and packed. She was on the road home by seven, the sun in her eyes. By nine she was back in her secret garden, watering the pear tree and pretending all was well when someone knocked on the front door.

James and a short blond woman stood outside, behind the glass panes. Merle walked slowly to the door. This must be the ex-wife. She couldn't remember her name. She pulled herself up to full height, took a big breath, and opened the door.

"Good morning," Merle said brightly. The woman smiled back, warily. James threw up his hands in exasperation.

"Finally. I've been over here a dozen times, Merle. Worried sick."

"Really? Worried about me?" Nonchalance seemed the way to go.

"Stuff has been happening and you were—wherever you were." James frowned, smoothing his wrinkled shorts and yellow polo shirt. "This is Christine, my—"

"Ex-wife," the woman said, smiling, filling in his pause. Dressed in white capri pants and a striped sleeveless top, she looked the suburban mom she was. "You must be the Merle I've heard so much about." She held out her hand. "Nice to finally meet."

Merle shook her hand, feeling strangely favorable toward his ex. Beneath her cap of blond hair, she had kind, intelligent blue eyes. Merle invited them in, settling them in the garden and busying herself making espresso on the stove. Finally, she brought out a tray of coffee and cream. "No delicious French pastries, I'm afraid."

"We've had our share already," Christine said, cradling the demitasse cup in her hands. "Stress apparently makes you crave butter."

They'd met with the new lawyer in Bergerac on Christine's trip south from Paris. James complained long and loud about the trouble he had getting Michel Redier to let him leave the village for half a day to pick up his ex-wife. They talked in the garden, James back in his rapid, scattershot manner. He described the meeting with the new lawyer, Christine nodding along in supportive blandness.

Merle felt herself drifting off. She had lost interest. If indeed she had ever cared about James and his sleepwalking adventures. What did he expect her to do? He'd gotten himself into this pickle. He was a lawyer and he had a good French one. She just wanted them to leave so she could get on with finding Gillian and Francie. Could the women be together? Had Gillian been kidnapped too? No. Nor was Gillian behind Francie's kidnapping, she was pretty sure about that. They were friends, colleagues. It had to be those crooks who stole the dog in the first place. That was the only explanation that made sense, if anything made sense.

She was in the kitchen getting more coffee when the shadow passed the front window. Merle froze, thinking she had imagined it, delusions brought on by paranoia. They got very few passersby at this end of rue de Poitiers. Then a dark figure stopped in front of her door and peered through the glass. A large man dressed in black, muscular with broad shoulders, apishly long arms, a cigarette dangling from one hand. His dark hair was slicked back and he wore sunglasses. Tipping them onto his forehead he cupped his free hand around his eyes and saw her. In a flash he moved out of sight.

Merle set the tray down on the stove, heart thumping. She glanced back into the garden where James and Christine sat talking. He was waving his hands around, telling her she "just didn't understand." Merle crept through the dim living room, past the dining table, beside the window. She checked the window latch then flipped the deadbolt on the door. If only she'd locked the door shutters. She waited, looking for movement out in the street. The houses were built right up to the cobblestones in this old village with no front yards or sidewalks. She could see the large, broken stones at the end of the street, and her rental car parked next to them. She leaned out to see *Madame* Suchet's step, her flowerpots overflowing with color, across the street.

She listened, looking at her watch for a full minute, then unlocked the front door and carefully stuck her head out, looking one way, then the other. The man was gone.

"Merle?" James and Christine stood in the kitchen doorway, watching her. He said, "What's going on?"

She turned, trying to smile. "I just, ah, thought I saw somebody I knew. Can I get you more coffee? Sorry, I got distracted."

"We've had enough. Thank you," Christine said. "Jim has some things to show me around the village, don't you?"

"Ah, yeah. Sure. Can you meet us for dinner tonight, Merle? I thought Christine would like Les Saveurs."

"I'm sure she will. I'd love to join you."

A girl's gotta eat. She locked the door behind them.

After Merle checked her email and found nothing more from her sisters, she finished watering the garden and did a little cleaning in the house. Finally she went out the garden gate, down the alley, and around to Josephine's front door. The old woman was dressed in pearls, a red top, and blue skirt as if she was anticipating Bastille Day. She sat Merle down in a green brocade chair while she disappeared into the kitchen. It was no use telling a Frenchwoman you weren't hungry and not to bother setting out a spread. *Quel horreur.* How rude.

Josephine Azamar had lived in Merle's house briefly during the war. She'd only returned to the village recently after her second husband died. The bond of the house's secrets was strong between the two women. Merle took her tea gratefully with a slice of pound cake.

Josephine adjusted her white and red scarf, tightening the knot, before taking her own cup of tea. Merle waited then asked, "Have you talked to Albert?" Josephine shook her head and said not since he left. "Did he say when he'd be back?"

"A few days, I believe." She frowned. "I'm not sure."

They chatted about the hot weather, the grape crop, her grandchildren in Paris, her great-grandchildren in America. She'd had a rich, fascinating life. It was no punishment to listen to her. But Merle fidgeted. Finally she made her excuses, thanked Josephine, and left, walking up to Albert's house.

His door shutters were old like hers, repainted yearly until the thick blue filled every crack. Even the hinges were blue now. Not a sound from inside. She looked at the edges of the door. A small white corner of paper stuck out by the upper left hinge.

She leaned on the door but that made the crack tighter. She wedged a finger into the middle and pulled on the shutter, holding onto the note with her fingernails. Finally it loosened enough so she could inch it to the top and over. It fell to the stone step, a tightly folded square.

She held her breath and opened the note. The writing was different, blocky and childlike.

Meet on the plaza under the west arches.
9 pm. No police. Come alone.

Was this left last night? The night before? She looked around frantically for someone to ask, someone to show the note to, but the street was deserted. At least Albert was safe in the Languedoc with his family. Merle hoped he stayed there for a long time.

"No police." What if no priest came to the rendezvous?

28

Merle called Pascal and left a message about the note. She told him she was back in Malcouziac as he requested. She tried not to sound as anxious and lonely as she felt. She sat down in the shade of the acacia tree and tried to think. When no new action suggested itself, she went upstairs and lay on her bed, the iPad at her side. Tired as she was, sleep was out of the question. Her mind spun with scenarios, none of which made any sense. What had they planned to do to Albert? What would they do to Francie?

She put on her running clothes and headed out the back gate, putting the string with the large key around her neck and her cell phone in its usual snug spot against her chest. The afternoon air was still and scorching. She rounded the corner and headed out through the old bastide gate, setting her sights on a hilltop where the remains of an old hamlet rotted gently into the soil. As she got to the top of the hill, out of breath, hands on her hips, her cell phone rang. It was Pascal. She stopped in the shade of a gnarled apple tree.

"What's happening?" she blurted out without a "hello" and gasping from the exercise.

"We're still looking for her," he said solemnly. "No news."

"Shit." She wiped her face with her T-shirt. Jesus, it was hot. She was sick of these French cops. "No leads? Nothing?"

"There have been some leads about the farm truck. We have pieced together the probable license plate. It is not French, we know that much."

She blinked. "Is it Italian?"

"Possibly. It is white and we can see the blue stripe on one side but the other side is covered with mud or something."

"Gillian speaks Italian."

"Yes, okay." He sounded distracted.

"So focus on Italy, that's what I'm saying." Merle was aware that she was giving him orders and looked up at the blue sky between the branches of the apple tree. She wasn't going to apologize for her tone. Francie had to be found. "Elise thinks Gillian posted some photos online. They may help if we can recreate her last day in Malcouziac."

"Help? To find Francie?"

Merle dropped her head. He was right. What would finding Gillian do? She had probably sold the dog by now. But Merle had to do something or she would lose her sanity. She had to hold onto the hope that Gillian still had the dog. "If we find the dog, we can make the trade. That's my goal now."

He grunted, unimpressed, she supposed. She told him about the note left at Albert's door. "What about this new note? I didn't get one, just Albert."

"We don't know when it was put in the door, yes?"

"It could have been days ago."

He told her to keep it for analysis and to call if another one showed up. He had to go. She didn't blame him. He sounded tired and frustrated; so was she. She stuck her phone back in her bra and headed down the hill.

At Les Saveurs James and Christine were already seated, drinking wine poured from a large, brown earthenware pitcher that reminded Merle of the "Little Brown Jug" of American song. It was one of the country touches to the high-end tourist eatery. As Merle stepped through the tables, she remembered sitting right there with Pascal on the night he offered to whisk her away from Malcouziac. They ended up making a beach vacation in the garden instead, but you always remembered where you were when something happened between you and the man you—

"Have a seat, please," James said, standing. He and Christine sat across from each other at the table, leaving Merle with an awkward choice. She sat next to James out of courtesy. Somehow she'd rather be friends with Christine. Odd how easy it was between them, the ex-wife and the so-called girlfriend. Wine was poured from the pitcher, a cool rosé.

"Good choice," Merle said as they clinked glasses. What had she been thinking: *between you and the man you love?* She didn't love Pascal, not exactly. Did she? "Have you been here long?" She checked her watch. She was rarely late.

"My fault," Christine said. "My inner clock is off. I get hungry at weird times."

"We had a small plate, the meats and cheeses," James said, smacking his lips. "All gone. Sorry!"

"This heat kills my appetite," Merle said. "Except for wine."

They ordered after a long discussion about the various dishes. Merle found she'd sampled almost all of them. It made her feel like a local, someone who belonged here. Then the memory of that thug at her window made her stomach go sour. She glanced around the room at the diners. Happy couples, lots of foreigners, blond Dutch and booted Germans: nobody muscled and suspicious.

They had finished their first course, cold shrimp for Merle, when she checked her watch. It was five until nine. Was tonight the night the kidnappers wanted to meet Albert? What was the meeting about? She wiped her mouth, setting her napkin next to her plate.

"My stomach is feeling a little off. I'm going to get some air," she told the Silvers who hadn't stopped talking about James's legal problems since she arrived. They squawked in concern but she reassured them. "Ten minutes of brisk walking usually does it."

The plaza was not quite dark with evening stars glowing in the twilight. The old market colonnades, a series of covered archways, stretched along two sides of the plaza. In the center was the ubiquitous

French fountain, wide, golden, and moldy, the water still now as the light faded from the sky. A lavender glow shone from the cobblestones as couples walked arm-in-arm through the warm night. Merle let her eyes adjust to the shadows.

Walking to the left, she approached the south end of the arcade. These buildings were some of the oldest in town, weathered stone, two- and three-story, at least four hundred years old. They stretched in an unbroken line, shoulder to shoulder though the styles didn't mesh. Some mansard roofs, some tile. Some half-timbered walls in the English style. She leaned into a doorway without a sign or plaque. The windows were shuttered and dark. She'd often wondered what went on in these old buildings. They were probably uninhabitable.

She pulled her wrist up to her face: nine o'clock on the dot. A foursome entered the plaza on the far side, laughing on their way to dinner. A couple with arms wrapped around each other walked the other way. Then silence. Her watch ticked. Merle bit her lip, trying to be still and patient. A single man came swinging through, hurried, slightly drunk. Silence again. A dog barking in the distance. A car engine. A garbage can. A door slamming.

Ten after. She had to go back. She didn't want to tell them about Francie or Gillian or the dog. They had their own problems. She didn't want James involved. This was a family matter. She sighed, defeated, and returned to the restaurant.

James and Christine were drinking red wine now, the bottle open at the table. Maybe wine was all they had in common these days. Weirdly, she understood that. Merle slipped into her chair and apologized. James said, "We told them to wait on our main courses until you got back. Ah, here they come."

"Feel better?" Christine asked. "I get tummy things when I travel."

Their stomachs appeared to be functioning quite well as they attacked their main courses: filet of roast duck, *l'agneau en coque d'argile*, a lamb dish baked in clay, and for Merle, the fish of the day, *dorade royale*. By eleven they had cleaned their plates, sampled the cheese, shared a crème brulée, and enjoyed a coffee.

"That was amazing," Christine said, eyes wide. "How do you keep your figure, Merle, with all this fabulous food?"

"Merle's a jogger, Christine," James said pointedly.

"And a worrier," Merle added.

"Worrying doesn't help my waistline," Christine replied. "You're not worried about Jim, are you? Should I be concerned that my children will never see their father again?"

"I wouldn't be," Merle said. "The French are very strict though. Keep apologizing and you should be fine. They like it when you grovel. They will make you pay somehow, James. Probably just by sending you home and telling you to never come back."

"Really?" James said. "You don't think they'll put me in jail?"

"For a fist-fight? No."

He looked relieved. "The lawyer from Bordeaux called this afternoon. He said the priest didn't show up for a meeting with investigators."

Christine frowned. "What does that mean?"

"Maybe he's dropping the charges," Merle said. "On the other hand, he moves around from village to village. He might just be hard to locate." She leaned back in her chair and asked Christine, "You live in New Jersey, right? Do you know the town of Florence?"

"I have a cousin who lives there." Christine glanced at James. "What's this about?"

"Just curious. I was wondering what sort of place it was."

"Very small. It's downstate, near Trenton."

James added, "We drove through there once on the way to Philadelphia. Stopped to see Eddie. It's very Italian, I remember. Fredo this and Spumoni that."

"Of course it is, Jim." Christine rolled her eyes at Merle. "When you call a place Florence, you know it was founded by Italians. That part of the state is thick with them."

Merle hadn't thought of Florence as the Italian city, just as a first name. She went to Florence, Italy, years ago, after college. James—whose ex-wife called him Jim—squinted at her. "What's the connection? You thinking of moving?"

She smiled. "Who knows?"

When Merle returned home from dinner an email awaited containing a link to Gillian's online folder of photos. Elise's hacker friend was an evil genius. Nestling into bed with the iPad Merle opened the last album of photos, hopefully Gillian's last day in Malcouziac.

The first photos were roses in bloom around town, growing out of impossibly small holes at the bottom of downspouts and next to the church steps. Merle looked for shots of buildings and people, something recognizable. A photo of Place de la Victoire, the central plaza, with its old fountain, was first. Gillian had gotten creative, taking a variety of angles, reflections off the water, the spray against the sky.

Merle felt her eyelids droop. It was close to midnight. Then a rattling downstairs sent a cold shiver down her back. She sat upright, listening. The night air coming through the back window was moist and warm. A sliver of moon hung over the hills. There: a scraping sound, metal on metal. She threw back the sheet and swung her feet to the floor. It was coming from the front of the house. She stood up, looking around for something to defend herself. Next to her bed was Francie's camera. She grabbed as she tiptoed into the loft.

She padded to the window that overlooked the front door, at the top of the stairs. It was locked, the shutters closed. Easing the latch she swung back the glass. The shutters were trickier, brittle and creaky.

She raised the old wrought iron latch and pushed open both shutters an inch. Leaning out she could see two men on her step, doing something to her door. She turned on the camera, pointing it down, then pushed the window shutters wide. They were miraculously un-creaky tonight. The business at the front door continued. Whispering, sawing, elbowing. Merle positioned the camera right over them.

"Hey!" she yelled. The flash of the camera went *flick-flick-flick* as she held the button down. The men looked up in surprise, dropping their tools, pushing each other as they ran down the street. Merle kept shooting as they skidded around the corner and out of sight.

A light came on at *Madame* Suchet's house. Her front door opened an inch. Merle called from the window: *"C'est okay, Madame. Dormez-vous."*

Downstairs Merle stood in front of the door, rechecking the locks.

On the threshold between the door and the shutters lay a hack saw. The thick chain that held the padlock on the shutters hadn't been cut through but she could see the link they had been working on, a silvery notch on the rusty chain. It would have been easier to unscrew the hasp that held the chain, she thought, retrieving the saw. She laid it on her dining table and relocked the door.

Common thieves? She wanted to think so. She stared at the hack saw, a rusty tool with a grubby, notched wooden handle. Fingerprints were probably impossible. She sat on the horsehair settee and looked at the screen on the back of Francie's camera. The first shot caught them in the act, but just the tops of their hats were visible. In the second, the man in the back looked up. He wore a black knit cap, dark T-shirt, and jeans, and looked suspiciously like the thug who peered in earlier. She clicked the next shot, holding her breath. The man with the saw glanced up so quickly she caught only a third of his face but his hair stuck out from his hat. It was black. He was shorter than the thug, older and stockier. But she had no idea who he was.

She stood up, summoning her courage. There was nothing in the house to steal. Still the feeling reared its ugly head. *This house is for guests.*

She couldn't stay here alone. Not tonight.

29

Forty-two. Forty-three. The pain was awful. Francie grunted to finish forty-five sit-ups on the lumpy straw bed in her "deluxe single." She took a breath, unhooked her feet from the metal rail at the foot of the bed, and rubbed the spot where the rope was tied to her ankle. She'd recovered from the initial shock and humiliation of being held captive. For five days she'd slept little. Then she'd discovered the simple exertion of sit-ups twice a day expended enough nervous energy to let her rest at night. And couldn't hurt her cheesy waistline.

So far her captors had been, well, not decent, but not indecent either. She couldn't understand them and didn't know what they wanted. Presumably this was a ransom deal. Her father would come through with the cash eventually. They were keeping her fed, mostly, and wall-eyed Milo slipped her enough wine to keep her from completely losing her shit.

But damn. This was getting old.

And then, the surprise last night, the arrival of Father Cyril. At first she thought he was connected to the kidnappers somehow. She didn't trust him. But he swore in several languages, it appeared. He thrashed around until they tied him to a chair and gagged him to keep him quiet. She heard most of this through the locked door but saw glimpses once or twice when Milo brought her something.

Francie assumed the kidnappers got tired of her—or irritated that she wasn't fluent in Italian—so they turned to a new victim. Why kidnap a priest? Would the Vatican pay a ransom?

She pulled her knees up and hugged them. Her clothes smelled awful but there was nothing for that. The little stone room, her prison, was stuffy with only a small window high on one wall. It smelled of hay and horses. This must be a barn. She'd awakened here, roped to the bed. The last thing she remembered was struggling with some man in Malcouziac. He put a cloth over her mouth and nose and knocked her out. It made her sick for a day or two, whatever it was.

By the golden glow of sunlight on the window, it must be late afternoon. Voices came through the door, but she couldn't tell who was talking. Had they taken the gag off the priest? What was his game anyway, pressing charges against Jimmy Jay? That was a bizarre night. If only she'd known how completely bizarro things could get.

Gillian and her stupid dog. Was that how it all started? Was all this somehow connected to Gillian? But what could Cyril have to do with that?

No answers, just the whirling of her mind. God, she was bored. If only she had a book to read, anything. Or her iPad. The square of sunshine lit the scratchy blanket as she lay back. She would write a blog post in her head. Anything to not go totally bonkers.

Lawyrr Grrl

BLOG—Cherchez moi
posted no clue bluesday

Forget the cheese, *mes amis*. *La fromage* is delightful and delicious, but right now I need a different sort of search. For me. Yes, Lawyrr Grrls, I am lost.

[*Hold on.* She hadn't crashed on a desert island, for godssakes. Sooner or later someone would find her. Merle would be looking at least. Start again. *Ahem.*]

The search for That Girl, my colleague, has turned up nothing. It's like she disappeared, willingly, willfully. Not that I totally blame her. After the last few days walking through the French countryside with my sisters, I considered never going home again. Never staring at a towering stack of documents waiting to be parsed and analyzed. Never sitting through another tedious meeting or twelve-hour deposition. Never again going before a judge to explain why a man's wife wasn't due a penny of his fortune because she had too many wrinkles.

Life seems vast and thrilling, full of opportunities. A smorgasbord of choices to entertain you while you count your birthdays. I'm an optimist, that's how I roll. But is this accurate? Your opportunities whittle down as you make choices, follow paths, find a mate, put down roots. And while limiting you, these are things you desire, these conventional life choices, sometimes more than you ever realized. Having too many possibilities can be paralyzing. Why fight the biological urge to have a home filled with people you love?

You don't have that urge? You're just fine on your own, tripping the light fantastic and keeping it loose and fresh? Good for you. But consider that you will not be 30 forever. You will not be the lovely flower you are today in 25 years. You will have gray hair, bad knees, a shot liver, and—baggage. The weight of your take-no-prisoners youth may drag you down, keeping you from being anywhere near "fresh."

Yes, you can fly solo all the way to the grave. Many have before you, many will follow your path. Many have no regrets (or wouldn't tell you if they did). If it's for you, if you've thought hard and long about it, as much as you have about any malpractice lawsuit featuring eight surgeries and sixteen defendants, then *brava*.

Just make sure it's your decision, not your *non*-decision. Choose out of fear if you must, but choose.

Francie stared at the wooden beams. Where was this coming from? Was this how a person cracks under strain? Hallucination by introspection? Was she thinking she had blown it with Richard? That she should have given him a second chance, had the babies, done whatever it took to keep him? She closed her eyes. *No.* He wasn't the one, the cheating bastard. Was she thinking she should find somebody else, someone to grow old with? Maybe, a little. She'd certainly run through enough hottinghams. And 40 was in the rearview mirror.

But she wasn't thinking about herself. She was thinking about Annie. The matriarch in the family of girls, a shining beacon of all that was virtuous, wild, and free. How Annie had glowed when she finally confessed about her boyfriend. A little surprised, maybe even embarrassed, that she felt so deeply for him. What a wonderful thing. What was his name? Callum. A very sexy name.

A vision floated into her mind, Annie and Callum. Maybe he was wearing a kilt, maybe not. Whatever, he wore an enchanted smile when he saw her. He picked her up at the airport, hugging her tightly as they reunited. The sun on her hair, his arms around her. A simple, happy moment. No drama, no pretense. Just love.

Francie clung to that, the knowledge that goodness exists in the world, that love is possible at any age, as the sun lowered in the sky, the room darkened, and the voices began again outside the door.

30

Merle awoke with a start, wondering where she was. By coincidence she had been given the same room in the Hotel Quimet as last year. *This room.* Malcouziac seemed to be giving her a message: *you're not safe here.* She sat in the short bed with its questionable bedspread and rubbed her eyes. It was after midnight when she'd checked in. She'd brought only small valuables: camera, iPad, jewelry, sunscreen. She'd go back for her clothes this morning, right after she figured out what to do next.

Francie had been missing for days. Capable, smart, and brave but she might be getting despondent after so long. Merle dug out her phone and called Pascal. She left a short voicemail asking him to call. Her voice sounded even and strong. She would join the police search, one way or another.

She packed her backpack and headed downstairs to the dining room. It was just seven and only two groups of tourists were at breakfast. No James or Christine, she noted with relief. She ordered coffee and picked up yogurt and an orange from the buffet. Eating quickly she lingered over her coffee and turned on the iPad. The French frowned on technology at the table but she was alone. And goddamn it, her sister was missing.

Elise and Annie had written. She opened Elise's email first.

Hi Merle & Francie: Hope you're feeling better, Francie. I wanted to point out one photo in that Flickr stream that seemed out of place with all the pretty ones. It's #526, the two men at the café table. Check it out. Miss you! E.

Merle hadn't finished looking at the photos last night. She went back and scrolled to the photo 526. It was the sidewalk café on the Place de la Victoire. Right before it, a shot of coffee and croissants on a plate. This was where she'd seen Gillian on that last day, on the plaza. Merle recognized the wrought iron tables. There were two photos of the men. They were dark-haired and tanned, one large, one small. The small one had a weak chin, wide-set eyes, and shaggy hair that covered his ears. The larger guy had broad shoulders with a large nose and drooping eyes.

In one they were talking, the taller man waving his hands around. In the next photo he read a newspaper while the small man drank coffee. Why had Gillian singled them out? They didn't look like tourists. They were dressed similarly in navy shirts and black jackets. Their fingernails looked crusty and their beards unshaven.

Could one of them be the man with the hacksaw? She got out Francie's camera and looked at the photo again. The coloring was right but otherwise she couldn't tell.

On the iPad Merle enlarged the second photo to read the newspaper. Only a headline was readable. *"America per lanciare Marte spedizione."* Was that French? She read it aloud in a whisper. Italian?

Merle plugged the phrase into an online translation program. Well, Gillian hadn't taken an expedition to Mars. But yes, it was Italian. They were reading an Italian newspaper. So they must have been speaking Italian in the café. And Gillian overheard them.

Merle felt her hope rise. Gillian spoke Italian. She might be in Italy. And these two Italians, who looked like shady operators, might be involved in Francie's abduction. She shot off copies of the two photos to Pascal's email, explaining the connection. Why didn't he return her call? Where was he?

Merle ordered another *café au lait*. She'd be buzzing but that's what she needed today. Her mind wanted to make some connections; she could feel it as she stared out the window. Would the two men be identified? Were they in some criminal database? Were they still in France? Was there a way to track them?

She sighed and clicked on Annie's email.

Merle: You won't believe this—and let's hope the NSA isn't monitoring our email. I found out Gillian Sargent was in WitSec as a juvenile. I know, don't ask about my methods. Her birth name is the only thing I got: Giulia Biondi. Lexis-Nexis to the point: Twenty-five years ago, a Long Island mob boss named Renato 'Max' Biondi was indicted for racketeering and a shitload of other stuff like tax evasion, obstruction, perjury, and narcotics. He went to prison and is still there.

He had a 15-yr-old daughter, a 22-yr-old son, and a wife named Carole. The wife testified for the government against her husband. She and the daughter disappeared after the trial but the son went into the life. He wound up in prison, convicted of conspiracy, promoting gambling, and money laundering twelve years ago. He was released on parole last year and lives in Florida—where everyone knows it's easy to stay clean.

It gets better. Max Biondi's parents didn't take witness protection and were harrassed so badly they emigrated to Europe. To France. Anthony and Lucy Biondi.

Go get 'em, Merdle.

31

Merle was careening through the second roundabout in Cahors, watching the direction signs, when Pascal called. She nearly hit a farm truck but managed to pull off and answer.

"*Allo*, blackbird. How are you today?" His voice was back to smooth and sexy.

Merle babbled for a minute, bursting with information about Gillian, her grandparents, Francie, the men in the café. "I just know she's gone to her grandparents. It makes perfect sense, why she was so secretive all the time."

"Whoa," he interrupted. "Where are you?"

"Driving to Montpellier to join you. I'm in Cahors. I have to talk to the police, Pascal. Did you get the photos I sent? Of the men at the café?"

"Yes, I got them. But you should not go to Montpellier."

"She's my sister, Pascal! I'm done sitting around waiting for the Keystone Cops to find her. If they won't—"

"Stop, blackbird. I meant the investigation has moved. We are in Arles now."

"Arles? Have you found her?"

"Not yet. But the truck used in Montpellier was abandoned outside the city here."

Merle wrestled to unfold her guidebook map. Arles was east of Montpellier, around the coastline of the Mediterranean. "Okay, I'm headed that way." She tossed the map onto the seat. "I need you to do something for me, Pascal."

"Yes?"

"I need an address of two Americans living in France. Their names are Anthony and Lucy Biondi. Possibly Italians but they should have American passports. They emigrated to France about twenty or twenty-five years ago."

"And they are?"

"Gillian's grandparents." She didn't want to beg. But she would.

"Biondi, got it. I will call as soon as I find anything. And you call me when you get to Arles?"

"Right. Thanks." She hung up, already pulling into traffic. She checked the gas gauge: half-full. Some would say half-empty. But not a Bennett sister.

She retraced her route over the forested hills to Rodez then into Millau. She filled up the gas tank there and headed out again, her hands aching from gripping the steering wheel so tight. The phone rang again as she crossed into the Languedoc-Roussillon province.

"Pascal?"

"Can you pull over?"

Such a policeman. "Hang on." She set the phone on the seat as she sped up, looking for a driveway on the narrow road. A farm gate with a dirt drive served. "Okay. I'm parked."

"You have something to write on?" She scrabbled through her backpack, locating her notebook and a pen. "There is an Antoine and Lucie Biondi listed living near Caveirac. A village west of Nîmes. The number is twenty-eight, Chemin de Calvisson." He spelled the names, the villages, and the street. She read them back, making sure she had it all correct. "May I ask what you intend to do, blackbird?"

"You may." She was staring at the map, trying to find the village. "But you may not like it."

"As it were," he said with a sigh.

"Gillian might be there. With the dog. When you find Francie, I'll have the dog for the exchange."

"You're coming to Arles then?"

"If I can. Find her." *Before it's too late.* Merle threw her phone on the seat and bumped off the farm lane back onto the blacktop. Before she got a half-mile her phone rang again. "What is it?"

"Merle?"

Her heart leapt into her throat. "Mom? How are you?"

"Fine, dear. How is France?"

For a second Merle thought she said *Francie.* She swallowed, hoping to sound cheerful and not frantic. "Beautiful. Gorgeous. Roses blooming. I'm driving around, seeing the sights, taking pictures. Touristy stuff."

"Is Francie with you? We heard she was sick."

"She's better. But she stayed back at the house." Merle pinched herself for lying. "She's a little tired from all that tramping around we did."

"We were hoping to talk to her but she's not answering her phone. Her landlady called here. Francie missed her rent payment. We sent it on for her, but that doesn't seem like Francie."

Whispering then her father came on the line. "Merle? What's going on over there?"

"Nothing, Daddy. Just, you know, ooh-la-la French stuff."

"What about Gillian Sargent? Annie won't tell me what's going on, even after I did some sleuthing for her."

"Gillian's still on the lam, Daddy. I wish I knew where she was. But I have a feeling it will all work out. I mean, she's got to come home sometime."

"So does Francie. I don't buy this sick thing for a second. You sound funny. You two are up to something over there, aren't you?"

"Yup. We're secretly working as lavender sachet stuffers."

Her father sighed. "You're not missing work too, are you?"

"No, I have six weeks off. Pretty nice racket, huh?"

"Tell Francie to get herself home or she's going to damage things at Ward & Baillee. I mean it. They don't like this sort of slacking off."

"Are they gossiping about her at the golf course?"

"Just be careful, Merle."

"I will. Love you. Kisses to Mom."

The road wound along a river bottom and up over a hill. *Great.* Now she had her parents to worry about. *Bring it on.* She would take it for all of them. The worry ship was filling up. It had to land somewhere.

Pascal d'Onscon sat in the back room of the police headquarters in Arles, fingering the address he'd given Merle. Around him several officers worked phones and computers around the long, rectangular table while the captain, finally divesting himself of that ridiculous uniform, went from man to man, getting reports. The morale in the task force was mixed to bad. Some officers were pessimistic, whispering that the woman was likely dead by now since the exchange of the dog in the shopping center had been so badly botched. Others were more imaginative, piecing together the latest disappearance in tiny Malcouziac of the traveling priest, Father Cyril Fabre, with the abduction of Francine Bennett. Such a small village, these officers said, the two had to be connected. How they were connected hadn't been discovered. Pascal had yet to mention his knowledge of the priest's charges against Merle's boyfriend. He had a bad taste in his mouth, thinking about King James. He had checked with the Périgueux authorities. James was wearing an electronic anklet. He hadn't left Malcouziac without permission. He didn't want to involve Merle even more. He could hear the near-panic in her voice, normally so clear and rational.

He looked at his watch. If Merle had been in Cahors when they first talked, she'd likely be in Caveirac within the hour. He had no faith that the dog or Gillian would be there. It seemed unlikely that the American still had the dog. She could easily have sold the truffle dog on the black market as she was worth, he estimated, 25-thousand euros. Some officers scoffed at such a figure, especially after seeing the dog's photograph. She was no show dog. But in his line Pascal came across some expensive wine scams, the sort that make you wince at the greed and stupidity of buyers. A proficient, well-trained truffle dog could easily make that much for its owners in a single season, possibly many times that. Truffle prices in the spring were nearly 2000 euros per kilogram, $1200 per pound. Hot summer weather without soaking rains was predictor of a bad crop this winter and even higher prices.

A young officer down the table shouted, "We have found the priest!" Pascal stood up, rounding the large conference table. The officer, a short man named René Hellenes, was speaking rapidly to the captain. "Seen last night, or possibly two nights ago, at a gasoline station in Montauban. The priest inside, tied up. Two men with him, not identified."

A flurry of excitement was quickly dampened when it appeared the vehicle was the same one found abandoned outside Arles. No trace of the occupants. Hellenes went back to his computer.

Pascal stepped up to the map tacked to the wall, looking at the routes and possible hiding spots around Arles, Montauban, Malcouziac, and now, the village of Caveirac. He examined the pencil sketches of the two men wanted for beating the old man in the Lot. They looked very much like the two in the photograph that Merle had sent, now blown up and posted next to the sketches. Unfortunately, they hadn't been located in any criminal database. Another photograph was tacked up, the abandoned farm truck, dirt covering the lower half, the hubs, the bumpers, license plates removed.

Carefully Pascal stuck a blue-headed pin in the center of Caveirac. So close to Nîmes, just eight kilometers, probably a bedroom community for the larger town. He turned to find the captain watching him. He cocked an eyebrow.

"The sister of *Mademoiselle* Bennett has some new information," Pascal explained. "The American who took the dog has relatives in the village of Caveirac. Grandparents." He gave a half-shrug. "As far as we know the kidnappers don't have this information."

"Or they would have the dog themselves by now," the captain said. Pascal nodded. "Question the grandparents anyway. See what they know."

Pascal went back to his chair on the far side of the table and got out his phone. He thought of Merle, driving there like a mad woman. Was she hoping the element of surprise would work in her favor? Would calling these Americans tip them off, make them run? Were they very old perhaps, non-French speakers, or just easily frightened? He put his phone down and stared blankly at his computer for a moment. He went back to the report from Paris about the old couple. No telephone number was listed anyway. Maybe they were part-time residents, or simply very careful. He did another search for "Biondi" in the province, then in all of France. Nothing promising.

He picked up his phone again and rang the number of Claude LaFleur, the *gendarme* in the Lot, the one closest to the case of the assault on the dog owner. It took a few tries to find him out in the field.

"What news of *Monsieur* Poutou?" Pascal asked. The *gendarme* had shepherded *Madame* Poutou through the process for the sketches of the assailants and had taken the old couple under his special care.

"He improves. They expect to release him from the hospital in a day or two."

"Do you see anything strange around there? Anything related to *le chien de truffes*, the truffle dog?"

The officer said all was quiet in the area since the assault. *Madame* Poutou was staying with a relative nearer to the hospital but the *gendarme* had been driving by the farm each day to make sure everything was secure and that someone was feeding the chickens.

Pascal asked him to call if he saw anyone suspicious. He took his jacket off the back of his chair. He had to move, to do something. Could Gillian Sargent be meeting these miscreants to pass off the dog herself? What if Merle got caught in the middle of it? Why had Gillian taken off with this expensive dog? Why didn't the grandparents have a telephone?

As he shrugged into his jacket, the captain gave him that look again.

"Going to check out Caveirac myself, sir."

32

When the tall priest walked into her room that morning, Francie was confused. Why was Father Cyril, the gangly, stoop-shouldered priest with dandruff, walking free now, palling around with the Italians? His eyes still bore the shadows of Jimmy Jay's wallop plus some fresh scrapes. His black jacket was dusty, his slacks wrinkled. He slouched in behind the major domo, the gray-haired slapper, the chieftain of this band of nincompoops. Behind him Milo and the other unshaven malcontent lurked in the doorway.

She scooted back on her bed, pressing against the wall. The rope burned on her ankle where it had rubbed the skin raw. She crossed her arms and threw back her hair, glaring at the chieftain. He stepped aside and let the priest move closer, muttering something.

"Miss Bennett, I presume?" Father Cyril squinted at her.

"What are you doing here?" she asked.

The priest glanced at the older man and raised his eyebrows. "They seem to think I know something about this lost dog. I believe they have mistaken me for *Père* Albert. I have tried to explain."

"Good luck with that. You speak Italian?"

"Just a little. One of the men has French. Hector, I believe is the name." The priest looked around the room. "May I?" He pointed to the end of her bed.

"No, you may not. What's going on? I haven't been able to talk to any of them."

"They believe you know the whereabouts of this dog. The truffle dog. Yes?"

Francie frowned. "The dog we found by the side of the road?"

The priest gave the chieftain a small nod. "That's the one. The one you took to your house in Malcouziac. It belongs to these men."

She shrugged. "I don't know anything about it."

"Come, come, Miss Bennett. The dog was sheltered at your home."

"What home? You mean my sister's house?"

The priest startled, blinking madly. He glanced at the chief. "Mademoiselle, what is your full name?"

"Francine Eloise Bennett. What's yours?"

"You own a holiday house in the Dordogne?"

"No. My sister owns a house. You've been there."

"What is your sister's name?"

"Merle 'Danger' Bennett. What's going on? I'm not going to let you and your friends kidnap my sister. She had nothing to do with that dog. The dog was snatched by another woman. She ran off with it. She stole our rental car."

Father Cyril stared at her. "Repeat that please. Slower. The dog was—?"

She obliged him and waited as the information was relayed through two languages. The chief was now yelling at the men in the doorway.

"Did they think I was Merle?" She gave the chief a sneer. "Just like they thought you were Albert." She laughed. It was just too much, these imbeciles. The chief stepped closer with a thunderous look and raised his hand. The priest took hold of his arm and forced it down.

"Who is this woman, the one who took the dog?" Cyril asked.

"Her name is Gillian Sargent. She disappeared without a trace." She frowned again. "Why don't you call my sister? She might know where the dog is by now."

"You have her phone number?"

"No." The number was in her phone which she obviously did not have. Merle had to find Gillian. She had to get the damn dog for these morons. "Have they been to her house? She should be there."

The priest said something to the chief which was translated by the man Hector. "She is not at home," Cyril said.

"Why are you here again?"

"They wanted *Père* Albert but got me instead. Possibly not the brightest of criminals." He smiled brightly to the men. "How can we find your sister, Miss Bennett? You and I should help each other. They will not let us go until they get the dog. She is worth many, many euros. They appear to be sparing no trouble to find her." Cyril lowered his voice. "I believe the big man is a wealthy truffle merchant."

Francie squeezed the bridge of her nose, thinking. "Albert must know how to find Merle. Do you have his number?"

There was a flurry of Italian and French. The chief fished a cell phone from his trouser pocket. They all looked at it until a button was pushed and Hector took the phone. After twenty seconds of ringing he handed it back and said, "*Non.*"

"Does he have a mobile?" Francie asked. Cyril stared at his phone again.

"Ah, here." He handed it to Hector. Francie could hear it ringing. Hector listened then and passed the phone back to Cyril. "*Vous.*"

"Albert? *Cyril ici. Comment ça va?*" The priest listened then spoke haltingly in French, waving his hands. He seemed to be making up a story that included Merle and her *jardin*, her garden. He motioned for a pen. The chief passed him one and he wrote on his palm. "*Bon, merci. À bientôt.*"

"I have it," Cyril said triumphantly. His hands were shaking as he punched in the new set of numbers, reading from his hand. The chief stopped him, hand on his arm, saying something and motioning to Francie.

"They want you to speak to your sister," Cyril said, punching in the last two numbers and handing over the phone. "You must tell her to bring the dog to exchange. And no police. Wait." Cyril punched the speaker button so all could hear the conversation.

"Hello? *Allo?*"

"Merle? Is that you?" Francie said, her heart beating fast. She felt the blood rush to her face at the sound of her sister's voice.

"Who is this? Francie!"

"It's me. Listen, I'm fine, more or—"

"Oh, my god, Francie. I've been worried sick. Are you okay? Did they hurt you? Where are you?"

"They've still got me. I don't know where we are, some barn. They want the dog, Merle. Have you found her yet?"

"I'm close. I found Gillian's grandparents. I think she's there." A strangled sound. "Are you sure you're okay?"

"Not bad for being held against my will by a bunch of brainiacs. Just a second." Francie looked up at the men. "What now, assholes?"

Cyril spoke to Hector in French who relayed the message in Italian. Francie closed her eyes in disgust. Finally Cyril bent down to the phone and spoke: "You will receive a text for the location to bring the dog. No police."

"Did you hear that, Merle?" Francie asked.

"Yes, I'll wait for the text. Who was that?"

"Father Cyril, believe it or not. This is his phone. I feel like you're close by. I don't know why I said that, but I like to think you're nearby, Merle."

"Oh, Francie, I am. I'm right by your side, never forget it. Hang in there, sister. I love you."

The chief snatched the phone and ended the call. The men filed out and the lock turned in the door once more.

Francie let her head fall back against the stone wall and shut her eyes. Her heart was still beating furiously. She willed it to slow down.

This wasn't over yet.

33

Merle held her breath to stop hyperventilating. The call from Francie had rocked her. She had to hold it together, find the dog, make this happen. But she felt like she was flying apart in all directions. She had just come through an intersection where she had to consult her map again when the call came. Now she glanced at the map once more, grounding herself. She wasn't far from Caveirac now, just minutes away if she didn't get lost again.

The poorly marked back roads were picturesque, winding through fields of poppies and waving grains. She wished she was walking them with her sisters, with Francie—No, must not get mushy. Forward, on to Caveirac. *Stay on task, Merdle.*

She reached the village just after one in the afternoon. The town seemed deserted. When she parked and got out of the car, she realized why. It had to be close to a hundred degrees. The Mediterranean sun beat down fiercely. She looked back in the car for her sun hat but it wasn't there. The name of the road she was looking for, Chemin de Calvisson, wasn't on her map. She had to find a local. She walked down one side of the village main street, looking in shop windows. Everything was closed for lunch: the *patisserie*, the *boulangerie*, a dress shop, a pharmacy. She crossed the road. Not much on this side. A doctor's office, real estate offices, a small hardware store, a tiny grocery, everything shut tight. Back in her car, Merle drove slowly down the street. On the left rose a large stone building with a parking lot in front,

something modern. She raised a hand against the sun. *Maison du Vin &*
Tourisme. She parked and turned off the car.

A cool blast of air dried the sweat on her face as she entered the
building. She'd been in tasting rooms like these before, a cooperative for
vintners where you could taste and buy local wine. This one combined
the tourist office and was staffed by just one pimply-faced young man.

"*Bonjour, madame,*" he called cheerfully.

"*Bonjour, monsieur,*" she replied although his days as a man had only
begun. Gangly with a prominent Adam's apple and a bad haircut, he
rattled something off in French. She hoped she didn't have to buy a
tasting. She could see from the board they were pricey, and she didn't
want to make excuses for hurrying. Merle smiled and asked him if he
spoke English. He frowned, disappointed in himself, and said no.

"*Ça fait rien,*" she reassured him, telling him she spoke a little
French. "*Je cherche une famille Americaine.*" She told him she was searching
for an American family who lived on Chemin du Calvisson. He
brightened immediately.

"But I live on Chemin du Calvisson," he said, smiling again. "You
mean the Biondi family?"

God love small-town people, Merle thought as she ran across the
hot asphalt to her car. The boy had shown her exactly where they lived.
He said the house was behind high hedges and hard to spot but there
wasn't a wall or gate, to just park next to the hedge and walk around to
the left, under the olive trees.

It was just as he described. Within a minute Merle had pulled off
onto the verge, next to a dense thorny hedge, the sort that said "keep
out." It was well-trimmed and nearly fifteen feet tall. She grabbed her cell
phone, backpack, and keys and locked the car. The hedge had an
advantage to the unexpected visitor as well. The car wouldn't be seen
from the house.

She walked down the hedge to the far end where it thinned in the
shade of an enormous tree. It looked like one of her oaks at home.
Beyond a row of smaller, pale green trees were grouped, hanging with
tiny round fruit.

The house was plain, a low-slung rancher with white stucco walls, dull green shutters, and a red tile roof. The lawn was dry and yellow. Somewhere she could hear a sprinkler going *cha-cha-cha*. Otherwise, quiet reigned. The blinds in the house were drawn. She walked next to the olive trees, around the side of the house. A cement patio sat blazing in the sun, a green umbrella in a picnic table tightly closed. Beyond the patio, more grass, greener here, and two outbuildings. Garages or farm sheds, she couldn't tell from this angle. They matched the house in style but were smaller, the size of double garages. No cars in sight.

An air conditioner kicked on behind the house. Merle retraced her steps, making her way over the crunchy lawn to the front door. There was no doorbell or screen door. She knocked. She rapped again, harder, and called out, "*Madame* Biondi?"

Suddenly the door opened. An old woman stood there, a half smile on her wide, wrinkled face. She paused, staring at Merle as if she might know her but not placing her, the smile frozen.

"Hi, hello! *Madame* Biondi? *Bonjour!*" Merle stuck out her hand. The old woman blinked, then shook it. "I'm Francie Bennett. Gillian's colleague in the law firm. Back home? Ward and Baillee? In Connecticut? She must have told you about it. We work together. She's a fantastic attorney. Anyway I was just passing through and she told me about you, her grandparents, living in France. My sister has a little place near here. Well, not so near, over in the Dordogne. Do you ever get over there? It's a ways, through the forest, over the hills. Whew, it's hotter here than in the Dordogne, isn't it? It must be ninety-five degrees. A dry heat but still. Hot is hot."

Merle stopped babbling abruptly, the lilt still in her voice as if she could go on for days. She stared at the old woman, grinning like a traveling salesman, friendly as the day is long. When the woman still didn't speak, Merle glanced behind her for the grandfather. Maybe he was out. That would be lucky.

"Sorry. You speak English, don't you? You've been over here a long time, but I didn't even think—" Merle put a hand on her throat. "Do you still speak English?"

The old woman shook herself slightly. "Yes. Of course. Won't you come in?" Her voice was thin and reedy. She looked to be on the dark side of eighty, with wire-rim glasses and a thick shock of white hair she pulled back into a bun. She was short but sturdy, wearing a cotton shift and a flowered apron. She led Merle into the front sitting room. "You must be hot. Can I get you something to drink?"

Merle sat down on a worn armchair. "A glass of water would be fabulous. What a great place you have here. I often wondered what it would be like to live in France. Do you like it? I think I would adore it."

The old woman was in the kitchen, running water into a glass, and didn't answer. She returned, handing Merle the water. "Who did you say you were?"

"A lawyer with your granddaughter, Gillian. Back in Connecticut."

The old woman stiffed. Her demeanor had changed. Her features shifted and she no longer made eye contact. "I don't know who that is."

"You don't know your own granddaughter? Is she here?" Merle downed the water and set down the glass. "I thought I saw her out back."

"Who?"

Merle stood up, making the old woman take a step backward. She tipped her head, trying to look both non-threatening and threatening at the same time. Lawyer stuff.

"You may call her by a different name, Mrs. Biondi. Giulia. Your son's daughter."

The old woman was blinking hard and fingering the edge of her apron. "I don't know anyone by either of those names. I d-don't have a son. You've got the wrong person. You must leave now."

Merle picked up her backpack from the floor and unzipped it. She took out the wrinkled picture of Gillian and the dog in Loiverre. "We call her Gillian. But before all the, ah, bad stuff went down, you called her Giulia. Such a pretty Italian name. Here she is with the dog on our walking tour. We had such fun. She's crazy about that dog, isn't she?"

The old woman's mouth dropped open as she glanced at the photograph. She couldn't speak. An old clock in the corner ticked off the seconds. Merle waited. Time was her weapon of choice. Thirty seconds passed, then another thirty. An eternity. A trickle of sweat made its way down her back. Finally Merle whispered, "Is she here?"

The old woman's face was white. She grabbed the back of a chair for support. She glanced up, then looked toward the back of the house.

Merle tiptoed across the tile floor, her running shoes squeaking. A short hallway ran to the left. Two doors were open, a bedroom and a bath. Two doors were closed. She turned back to Mrs. Biondi. "This way?"

The woman was mute. Merle stepped up to the first door, turned the knob and looked inside. An office with a computer, rolling chair and lounger, venetian blinds shut. She looked behind the door and moved on. The second door creaked as she opened it. In the dim lighting she made out a bed, lamps, dressers. She paused, wondering if she should search the closet, when the barking of a dog somewhere came through the house.

She froze in the hallway. There. Outside.

She retraced her steps through the tidy kitchen to the back door. She wondered again about the grandfather. Was he waiting with a machete in the garage? Merle straightened her shoulders, throwing open the kitchen door. The heat blasted her face and chest. She stepped into it, leaving the door ajar.

The two outbuildings, from this angle, were not identical. One was a two-car garage, its gray metal door shut. The other looked the same from the side, but from the front, it was obviously an apartment or vacation *gîte* with a pot of geraniums and a wooden bench by the door. At the very least a workshop. Big enough for a woman and her dog.

The green shutters on the building were shut on the south and west sides. But to the east, the front, the door had no shutters, only a lace curtain. Merle sidled up to the side, close against the stucco, and stopped to listen as Mrs. Biondi stepped onto the patio. She had a fierce look on her face now, as if Pompeii was ready to blow.

Go back inside, old woman. She doubted Gillian would try anything, but whatever happened might be traumatic for her. Merle didn't need a heart attack on her hands. She waved as if pushing Mrs. Biondi back inside but the woman put her hands on her hips and opened her mouth.

"Giulia!" Mrs. Biondi had found her voice. She called once, gathered her breath and yelled again at an even higher register, "Giulia!!"

Merle's heart skipped in surprise. She stepped back from the edge of the door, around the corner of the building. Inside, there were footsteps, scrabbling sounds, woofs. The door opened and a brown-and-white dog rushed out, streaking toward the old woman who backed into the house. "Shoo! Get away!" She batted her hands at the dog, which only seemed to make it bark louder.

And finally, Gillian. Running after the dog, calling to her, speaking another language. Italian? French? It happened so fast. Merle stepped away from the house.

The dog was under control, barely, dancing around as Gillian held its collar. Mrs. Biondi crossed her arms, annoyed. Gillian said, "It's okay, Nonnie. Shhh, Aurore. *Calmez-vous, petit.* You shouldn't yell like that, Nonnie. It scares her."

Mrs. Biondi was staring over her shoulder. Gillian turned, flinching as she saw Merle. "What are you doing here?" The dog twisted out of her grasp.

"Hello, Gillian. We've been so worried about you since you disappeared." Merle crouched down to the dog's level and was rewarded with a sloppy lick to the cheek. "Ah, sweet dog. She remembers me." Aurore was clean and soft. She still had a bare spot where she'd been injured but it was healed now. Merle rubbed her curly head then stood, getting her first good look at Gillian. She looked no worse for her adventures, in khaki shorts, flip-flops, and a Mets T shirt, hair pulled back in a thick ponytail. Her cheeks were rosy from the sun. She crossed her arms and stuck out her chin.

Merle stepped close to her and whispered. "We need to talk."

34

Slumped in a chair in the darkened apartment, Gillian stroked the dog's ears, her eyes facing the floor as if she were a child being chastised. Merle couldn't blame her. She'd been found out and her beloved dog discovered. Above all, her Big Secret, the identity she'd kept underground since she was fifteen, was out, whether she realized it yet or not. Merle wondered how she would feel if the burden of such a secret were chucked. There had to be an element of both release and anxiety. You didn't change your identity unless there were some very bad people after you.

The *gîte* behind the grandmother's house was sparsely furnished with cast-offs, a sagging bed, a rickety table with one chair, dishes in the sink. They sat in a small parlor with only a dusty plastic houseplant separating it from the bedroom. The parlor chairs were upholstered, holes worn in the arm rests. Merle was surprised at how depressing it was. Something about Gillian said "class" and "self-respect." It had not said "yesterday's hamburger grease."

"How did you find me?" she asked in a small voice.

"Through your grandparents," Merle said. Gillian looked up. "Yes, I know who you really are, Giulia."

"That's impossible."

"It's the government. What can I say? It was a good run. You didn't expect to stay under the radar forever, did you?" Merle gave her a small smile. She needed Gillian soft and pliable. "But this is not about you."

"What do you mean?"

"Remember those Italians in Malcouziac? The ones at the café? They kidnapped Francie. She's being held somewhere because they want this dog. You know she's worth a lot of money."

She nodded, petting the dog's fuzzy muzzle.

"Did you see the reward poster?" Gillian nodded again. "Then you know she doesn't belong to you. She was stolen from an old man who was beaten and almost killed."

"By who?"

"Probably the same dirtbags who kidnapped Francie and stole the dog in the first place. She got loose from them, that's when we found her. They went back to the farmer to wait for somebody to return her for the reward."

"I wouldn't do that." Gillian looked angrily at Merle. "She's not for sale."

"She's a dog, Gillian. A highly-trained dog, no doubt sweet, but a *canine*. She's worth thousands of dollars, even more if you're a truffle hunter. People buy and sell dogs every day. It's not like human trafficking." Gillian acted incensed at the whole idea of money exchanged for dogs.

"To me she's priceless."

"To me too. Because she will get my sister back."

Gillian tossed her head, her thick hair grazing her shoulder. "It's all set. In a week I'll have all the paperwork. And I'll take her home."

"She doesn't belong to you, Gillian, no matter how much you love her."

"I can't give her back. I won't." Her words were strong but her voice was faltering.

"Look at me," Merle said with steel in her voice. "Do you want me to tell my mother and father that Francie's best friend at the law firm chose a stray dog over her *life*? Are you going to bring your dog to Francie's funeral and tell everyone that your little lost dog was more important than Francie? That you let my sister—your colleague, your friend—die?"

Gillian kept her head bowed, silent.

"How's that going to work, Gillian? Or should I say Giulia, daughter of 'Max' Biondi, racketeer and convicted felon and no doubt the sweetest Mafia Don to ever grace the halls of Sing Sing."

Gillian winced then tried to look defiant. "You don't know what you're talking about. And you won't tell anyone. You got that information illegally. Nobody will believe you."

"Watch me." They stared each other down for a moment. Then Merle said, "I bet old Max still has enemies out on Long Island. No, wait. He's got *friends*. Friends who'd love to find your mother and get reacquainted. How is Carole?"

She sounded like a character from "G-Man." But it worked. Gillian slumped against the head of the dog, arms around its neck, and began to wail. "I love you, Aurore. I won't let them take you."

But the die was cast. Her crying ended as quickly as it began, as if it was an act. Maybe everything about Gillian was an act, from her name and her background, her law degree, her fancy clothes, and her love of dogs. Maybe she identified with stray dogs, lost and alone in a big, bad world. At this point Merle didn't care. Gillian could win an Oscar. It didn't matter. Because they were going to exchange the dog for Francie.

Tonight.

It took close to an hour to get Gillian into the car. She had to explain and argue with her grandmother for a long time. Merle held the dog, listening to Gillian say she was going to return the dog to her owners, that she realized someone else loved Aurore as much as she did and she should go home. It was mildly convincing. Nonnie took it in, frowning, letting loose some Italian, then threw up her hands in surrender.

Gillian wanted to pack a bag, but Merle would only let her bring dog food, water and a dish for the dog. They weren't spending the night together. On the way out, Gillian strapped a leash to Aurore's collar. "Likes to follow a scent," she muttered darkly.

They all piled into the front seat, the dog between Gillian's knees in the passenger seat. She put on her seat belt and sighed as Merle started the engine and turned on the air conditioning. Merle didn't have much of a plan from here on, but she didn't want Gillian to know that.

"Where's your grandfather?" Merle asked as they got on the road.

Gillian stared at her, stone-faced. "None of your business."

Merle shrugged and drove back through the village. As she turned toward Nîmes, Gillian said softly, "He died two years ago. I hadn't seen him for years."

Merle glanced at her. "I'm sorry."

Nîmes was larger than she expected with suburbs and highways going in every direction. She got lost and wandered into the old part of town, rounding the ancient Coliseum with its bullfighting posters, passing a columned Roman Forum, then righting herself to go south. The afternoon sun beat down on the streets. Outside the city Merle pulled into a parking lot to consult her map again.

"Where is she? Francie," Gillian asked.

"If I knew that, I wouldn't need the dog, would I? The police have been looking for her for days." Merle glanced over, hoping to see some regret on the other woman's face. But she was just petting the dog, dreamy-eyed.

"I had a dog when I was a kid. Her name was Trixie." Her voice was wistful.

"Did you have to leave her behind?"

She nodded. "She was a Jack Russell. Little but with so much spunk, so much heart."

"Like Aurore," Merle said. She looked on her phone for a message. Nothing. She stared at the last call, the priest's number. Maybe they could trace it. She called Pascal and it went to voicemail. Quickly she explained about the call, giving him the number and where she was when she got it. She knew something about triangulating cell calls but wasn't sure they did that in France, how fast they could do it, or how well it worked.

"Did you bring your phone?" Merle asked Gillian. The small day-pack containing the dog food sat by her feet. "I know you have one."

She reached into a zipped pocket and pulled out a small phone. "Does it do text?" Merle asked.

"Of course."

"Turn it on. Then text to this number." She showed her priest's number. "Say this: 'Ready to exchange the dog. Tonight. Send location.'"

"My number is blocked. They won't be able to reply."

Merle squinted at her. "Okay. Add 'Text Merle.'"

Gillian worked her thumbs quickly. "Is that it?"

"Let me see it." Merle read it over. "Send it."

She watched Gillian to make sure she sent it, then looked at her watch. It was close to four-thirty. This would be over soon. She could hear Francie's voice, *I feel like you're near.* The courage and the trust in that moment. A shiver went down Merle's back as she steered the car out into traffic and headed toward Arles.

35

Lucy Biondi stood at the window, watching the two women talk in the back. They seemed to be arguing, gesturing at the dog and each other, voices raised. She didn't want to know. She'd had enough of this drama. Giulia had been here for over a week, demanding secrecy on all fronts just like her father. Nato was a very unpleasant boy who grew into a brute and a villain. Yes, he was her son—her only son—but she'd long ago wished for a different one. He had shamed her and the whole family. He was dead to her.

The dog was doing its business now on her lawn. Her carefully tended lawn. She bit down on her molars and made herself be calm. Giulia said the dog was special, had talents or something, but all he or she appeared to do was run around barking and shit on the grass. Lucy rolled her eyes in disgust. If they left, it would be none too soon. She loved her granddaughter of course but being here only made things more difficult than ever. She saw much of Nato in Giulia, in her looks, the stubbornness, and even meanness.

The women and the dog went inside the cabana. Tony had called their holiday rental a "cabana" and the name stuck. It made them a little money and cost very little. He had loved having guests back there, even if he couldn't speak their language.

Lucy walked through the living room. She pushed aside the curtains to see the woman's car outlined against the hedge. She glanced to the backyard again then slipped out the front door, taking a pencil and scrap of paper in her apron pocket. In the olive grove she pretended to check them for the crop although everyone knew it was too early.

Under the oak tree she paused, wiped the sweat from her eyes, and drew out the paper and pencil. *Gray Peugeot, four door.* She wrote down the license number. Shoving the utensils back in her apron, she scurried through the afternoon sun, back into the cool air of her house, locking the door tight behind her.

In the kitchen she shuffled through the mail on the table. At the bottom was the reward poster Giulia had brought, the one for the dog. The one that made Lucy think Giulia had stolen the dog herself, although she denied it. She said she loved the dirty old thing, that someone else had stolen it. As if that were an excuse. Lucy looked at the poster, thinking what ten-thousand euros would mean. She could travel again. Go see her sister in Florida. Not live like an outcast, a fugitive in a foreign land.

She leaned against the table. *Ah, Tony. Would that we never had to leave New York and all our friends.* But, as he said in a rare correct use of French, "*C'est la vie.*"

36

The park on the banks of the Rhône River was dry and weedy, the perfect place to hide in the shade and let the dog have a break. They'd stopped at a grocery and bought goat cheese and a baguette and an assortment of olives and sat on the ground. Gillian got up to let Aurore sniff every tree. She walked with her on the leash. She was too precious to run free.

Merle had debated where to wait for the kidnappers' text. The outskirts of Arles seemed the best bet. According to the map, the interior of the ancient city was a rabbit warren of narrow streets and awkward plazas. A quick getaway would be impossible.

The Rhône was wide and lazy here. Upstream, the remains of an ancient bridge, complete with imposing white lions, watched over the water. The banks of the river were mostly built up with high stone walls to control flooding, with walkways along the top. This tiny green space was a rare wild area.

An hour passed slowly. Merle tried not to keep looking at her watch but her inner calendar did the job of ticking the minutes. At seven, as clouds gathered in the western sky, obscuring the sunset, Pascal called.

"Are you in Caveirac?" His voice was tight, anxious.

"No, Arles," she said. "Did you get my message about the phone call from the kidnappers?"

"Not until half an hour ago. I was on my way out of the building to meet you in Caveirac and I got caught in a meeting with my superiors."

"Were you able to track the call?"

"Not yet. The permissions take the longest." He caught his breath. "What are you doing in Arles?"

"Waiting for the text. I have Gillian and the dog."

"I know. Listen. There was a tip about the dog. Your rental car was identified. The description of the car and the license number have been broadcast. You'd best come in, Merle."

She looked back at the car, the only one in the lot by the road. She jumped to her feet as if being upright would help her hearing. Gillian looked over, the dog straining on the leash under a small tree. "A tip?" She tried to recall anyone paying attention to the car. "From where?"

"Someone in Caveirac. She's hoping for the reward. I spoke to her. The *gendarme* in the Lot sent her on." His voice dropped. "It's the woman you were looking for, Merle. *Madame* Biondi."

Merle swore under her breath. "She didn't waste any time." Turning in her own granddaughter. Classy. "Do you have any idea where the call from the kidnappers came from?"

"Possibly west of Arles, up in the hills. Merle, go to the police headquarters in Arles. I will meet you there."

She was throwing cheese and bread crusts into the paper bag. "I have to get Francie. The dog is the only way."

"The police have something to work on now, thanks to your call. Let us do our work, blackbird. Be safe. These are desperate men. They have kidnapped your sister. You can't go into those hills alone and expect to just hand over the dog, can you?"

Merle bit down on her molars, trying hard not to tell him to stop being such a chauvinist. He wasn't one, or at least not more than most Frenchmen. She swore again then covered the phone and called Gillian. "I have to go, Pascal."

Back in the car, Merle consulted her map again and plotted the route to the train station. Gillian looked at her curiously but asked no questions. Five minutes later Merle pulled into an alley near the station and put the car in park.

"Hand me your pack," she said. Gillian gave it to her. Merle took out the bottle of water, the dish, and the bag of dog food, throwing them into the back seat. She zipped up the day-pack and gave it to Gillian. "Get out."

The younger woman frowned. "What do you mean?"

Merle took the dog's collar, pulling the animal up into her lap. "I mean, you're done. Say good-bye to Aurore and get out of the car. Get on a train and go somewhere."

Gillian's nostrils flared. "What the hell?"

"Your grandmother turned us in. The cops are looking for this car. For us."

"She wouldn't."

"I guess she wants that reward." Merle gave her shoulder a little shove. "Get out of here. They are going to think you stole her. Unless you aren't in the car and don't have the dog."

She opened the door. "What about you?"

"Don't worry about me. Worry about Francie."

The light in the sky faded to black as Merle wound her way out of Arles. The dog had curled into the passenger seat after a frantic yipping episode as they drove away from Gillian. Merle patted her head, using Gillian's words: *"Calmez-vous, petit."* *Be quiet, be calm, little one.* The dog looked at her with big brown eyes, listening, then miraculously fell asleep.

She had plotted a simple route on the back roads out of Arles, the slow streets, off the motorways. Across the Rhône once, then again, merging into traffic on bridges then off again onto the old byways. Under the train tracks and over a canal, the moonlight flashing on the surface of the water. Barges lined up, pleasure boats and working craft. She left them behind, circling Saint-Gilles on the *Chemin du Vin* and on to other *chemins*, the old roads lined with farms and crumbling churches and storefronts boarded and abandoned.

West, toward the hills.

As she drove, Merle's mind whirled with the events of the last two weeks, from arriving in Paris with her sisters, Tristan, and Gillian, to the awkward moments on the hike, the arguments over whose turn it was to buy the wine, the late-night laughing and bouncing on beds like children. The birthday party for Merle and Elise complete with chocolate cake and candles. The truffles, the *foie gras*, the wine. The annoyance with Francie at first, her princessy reluctance to walk faster than a stroll, her long morning beauty routine followed by her long evening beauty routine, hogging the bath tub.

Francie unwound during the trip, let her hair down literally. Her pigtails as she left that last time, her auburn hair bouncing. Her blog. That was a surprise, that Francie could be so incisive, so shrewd. And cutting, of course. Witty barbs were her forté. But she was more than that. The blog was obviously an outlet for her bitchiness, but it also offered advice to women lawyers. In an early post, before the trip, she'd called them the "slave class." They hoped working eighteen hours a day would ingratiate them in the partners' eyes. Male law grads did it too, of course, but it was different. Subtly and very un-subtly in the bastions of male power. Francie understood that thin line between being admired and being taken advantage of.

Francie: talking on the phone, waving her hands around, pacing the gravel walks of the garden, making her points with a kiss of sweetness and a jigger of *don't-cross-me*. She really should be on the stage. She didn't know who Gillian really was. Would the entire firm find out? Would the girl nobody knew now be seen as a real person, warts and all? Would she even come back from France? Start her life over with her real name? Or reinvent herself with a new identity?

Merle would tell Francie everything. She wished she could tell Annie. She was the one who'd broken through the wall of secrets. But her oldest sister still knew nothing about the abduction. Their parents' voices from this morning rang in her head. It was all Merle could do to keep it inside. All her life her sisters had been there for her, helping her, prodding her, maddening her, encouraging her. But she had to do this alone.

Bucket of balls, case of courage.

Merle smiled, remembering happy days together, their voices over the years cheering her on as she merged into a crowded roundabout, dodging a rusty Deux Chevaux and a sleek Mercedes, hoping to make it out alive. She missed her exit and made another round, whipping her head from side to side, changing lanes, turning sharply. She would go round and round until she found her sister.

37

The back roads took their toll on her nerves. The endless rows of vines, the flat, monotonous farmland, the moon over the marshes, the wrong turns. She finally had to get on a more major byway to avoid the dead-ends and unmarked lanes. Then it was a straight shot through the darkness. Every passing car amped up her anxiety. Every village had the potential for a *gendarme* on alert. The dog began to whine. Merle pulled into a weed-choked spot near a train overpass and let her out on the leash. She was waiting for the dog to finish, staring at the navigation map on her phone when it rang.

She stared at the number. It wasn't Pascal. It wasn't the priest.

"*Allo?*"

"Merle? Is that you?" A man's voice, and so obviously James. "Where the heck are ya?"

"Out of town."

"No shit. You keep disappearing on me. I'm startin' to take it personally, sweetie."

Merle winced. "How's the legal case?"

"That's what I wanted to tell ya. That new lawyer is the bomb. He's been working with the prosecutors. Since the priest disappeared, they can't get him to testify so the lawyer is working on them to dismiss the charges. Pretty cool, huh?"

"Right." Merle pulled the dog away from a bush and walked back to the car. "I'm on the road. Can I call you later?"

"Oh, sure. Christine went home. She likes you, Merle. She told me."

"Great, um. I'll call tomorrow." She ended the call before he could say anything else. Merle opened the car door for Aurore and threw the leash in after her. She really was a well-behaved dog, so smart.

Back on the road, Merle turned north, skirting a number of villages at the edge of the foothills. James and his annoying accent had distracted her for a moment. She had her own problems, something that never occurred to him. It was all about James Jeremy the Third. He was like many men she worked with. Not vicious or mean, just self-absorbed.

She opened her window a crack and blew a big sigh into the passing air. The dog perked up, staring at her. "Out with the bad vibes, Aurore." She patted her curly head and the dog quieted again, laying her chin on the console, worry in her trusting eyes. "I have a plan, little one," Merle told her. "You will go home soon if all goes well."

At nine-thirty she pulled into a dark lot by a gas station somewhere and closed her eyes. She was beyond tired, living on anxiety. Finally the text came.

Drive to village of Guzargues. Await instructions

Turning on the overhead light, she consulted her map again. It took a moment to find Guzargues. Where was she now? She turned on her phone's navigation, put in 'Guzargues' and got directions. It was only twenty kilometers to the west.

As she drove she wondered if the kidnappers knew where she was. How could they? They appeared to be idiots but she didn't want to underestimate them. They had managed to kidnap two people. Over a hill and down the other side and there was Guzargues, a sleepy village with few conveniences. A bar was still open but everything else was dark. She pulled into the parking lot near the city hall, parked under a street light, and turned off the car to wait.

Ten-thirty passed. Merle took a photo of the dog with her phone and texted it to the kidnappers.

If you want the dog, release my sister. Bring her to Guzargues and leave her unharmed in the center of town

No answer for ten minutes, then:

If you want to see your sister again, follow instructions. No negotiations

So much for the bully. What would the police do if they got a message like that? She hated to think. They apparently thought they were smarter than all criminals. That was a dangerous assumption. The fiasco at the Polygone proved that. She had no choice but to wait, and she hated being out of options.

She gathered the dog into her arms. Aurore was trembling, fear radiating out of her. Merle buried her face in her curly ears and tried to calm her. When would they call? How would they exchange their hostages? She stared out at the stone houses, the ornate lights, the stars. She punched in Pascal's number even though she'd promised herself she would handle this alone.

"Merle?"

"They told me to go to Guzargues. A small village."

"Near Montpellier, yes. Where are you now?"

"In Guzargues. I wasn't far." She squeezed the dog to her chest. "How will this work, Pascal? I can't. . . . I can't figure out how this will work." She wanted to tell him how afraid she was that something would go terribly wrong, but she didn't want to say that. Being afraid never stopped a person from doing what they had to do. Annie always said that courage was doing what was necessary in the face of fear. Tonight she would be brave.

"They must be near there. Maybe watching from a hilltop location. I am on my way. There is a *gendarmerie* near the *hotel de ville*. Go there and wait, blackbird. Please."

"I have to see this through, Pascal." She pressed "end" as his voice trailed off. If she talked to him any more she might lose her nerve. "*Ah, petit. Calmez-vous,*" she repeated to Aurore, settling her back on the passenger seat. As the dog relaxed, she felt her own reserve of courage rise. "I can do this," she whispered. "I can."

The next message came ten minutes later.

Drive north on Camp Paillas. Take the third right turn. Drive to the top of the hill. You will see a lantern by the road. Stop and await instructions

Merle turned on her overhead light and looked at the map. The type was miniscule and her eyes were tired. Squinting, turning it to read the street names, she had just located a road called Camp Paillas when the *gendarmes* arrived.

Two police cars drove up silently, lights off, gliding into place in front and behind her car. The one in front turned a spotlight on her. As he made his way toward her, with a swagger and a scowl, Merle sighed, placing both hands on the steering wheel.

The dog began to bark.

38

The *gendarmes* took her and the dog to the small police station behind the city hall. Similar to the one in Malcouziac, the interior was institutional gray. Someone had painted a colorful mural on the outside walls, sunflowers, lavender, and sunshine. None of that warmth could be felt in the small, dark cell where Merle sat on the cot, staring at the floor. Aurore could be heard barking behind closed doors somewhere.

She was being charged with stealing the dog. Because Aurore was so valuable it was a major crime, the *gendarmes* explained gravely. They took her passport and identification, rifled through her backpack then left it with her. Merle curled into a ball, pulling her knees into her chest on the cot, and pounded the blanket with a fist. Damn Pascal. He had done this. The French police were so incompetent she wanted to scream. Pascal knew she didn't steal the dog. Why had he told them that?

Damn him!

She jumped to her feet, fuming. She paced the small cell, rattled the stupid bars, a caged fury. What about Francie? It made her sick to her stomach. She was supposed to be up on a hill, arranging the trade of the dog. She bent over, nauseous with anxiety, when she heard the *ping*. It took a moment to realize it was her phone. And that the *gendarmes* hadn't confiscated it.

They took her ID. Why not her phone? More incompetence. She looked up and down the empty hallway. Another *ping*. She scrambled through her backpack, searched the pockets of her pants, then her shirt.

It was in a chest pocket, almost in plain sight. She pulled it out and stared at it.

Proceed to the top of the hill immediately if you value your sister's life

Merle tried not to groan. How was she going to get to the hill? How was she going to turn over the dog? What was Francie doing? Was she okay?

She sat down on the cot again and willed herself to think. *Calmez-vous*, she told herself. She needed to buy some time. She texted again.

Seem to be lost. Very dark

When she looked up, the less swagger-y *gendarme*, a young recruit by his fresh-faced looks, was standing outside the cell. She pushed the phone under her leg but there was no chance he hadn't seen her texting. He said something complicated in French, with an unusual accent, and she shook her head.

"*Je ne comprend pas.*" She asked for a translator. It was nearly midnight. It would take some time to find one. He nodded and disappeared through the hall door.

Why hadn't he taken her cell phone? It made another beep.

They texted: *Give your location*

She replied, *If I knew that I wouldn't be lost*

Then the battery died.

Merle closed her eyes. Hadn't she plugged it in? The dog got tangled in the cable in the car. Unfortunate beast at the center of this mess. She bent double, lowering her head to her knees, trying to think how this might go, how to get Francie away from those criminals. How frantic her sister must be, how scared.

She must have dozed off. She'd hardly slept for days. The crack of the metal door in the hallway made her jerk awake. She dropped her phone to the cement floor. Cursing she snatched it up and hid her hand behind her back.

"Blackbird? Are you all right?"

The sight of Pascal sent a flood of relief through her. His black T-shirt and wrinkled jeans, his cowboy boots, his broad chest and tanned face: she'd missed them. Then she remembered he was the one who had her arrested. But the young *gendarme* had his keys out and was unlocking the cell door. Merle stood, her head still fuzzy with sleep. Pascal stepped inside and took her hand. "Come on now. We have to find Francie."

In a back room, sitting around a table, he explained that he had her arrested so she didn't go meet the kidnappers on her own. She opened her mouth to protest and he raised his hand. "I know you think you can handle everything yourself, Merle. Oh, I know." He smiled wearily. She sat back. This wasn't about her pride. This was about Francie. "We have a helicopter coming." He looked at his watch. "In fifteen minutes."

"They texted again," she said. "I need to plug in my phone to show you."

Pascal went to the door and called something to the *gendarme*. He turned back to her. "What did they say?"

"The third right turn off Camp Paillas. Go to the top of the hill where a lantern sits by the road."

A *gendarme* arrived with a phone charger. Merle plugged it into the wall and her phone. Pascal said he'd be right back and disappeared, shutting the door. Merle checked her watch, waited three minutes, then turned on her phone.

There was one more text.

Bring the dog to the lantern at the top of the hill and stand in the headlights at exactly 1 a.m. or your sister dies

Merle burst out of the room. One a.m. was less than a half hour away. She opened the hallway door to the reception area and stopped short. The room was full of policemen with large guns, and a woman with a small beagle on a leash. The woman looked at her then down at her black slacks, white blouse and dark jacket.

Pascal turned from a lecture he was giving to the officers. "Go back inside, Merle."

She held up her phone. "There's another text. I need to be at that hilltop with the dog at one."

Everyone looked at their watches and shifted uncomfortably. "Wait in the room," Pascal said. "Plug in your phone."

"They said—or my sister dies." She looked at Pascal. His cheek muscles clenched. Then her phone beeped again. She read the text. "And now they say—the priest dies with her."

Pascal stood in front of her. "They're bluffing, Merle. Francie and Father Cyril are their only cards to play. They'll never get the dog if they harm them."

"Maybe they've given up on the dog. Maybe they know you've got a bunch of cops ready to arrest them."

"Then they wouldn't be texting you, would they? They would just run." He touched her arm. "They want the dog. Trust me."

"So what's the plan? Another switcheroo? Because that worked so well last time?" Merle glanced at the woman with the dog. She wore a wig, brown like Merle's hair. She frowned at Merle as if she didn't understand. "How is this person going to communicate with the kidnappers?"

Pascal asked the woman something about '*parler anglais,*' speaking English. She shook her head. "You will have to text for her, Merle."

"Am I going to be there? Hiding in the car? Dropping from a helicopter? On a walkie-talkie?" Pascal was not liking her tone. "And that dog? It looks nothing like Aurore. They're going to see it in the headlights. They'll know it's not the right one."

Merle stepped closer to him. "I can't take another chance that it gets botched. I have to do what they say." She looked at her watch. "And I only have minutes to get there."

Outside, the heavy chop of a helicopter cut the night. Merle looked around the room at the team of policemen in combat gear, weapons at their sides. The beagle whined then barked at the noise. Merle looked down at the dog then back at Pascal.

"I have an idea."

39

The third right turn off Camp Paillas was a fork in the road, easing uphill toward the wilder outskirts of Guzargues. The area was a wealthy suburb of Montpellier, it appeared, with lavish country houses behind gates. A new moon rose in the east, a slant of silver across the dirt road. Merle drove and Aurore rode shotgun, watching the dark trees go by.

"Which hill do you think they're on?" Merle asked. Pascal was in the back seat with the beagle and the woman, a police dog handler named Giselle. They crouched low as she drove out of the village and into the dry hills dotted with scrub and stone.

"To the West probably. Get the dog from the passenger side."

Merle gripped the steering wheel, driving as fast as she could around potholes on the narrow country road. It wound upward, past a compound of buildings, dim shapes against the night sky, a stand of pines, and dry, empty ground, away from civilization. She rounded a bend and saw the lantern ahead on the right, lighting a yellow circle on the ground. "There it is," she told them, bouncing off the road onto hard dirt. Her heart began to flutter. Aurore pricked up her ears and whined.

"Leave the car running," Pascal said.

The location was treeless and open, not even shrubs growing in the dry soil. To the west the hill dropped to a bottomless ravine, then another hill rose, barely visible in the moonlight. To the east no hills could be seen, just blackness and a smattering of stars. It looked like the perfect place to get hit by sniper fire.

"*Allons-y*," she whispered to the dog. *Let's go.* "Time to show ourselves to the bad men."

The dog began to tremble again and struggled against the leash as Merle pulled her over to the driver's side. She barked as Merle tucked her under her arm and shut the car door. Pascal whispered through his open window. "Can you hear me, blackbird?"

"*Oui.*"

"Check if there are more messages."

Merle got out her phone. It made a crazy amount of light. She wondered if the criminals could see her face in its glow. She hoped so. Unless they had snipers.

"Nothing," she whispered.

She set the dog down and held the leash tightly as they walked to the front of the car, into the bright stream of the headlights. She listened for the helicopter but the night was still. Not a breath of wind. Just the heat rising off the ground, releasing the stored sunshine. She tugged the leash and walked with Aurore out a little farther so her entire body was lit by the beams.

It was 1:04.

Merle held her sides, dancing from foot to foot. The night wasn't cold but she felt a chill anyway. Aurore leaned against her leg, shivering. She patted the dog's head.

At 1:07 the text came.

Drive to the first tree on the right. Tie the dog there. Your sister will be freed in one hour

Merle blinked, reading it again. She couldn't believe it. There wasn't going to be an exchange. This wasn't right.

She wrote back: *My sister must be freed now or I will not give up the dog*

The reply was immediate: *No negotiations*

Back at the car, Merle settled the dog in the seat. "They aren't going to exchange Francie. I have to tie up the dog at the first tree on the right." She looked back at Pascal, angry. "Can't you do something? Can't you tell where those texts are coming from?"

"Drive, Merle," he said. "We are working on it."

She cursed loudly and put the car in gear. This was going badly, very badly. Steering back onto the road, she drove slowly, her high beams on, scanning the rocky hillside for a tree. Finally, a lonely pine tree, long dead, came into view on a barren ridge. She stopped the car and put it in park.

"What about when they see it's the beagle?" she asked. This had been her plan but now she wasn't sure. How would they find Francie once the criminals were caught?

"We will have them by then, blackbird. Turn off the car."

She switched off the ignition. The headlights went out. It was very dark, moonless. She waited a moment for her eyes to adjust then got out. Inside the car, she heard yips and whining as the dogs were moved. She walked around to the passenger side. This was wrong. But what else was there? She had to go forward.

She took a breath to steady herself. "All set?"

"*Oui*," came the answer from the back seat from Giselle. "*À bientôt, Mignon. Soyez bon.*"

Opening the door quickly, Merle scooped up Mignon, the beagle, and shut the door quickly, dousing the overhead light. She set the dog on the ground and straightened, squinting in the dark for the tree. She wished she had a flashlight. The ground was strewn with rocks. That was out of the question; tonight the darkness was her cloak, her friend. She picked her way along, stumbling, until she reached the dead pine tree. She wrapped the long leash around a low branch and tied it securely. The walk back to the car seemed to take an eternity. The dog began to bark. Merle turned back, using the trainer's command, "*Silence, Mignon!*"

Poor dog, she thought, crossing the last of the stones. She hoped nothing happened to Mignon. She got in the car. "Now what?"

"Turn around and drive back toward Guzargues."

As she drove down the hillside, heart heavy, she saw two police cars hidden behind a stand of trees. Then another two, by a high wall. The kidnappers would be caught. Mignon would not be harmed. That gave her little consolation. Francie was still a captive.

The dog handler pulled off her wig as she got out of the car by the *gendarmerie*. She gathered up Aurore and disappeared into the building. "Come on," Pascal said, taking Merle's hand. They got in his BMW and headed back out of town.

"I'm going to text them again," she said. She wrote: *I did as you asked. Where is my sister?*

They passed the church and plunged onto the dark hillside. "Anything?" he asked. She said no, holding her phone tightly.

Pascal got a call and began talking rapidly in French. He braked hard, jerked the steering wheel, and made a U-turn. "*Enfin*," he said angrily. "The priest called the emergency number two minutes ago. Finally Paris gives approval to track his phone. They were worried about his privacy." He swore in French. It sounded very dirty.

"Did he give directions?"

"He had no idea where he was. Paris will call when they get a location."

As they pulled into the field on the edge of town where the helicopter sat parked, its rotors limp in the night air, Pascal's phone rang again. He listened then turned to Merle. "They need the GPS turned on the priest's phone. He's locked it. Call them."

Shaking now, she punched her phone. *Come on, Cyril.* It rang five or six times. She was losing hope when suddenly Francie was there. "Merle!"

"Francie, are you okay?" She gripped Pascal's arm.

"Yes. Well, sort of. We're locked in this room. I was tied to the bed and we got that off but we can't get out the door. And the window is tiny."

"*Le* GPS," Pascal hissed.

"You need to turn on the GPS on this phone, on Cyril's phone, so we can find you."

"I think they're gone. We saw some cars drive away. We've been yelling out the window but there's nobody out there."

"Listen to me, Francie. Turn on the GPS on the phone."

"Ah, right. Just a sec." She spoke to the priest, asking him how to work his phone. A minute passed, some discussion about buttons and functions and codes. Finally Francie came back on the line. "Okay, it's on. He didn't really know where it was, but I think we got it."

"Good, okay, now we can track the phone and—"

Pascal's phone rang. He said, "*Bon,*" and got out of the car.

"Hang on, Francie. We're on our way."

"Merle? I smell smoke."

40

The helicopter rose awkwardly, lifting into the night sky, sending dust and gravel flying on the ground. Merle clung to the seat, straining against the seat belt. Her first helicopter ride. She'd been given earphones for the noise but it came through anyway, a riot of percussion. Pascal, in front, was showing the pilot a map on his phone.

They didn't need a map once they'd cleared the hill. Yellow flames lit the scene against the black landscape like a beacon. Merle felt her stomach turn over. They circled once then set down in a pasture. The building was engulfed, the fire several stories high. The wind created by the helicopter didn't help.

Merle had to wait for Pascal to open her door, then threw herself out. They ran toward the building, a large barn, flames licking the outer walls. The noise was like a thousand lions roaring. The heat was intense, keeping everyone back. She lost Pascal in the crowd of neighbors who arrived carrying shovels, axes, and hoses.

Where was this window? Merle ran left, around the blaze, her eyes stinging from smoke. She called out for her sister but her voice was nothing to the raging fire eating up old beams and boards. She ran to the back where two men were cutting back shrubs between the barn and the farmhouse, a two-story stucco manse with a red tile roof and blue shutters.

She asked a man wearing pajamas if he'd seen a window on this side. He pointed to the opposite side of the barn. On the east and to the back the walls were whitewashed stone as if it was some ancient, original part of the structure. She rounded the corner and saw a tiny window about six or seven feet off the ground. Merle jumped, but couldn't see inside.

"Francie! Are you there?"

A hand poked out, then Francie's face emerged. "Merle? Thank God. Get us out of here. The smoke is getting bad."

"Are your walls made of stone?"

"Yeah but the ceiling is wood. We can hear it crackling. We're afraid it's going to fall in on us."

"Is Cyril okay?"

"I think he has asthma or something. Hurry!"

Pascal was helping throw water onto the edges of the barn to keep the fire contained. Without serious firefighting equipment, the barn was a loss, that was easy to see. The roof was tile but the wooden structure of it burned like a tinder box.

Merle grabbed his arm. "They're in the back."

Pascal grabbed an axe and followed Merle. He swung the tool wildly at the window. Glass flew in every direction but the stone held. After a few whacks, he told Merle he would have to go through the main door, and then he ran back to the front. Merle called to Francie, telling her they were going to come in through the door, then ran back to the front. Pascal borrowed gloves from a farmer, then picked up the axe again and chopped through the outside door. It shattered, half burnt. A whoosh of air sent a plume of sparks up to the rafters, feeding the fire. The skin on Merle's face felt dangerously warm. Her eyebrows might be melting.

Pascal disappeared into the smoke and flame. He shouted, his words lost in the chaos. The crack of the axe boomed. A cry went up as the west wall of the barn collapsed in on itself, sending everyone back. Merle called out to Pascal, her words evaporating. Fire was so unpredictable. She wanted to go in but knew it would just make things worse. Did the beams crush him? Would Francie burn to death? Had the smoke choked them? The scenarios ran through her head, the call to their parents, the trials for the kidnappers, the revenge she would extract, all hardening inside her.

No. It was too early for hate.

Around her, the work went on, the dousing of small flames, the digging of trenches, the wet trickle from an ineffectual hose. She waited until she was sure she would burst. Time during a calamity took on an elastic quality, stretching until you're sure it will break.

Finally figures materialized out of the smoke. Pascal was dragging a thin man dressed in black, his arm over Pascal's shoulders. Father Cyril, his hair, face, and clothes gray with ash. Was he alive? They stepped over burning debris, stumbling out of the barn. Pascal laid him on the ground. Cyril was coughing. A woman cradled his head her lap and gave him sips of water.

Merle let out a sigh. He would live. She looked back into the gloom and yelled, "Francie!"

Pascal turned to go back in, then paused as they saw her. Francie, high-stepping over embers and beams, hair flying, arms batting smoke and sparks out of her path, screaming very bad words as she leaped and ran. She plunged out the broken door and into Merle's arms.

"Oh god," Francie said, her face smashed into Merle's shoulder. "I don't want to do that again."

Merle and Francie sat on the ground, a blanket around their shoulders, holding onto each other. The fire burned on but they sat outside the active zone, spectators now. A fire truck lumbered up with its water tank but too late. The roof caved in fifteen minutes after Francie and Cyril got out. Pascal kept working tirelessly. He helped carry Cyril to the helicopter to be flown to a hospital.

Francie refused to go. She laid her head on Merle's shoulder, quiet now. There would be time to talk later. She had been wild to call Jack and Bernie and their sisters until Merle told her they didn't know about the abduction, that she'd kept it to herself so they could fly home together and tell the story with all the flourishes and drama. Francie's knees had given out then and she cried for a minute. The nightmare was over. The relief was palpable that no one had been stressed and worried, wondering if she was dead or alive. No one but her middle sister.

Merle wiped away tears on both their faces. They would recant the tale together with everyone there. It would become a moment of family lore, the telling and re-telling. It would morph into legend, or not. Whatever Francie wanted. For Merle, her arms tight around the sister she had underestimated and undervalued, but would never, ever do again as long as she lived, it was enough to be right here, right now.

Safe and sound.

41

As dawn crept into the eastern sky, turning the scene of the fire a smoldering, ghostly pink, Pascal put Merle and Francie into his car and drove back to Guzargues. He looked exhausted. They all did, gray smudges under their eyes, ash from head to toe. In the back seat, Francie laid her head back and was asleep when they pulled up to the *gendarmerie*.

Standing in the bright sun, Pascal turned to Merle. He began to speak but she put a finger to his lips and leaned in to kiss him. They wrapped their arms around each other silently. Finally, Merle pulled back and took his face in her hands. "Thank you," she whispered. *"Merci, mon chèri."*

He drove them home to Malcouziac in the afternoon. The sisters couldn't stay awake. Merle tried to stay alert to talk to him but kept nodding off. When she woke up, they were on rue de Poitiers again, parking beside the broken stones of the wall as they'd done so often.

Francie took the shower first. She was desperate, she said. Merle had asked if the men had hurt her and she said only that she was slapped a couple times. Nothing else, she said pointedly. "You know I would tell you, Merle," she said, giving her sister a hug.

Pascal stripped off his T-shirt and stood under the old cistern to wash his head and arms. When he'd dried off he and Merle sat at the dining table, trying to process what had happened. He pulled her into his lap and buried his face in her chest. They were sitting that way, silently, listening to the shower run, when the knock came on the door.

He looked over her shoulder. "*Merde*." James waited outside, wearing the same blue polo shirt and khakis he'd arrived in. "I'll get rid of him."

James startled at the sight of Pascal, shirtless and damp. "Is Merle here?"

"She's busy. What is it?"

Merle appeared at Pascal's bare shoulder. "It's okay. Hi, James."

"There you are." He looked back and forth between them. "I've been worried. So, ah, I'm going home. I'm taking the train to Paris tonight. The priest dropped the charges. They just called. He's in the hospital or something."

"Great. I'm glad," Merle said.

"You look—are you dirty or something?"

She wiped a swath through the gray ash on her arm. "I guess I am."

James pulled back his shoulders, eyeing the two of them. "I guess this is as good a time as any to tell you. We had some good times, Merle, and I hope you aren't crushed or anything. I don't want to hurt you. But, well, Christine and I decided to give it another try. We're getting back together. And not just for the kids although I did miss them a lot."

"Good news," Pascal said flatly.

"Yes," Merle said. "Good luck, James."

"She came to France for me. Must be something about France and, what do you call it, *l'amour?*" He smiled, pleased with himself, then squinted at Merle. "You're not angry or—"

"No," Pascal said. "She's not. She's happy for you. We both are. Very happy."

They watched James walk away, hands in his pockets. "It seems I reconciled a marriage," Merle said, pulling him close. "Or was it you?"

"It all worked out very well, blackbird. *Au revoir*, King James, *et bon débarras*. Good riddance."

Earlier, up in the hills, the police had appeared out of the night with flashers blazing to intercept Hector and Milo as they arrived to pick up the dog. Two other Italians including a prominent businessman were nabbed at roadblocks and taken into custody. Mignon, the beagle, emerged a little hoarse from howling but unscathed and was happily returned to her handler. Father Cyril enjoyed a long recovery from smoke inhalation on the island of Sardinia.

Aurore, the truffle dog, was returned to Jean Poutou and his wife amid much fanfare from the neighboring families. Newspapers carried the story of the heartwarming reunion. No one received the reward but not for lack of trying. In the autumn Aurore was sold to an Italian woman, a *Signora* Bettina Dellapiane, who had inquired about her availability. *Monsieur* Poutou would only say the price was adequate for a dog of Aurore's renown.

The rains began in the fall after a very dry summer throughout the Mediterranean. For the vineyards it was too late but for truffles it was just in time. After she found a French-speaking handler, *Signora* Dellapiane had an excellent season with her new dog. She made enough money to lease the prime truffle grounds of her debt-ridden neighbor for next year's season. Gianluca Gribaudi was otherwise engaged.

James Jeremy Silvers III and his ex-wife Christine got remarried in the autumn. It was a private ceremony. Annie Bennett and Callum Logan announced their engagement in September. No date for the wedding was immediately set.

Gillian Sargent didn't return to the practice of law at Ward & Baillee. Around the firm they said she had a nervous breakdown on her trip to Europe. Francie went pale when anyone asked about her so the questions stopped. One of the partners seemed to know all Gillian's plans except where she now lived. Francie never heard a word. She kept Gillian's identity a secret. Despite all she'd done, Gillian had helped Merle rescue her. She'd given up the dog to her rightful owners. She wasn't a criminal. She had a conscience after all. In the fall Francie spent many weekends with Tristan and Merle, working on a plan for a cheese importing business. She stopped writing her blog. For now.

Merle Bennett had serious regrets about leaving the Dordogne again. Before the chaos of the end of the trip, the walking tour with her sisters had been lovely. The countryside, the flowers, the wine, the family. They were together, celebrating life and birthdays.

And then there was Pascal. What was she going to do about Pascal?

She closed the house on rue de Poitiers, making arrangements for Josephine Azamar to tend the garden again. She hugged Albert and told him she'd be back. And then, saying good-bye to Pascal at the train station in Bergerac, she cried. Just a few tears.

She asked him to visit her. He whispered *"Blackbird"* in her ear and promised.

Read the first Bennett Sisters novel
Blackbird Fly
and more by Lise McClendon
lisemcclendon.com

Thrillers written as Rory Tate
PLAN X
Jump Cut

All Your Pretty Dreams - a new adult romance

The Alix Thorssen Mysteries:
Bluejay Shaman
Painted Truth
Nordic Nights
Blue Wolf

The Dorie Lennox Mysteries:
One O'clock Jump
Sweet and Lowdown

Made in the USA
Lexington, KY
03 November 2017